Out of the Corner Of My Eye

A Ghost Story

by

Liz McLoughlin

Dedication

To my late mother, Jeanne Byron McLoughlin, who engendered within me an absolute love of the written word from the earliest age and who surrounded me with books. I hope you would be proud of this.

Liz McLoughlin – Gloucestershire, August 2021

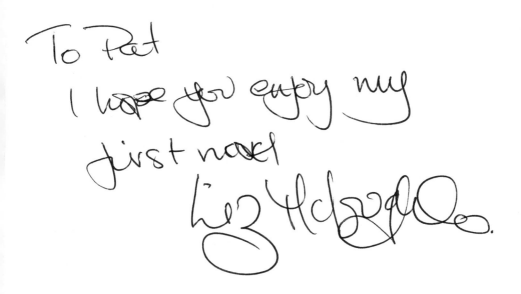

Contents

Dedication iii

Prologue 5

Chapter One 7

Chapter Two 20

Chapter Three 32

Chapter Four 43

Chapter Five 55

Chapter Six 67

Chapter Seven 79

Chapter Eight 93

Chapter Nine 104

Chapter Ten 117

Chapter Eleven 129

Chapter Twelve 141

Chapter Thirteen 153

Chapter Fourteen 169

Chapter Fifteen 185

Chapter Sixteen 199

Chapter Seventeen 213

Epilogue 222

Prologue

The house stands alone, empty, neglected yet defiant, as if waiting for something—or someone—to either bring it back to life or, perhaps, give it permission to return to the earth and the elements.

Blank-eyed, it watches, year upon year, like a brick and concrete Miss Havisham—its beauty eroded by the ravages of time.

The high, ornate chimneys seem to reach up, like skeletal fingers clawing at the sky, even as the roof slowly but surely crumbles and tumbles down into the dark, cavernous rooms below.

It has been a very long time since the walls rang with the sounds of the living, the last occupants having left with some urgency many years earlier, after only a few months' tenure.

Tales of ghoulish apparitions and strange, unexplainable occurrences abound in the surrounding area. These stories keep many away, but sometimes tempt the adventurous or foolhardy to venture close. None stay long.

A few, who refuse to acknowledge their fear, will say they got out before the roof fell in or the floor collapsed, but most readily own to being afraid for their lives—not because of such prosaic dangers as crumbling masonry, but because the house itself exudes menace. Those brave souls who have been inside variously describe a choking claustrophobia, as if the very walls are closing in. They talk of plummeting temperatures, even on the hottest summer days, and a hideously tangible sensation of being watched, and judged … and found wanting.

From time to time, there is talk of pulling the house down, developing the land, building luxury flats or affordable homes for local people. Nothing ever comes of such talk.

And so, year after year, the house becomes a little less habitable, a little more dilapidated. And just as human life is absent, the same holds true of any kind of wildlife. Where other such properties become overrun with rats, mice, foxes, pigeons, feral cats and the like, no animals seem keen to breach the perimeter; no birdsong can be heard, nor the muted snuffling and rustling of small creatures, intent on finding a meal or a home.

The house stands in dreadful silence, watching, waiting, biding its time.

And now, finally, it seems that time has come …

Chapter One

'Goddamn it to hell!'

I'd had enough. The shitty GPS in my rental car was driving me crazy. It seemed I'd been driving for hours, and I still had no idea where the hell I was.

'Turn left in two hundred meters.'

'There *is* no frigging left, you useless piece of shit!' I shouted, as the maddeningly calm, dyslexic Queen of GPS told me, once again, to take a turn that simply didn't exist. I had entered the exact location of my destination when I had collected the car at Heathrow, all as per the lawyer's email. At first, it had worked perfectly, but then I guess I must have entered some kind of GPS Bermuda Triangle once I crossed over the border into Cornwall. For the last twenty-plus miles, it felt like I was being taken on a wild goose chase, with the electronic read-out on the dashboard flashing on and off intermittently and spouting garbled and nonsensical directions in what was becoming an increasingly annoying clipped British accent.

'Turn left in one hundred meters.'

'Oh, for God's sake!'

I reached out to smack the damned thing but, as I did, I caught a glimpse of what looked like an opening in the thick roadside foliage coming up on the left. Slowing, I could more easily make out the turning; as I drew close, I could see that it was an unpaved road leading farther into the woods.

'Now turn left. Follow the road for half a mile,' the tiresome voice instructed me.

Maybe it was a shortcut back to where I'd gone wrong. You did hear stories about GPS devices instructing people to drive through fields and off piers, or some such nonsense, but you had to wonder if that stuff was merely apocryphal. I decided that, at worst, I would drive for half a mile and then have to turn and come back, so I indicated left and maneuvered the car onto the track.

'Follow the road for half a mile.'

'Yeah, yeah, I heard you. You better be right about this, or, so help me, I'm gonna have you ripped out and turned into an alarm clock!'

I continued slowly along the darkly shaded, woodland lane, growing ever more doubtful that it was going to lead anywhere but a dead end. Cursing myself for being a fool, I realized that there wasn't even enough room to turn around.

Then, two things happened at once: the sun, which had been languishing behind an enormous black cloud, suddenly broke free, illuminating a large clearing up ahead. And the GPS beeped.

'You have reached your destination.'

What the hell? What destination?

Up ahead, spotlighted by the sun, stood a seriously dilapidated house.

Without conscious thought, I brought the car to a standstill, turned off the engine and simply stared, torn by warring emotions.

On the one hand, I wanted nothing more than to get the hell out of Dodge and as far away from that crumbling wreck as possible. On the other hand, I felt myself being gripped by an irresistible urge to get out of the car and move closer. I must have sat there, peering through the windshield, for more than five minutes, trying to make sense of what I was seeing and feeling.

'You have reached your destination.'

I jumped in my seat, a loud squeak of surprise escaping me. What the hell was with the GPS? The coordinates I had entered were for the lawyer's office in Port Simon, which I knew to be a fairly busy tourist town on the coast. I didn't know where I was, but I was pretty damned certain it wasn't downtown Port Simon. And why was it repeating itself? To my knowledge, GPS units didn't randomly repeat themselves.

A shiver ran down my spine at just how weird things had become. I knew I was pretty close to freaking out completely, and took a couple of steadying deep breaths, willing myself to keep my shit together.

I looked again at the house, feeling my skin break out in goose bumps, despite the warmth which had now invaded the interior after turning off the engine and losing the air-conditioning. I had to question why I had even done that, but no answer was forthcoming. Neither could I fathom what forces might have been at work when, seemingly without permission from my brain, my body decided to get out of the car.

'Jesus, what the hell am I doing?' I whispered to myself. 'And why am I whispering?' I shook my head at my own foolishness, a nervous chuckle bubbling forth, as I moved around to the front of the car and gazed up at the house.

Immediately in front of me was an area of tall grass which had probably been a lawn at one time. The house itself was constructed with red bricks but was almost entirely swallowed up by the undergrowth. From here, I could smell the sea and realized I must be pretty close to the coast, but there appeared to be no way to reach the other side of the house to see exactly how close it was.

The windows were mostly broken, and the roof was pretty much gone—just jagged rafters sticking up haphazardly, like the wreckage of a sunken medieval ship at low tide.

The most striking features, however, were the chimneys—five tall towers of red bricks, all of differing designs, which jutted skyward. It seemed I was looking at the rear of the building, as there was only a rather unprepossessing doorway offering entrance. However, the undergrowth was so all-encompassing that it was impossible to see a way around to the front. I continued staring, my brain telling me to get back in the car and drive away, but my heart … well, my heart was saying something altogether different.

Again, my feet seemed to have a mind of their own, taking me closer. There was no way I could go inside—apart from the fact that the whole place looked ready to collapse, it was probably full of rats the size of piglets and God knew what else, just waiting to take a diseased bite out of me.

And yet, when my eyes fastened on the back door, I could see it was slightly ajar, and I found myself fighting an overpowering urge to yank it open. Moving ever closer, I finally stood in front of the opening and, with a will of its own, my hand reached out to grip the edge of the rough wooden planking of the door. I gave it an experimental tug, cringing as rusty hinges, long unused, squealed and protested, but it opened far more easily than I expected.

Inside, it was pitch dark, the light from outside barely seeming to penetrate the gloom beyond the threshold. I paused, weighing up my options. My actions were foolhardy at best, positively suicidal at worst, but I could no longer deny the extraordinary pull I felt to get a closer look at this remarkable house.

Making up my mind, I turned and trotted back to the car. My purse was on the passenger seat, and I quickly rummaged through it until I found what I was looking for—a small flashlight, which I turned on to check if it was working. As an afterthought, I also grabbed my phone … just in case. Satisfied, I hurried back to the house and took a tentative step inside.

Initially, I used the flashlight to scan the ground ahead of me, wanting to make sure there were no holes or obstacles to trip me up. I was mindful that if I stepped on a rotted floorboard, I might easily plummet into a basement, possibly breaking my legs or even my neck. I didn't even want to think how far the drop might be or what it might be like down there.

Shaking my head to rid it of such ghastly images, I swept the beam of light around the interior. The floor looked solid enough and I appeared to be in a large kitchen. From the small amount of illumination, I could see that it was a wreck. There was an old cooking range, smashed beyond repair, and what remained of the units must have dated back to the 1950s or '60s. Nevertheless, my designer's eye could immediately see how the room would make an amazing eat-in kitchen.

As that thought took hold, I suddenly felt an inexplicably warm, comfortable feeling envelop me, making me smile. Any trepidation I had felt on entering this intriguing house now fell away, and I found myself moving confidently and with a certain excitement as I explored deeper inside.

Unfortunately, my confidence evaporated pretty rapidly when I pushed the door leading into the main core of the building. At first, I thought it must be locked, but then realized that it was, in fact, blocked by debris. Shoving hard, I managed to move it far enough back to create a narrow gap through which I could squeeze, only to find my way barred. Filling what had clearly been the entrance hall of the house was the detritus from the worst of the roof collapse. Looking up, I could see light pouring into the rather dingy hallway through what had once been an atrium which had long since caved in, littering the floor with an ankle-breaking pile of splintered wood, rubble and shattered glass.

I sighed, glancing around the space to see doors leading off on either side of the foyer, and a once-elegant staircase sweeping up to the floor above. I judged that it might be possible to reach the stairs, but I didn't dare trust them. Even where the balustrade was still attached, I knew it was likely that the risers would be damaged or rotten, and it simply wasn't worth the risk. I would need a hard hat and steel-toed boots, at the very least, and the whole place would have to be scaffolded and shored up to provide adequate support for potentially unstable floors, walls and ceilings. With that in mind, I let my flashlight play across the interior, searching for major cracks in the masonry. I knew I would have to come back with better lighting and equipment, and that the place would need a full structural survey, but …

'Jesus, what am I thinking?' I muttered aloud.

Before the words had completely left my mouth, I caught a movement out of the corner of my eye. Turning my head sharply back to the stairs, I could feel my heart rate pick up as I swept the narrow beam of light back and forth, seeing nothing. Just as my heartbeat started to return to normal, I felt the softest sensation of being touched on my face, like the feather-light caress of fingertips against my cheek.

I shrieked, swinging the flashlight around frantically and stumbling slightly on the uneven ground. I backed up, holding my hand to my chest, willing myself to calm down. I didn't believe in ghosts or monsters, my mother having taught me from an early age to rationalize my fears by examining the cause, breaking it down and thereby demystifying whatever demon had upset me, robbing it of its power to scare me.

No, I had no fear of spectral incursion—my concern was for more corporeal threats. Although I didn't run screaming from bugs and spiders, preferring to trap them and set them free *outside* my living accommodation, I still wasn't keen on the idea of having them crawling on me. I swiped at my face and hoped I hadn't inadvertently walked into a cobweb, the mere thought of which made me shiver in disgust.

Sighing, I silently castigated myself for being a wuss and turned my mind back to what had so vexed me a moment earlier.

Had I really let myself think about what could be done with this house … or, more precisely, what *I* could do with it? Buying a house in England was definitely not part of the plan. Indeed, if there was a plan at all, it was to spend as little time in this country as possible. I would conclude my business with my late grandmother's lawyer, visit my dad in London, and then hot-foot it back home to San Francisco.

At no point had there ever been a suggestion of acquiring a property, either here or anywhere else in the UK.

Nope, not gonna happen. Zero chance.

'You hear me, House? No way am I interested in some random, broken-down old money pit, so forget it!' I called out into the darkness, feeling foolish that I was talking to a goddamned house.

I turned, pulling the kitchen door open as much as possible in order to squeeze back through. As I did, I heard a soft sound, like wind soughing through an open window, and once more I felt—or, perhaps, merely sensed—the brush of those ethereal fingers on my face. Inexplicably, I was a good deal less freaked out by it the second time, distracted as I was, once again, by the hint of movement in my peripheral vision. This time, I forced myself not to look, instead, yanking the door harder and easing through the opening.

From there, I made a beeline across the overgrown grass to the car, intending to simply get in and drive away. I needed to banish all thoughts of what could be done with this house; it wasn't mine, and even if it were for sale, there was no way I wanted—or could afford—to buy and renovate such a large, ramshackle property. I was in Britain simply to settle some family matters, see my father and then return to my life in San Francisco.

Nevertheless, as I reached my car, I found it impossible to deny the draw I felt to turn and look back at the old house.

Sighing, I sat on the hood and stared at what must have been a stunning property at one time. Its lovely proportions spoke to me, and as I continued to scan the blemished but still elegant façade, I could almost see how it would have looked in better times. Indeed, all of a sudden, my vision seemed to swim and, for the briefest moment, it was as though I was hurled back in time to when this extraordinary house had been whole and full of life.

Gasping, I shook my head, squeezing my eyes shut. When I reopened them, the house was once again the broken-down ruin I had first encountered.

The difference now was that I had an overwhelming sensation of being watched. My gaze swept the building, glancing from dark window to dark window, but there was obviously nothing there. I cursed my own stupidity and stood up. Determined to put an end to this foolishness, I walked around to the car door, got in and started the engine. Forcing myself not to look at the house, I swung the car around in a loop and drove quickly away from the property and back to the main road.

Reaching the end of the narrow lane, the GPS suddenly sparked to life, making me jump.

'Now turn right. Follow the road for one mile.'

'Are you freaking kidding me?!'

I stared in disbelief at the electronic display, letting the car idle at the junction while I rubbed my hands over my face and took a calming breath. It made sense, of course, to go back the way I had come, as I was obviously in the wrong place, so I pulled out onto the blacktop and accelerated up the empty road.

℘℃ℛ

Much to my relief—and a good deal of irritation—the GPS now guided me swiftly and unerringly into Port Simon and my original destination. I cast a baleful glare at the dashboard as it informed me that I had reached my journey's end, and then concentrated on finding somewhere to park. My detour had cost me over an hour, and my plan to give myself time for lunch before my appointment was shot to shit. Fortunately, as it was now the ass-end of the working day, I was able to find a spot quite close to the lawyer's office where my meeting was taking place.

Entering the small reception area, I glanced at my watch to see that I was nearly twenty minutes late, making me huff with annoyance.

The receptionist glanced up at me.

'Hello, can I help you?' she asked, giving me a friendly smile.

'Yeah, I've got an appointment with a Mr. Best. My name's Katherine Tregowen.'

'Oh, yes, Miss Tregowen,' she said, glancing at her computer screen and pursing her lips.

'Sorry, I know I'm late … I got lost,' I explained, hoping that after all I'd been through to get here, he would still be able to see me.

She nodded but didn't respond, simply picking up her phone and pressing a speed-dial button.

'Derek, Miss Tregowen is here … okay, I'll send her in.'

She put the phone down and pointed at a door toward the back of the office.

'Mr. Best will see you now. Can I get you a cup of tea or coffee?'

'Uh, yeah, coffee would be great—black, no sugar. Thanks.' I knew that, this being England, it would probably be some kind of instant shit, but right now I'd drink dishwater, I was so thirsty—and that's probably what it would taste like.

I headed towards the indicated door, pushing it open and entering.

Behind a rather pretentious oak desk which was far too big for the room, a short, dapper man stood and crossed the small distance, holding his hand out. He smiled, peering owlishly at me through round, wire-framed glasses as he took my hand.

'Miss Tregowen, it's a pleasure to meet you. I'm Derek Best, your grandmother's solicitor. Please, take a seat.'

He indicated one of the visitors' chairs and returned to his side of the desk, sitting back in his large, leather chair and folding his hands over his round stomach.

'I'm sorry to have kept you waiting. I'm afraid I got lost on the way here and ended up at some weird house about five miles outside of town.'

He frowned and leaned forward, resting his forearms on his desk.

'Weird house? I'm intrigued, Miss Tregowen. Can you be more specific?'

'Uh, well, it was a real wreck, practically falling down. A big, red-brick house, with five enormous chimneys. The damned GPS in my rental took me down some rutted road a few miles north of here.'

His eyes widened and he sat back again.

'Sounds like the old Merrick place—it's been empty for donkey's years. Oh, dear, I'm sorry you ended up there—that must have been a most unpleasant experience ... you didn't go anywhere near it, did you? It's a complete death trap and should have been pulled down years ago, but developers aren't interested in buying it because of all the covenants ... oh, but you didn't come here to talk about an old house. Let's get down to the business at hand, shall we?'

He pulled a file from a tray on his desk and opened it, glancing at the contents.

'Uh, of course,' I muttered. *The house was for sale? Oh, for God's sake, don't even go there!*

'You know, this could all have been sorted out by email and post, Miss Tregowen. I'm surprised you decided to travel all the way from America to deal with this personally, rather than let us sort it out with your own lawyers in San Francisco.'

He looked at me quizzically, and I sighed.

'Yeah, I know, but, to be honest, it was a good excuse for me to come to England to visit my dad. I couldn't get here for my grandmother's funeral as I was in the middle of a major project when she died, and I hadn't seen her since I was a child. But I had a lot of vacation time owed to me, so I thought, what the hell.'

'A major project?'

'Yes, I'm an architect and the project I've been working on was at a critical stage. But it's pretty much complete now, so it was a good time to get away. I haven't seen my father for a couple of years, and although I visited my grandmother here when I was a kid, I haven't been to Cornwall in a really long time. I do remember long summer days, the smell of the sea, and rich, yellow ice cream.'

I chuckled self-consciously, wondering if he would think I was being a sentimental fool, but he smiled indulgently as he peered at me over the top of his glasses.

'Yes, Cornwall does have that effect—once seen, never forgotten. Now, as to more prosaic matters, we should talk about your grandmother's Will. Your father, of course, got the London property, but as she signed that over to him more than seven years ago, it's not subject to probate.'

He paused when the door opened, and his receptionist came in with a tray of drinks and a small plate of store-bought cookies. Placing it on the side of the desk, she handed us our respective cups and then quickly withdrew. Taking a sip, I fought back my grimace at the insipid taste, putting the cup back down.

Best smiled briefly and returned his attention to the file.

'Which brings me to the details of your inheritance. Essentially, Mrs. Tregowen bequeathed to you, her only grandchild, the property known as Leigh Cottage, including all the contents. In addition, there is a cash sum of three hundred thousand pounds, made up of a life insurance policy, the liquidation of various stocks and bonds, and the contents of her bank accounts. The whole of your grandmother's estate, including the Cornish property, has been estimated at some four hundred and eighty thousand pounds, give or take. This means that, as the value falls below the five hundred thousand pounds threshold, it will not be subject to Inheritance Tax.'

Best finally looked up from the file in front of him and smiled at me, but I was having a hard time taking everything in.

Four hundred and eighty grand? That was, what ... six hundred and fifty thousand dollars? Jesus H. Christ!

'A very tidy sum, I think you'll agree, Miss Tregowen. Now, as probate was concluded last month, it's my pleasure to provide you with a banker's draft for the liquidated portion of the estate, in the aforementioned sum of three hundred thousand pounds.'

Referring back to the file, he unclipped a white envelope from the folder and slid it across his desk towards me.

It was at this point that he finally seemed to notice that I hadn't yet spoken and glanced up at me.

'Miss Tregowen? I believe you will find that everything is in order. The cottage, of course, is yours to do with as you wish. I'm assuming you will want to sell the property? I'm afraid house prices in this part of the world are somewhat depressed, and it is in need of a bit of a facelift, but you should get a hundred and eighty thousand for it, perhaps even a little more. I can put you in touch with an excellent estate agent who could sort all that out for you, if you wish.'

My head was spinning. I knew the house in London was worth a hell of a lot more than the figures Best was currently throwing around, but I'd long since had this discussion with Dad when he called to tell me that Grandma wanted to give it to him. I'd still been at Cornell studying architecture, and my father was funding my substantial tuition fees, so I'd had no problem with him having the house—it was his childhood home, after all, and I guess it would come to me one day anyway, although hopefully not for a long time yet. He'd mentioned then that I would get the house in Cornwall, but I really hadn't given it any thought at the time. In truth, it seemed the cottage wasn't worth a huge amount, but on top of the cash, it was way beyond my initial expectations.

'Is everything all right, Miss Tregowen? Would you like the number of Mrs. Jago?'

What? Who the hell is Mrs. Jago?

'I'm sorry, Mr. Best, you'll have to excuse me. I'm just a bit taken aback by the amount of money,' I said distractedly, still trying to make sense of it.

'Oh, I see. Well, your grandmother was comfortable, and the bulk of the cash sum is from her life insurance, so it's not really surprising. Now, would you like me to put you in touch with Samantha Jago? Her office is just up the road, and she could probably even see you this afternoon, if you're quick.'

'Sorry, what? Who's Samantha Jago?'

'She's the estate agent—I think you would call her a realtor.'

'Oh, right, to sell the cottage, you mean?'

'Yes, exactly. I have the keys here,' he said, rummaging through an envelope clipped inside the file. 'Here you are. And let me find that number for you.'

He pulled out a drawer and seemed to sift through the contents, but it became clear he couldn't find what he was looking for.

'Hmm, I could have sworn … let me just call Laura—'

'Look, don't worry about it. Her office is nearby, you said, so I can just swing by.'

'Yes, yes, that's a splendid idea. It's just three minutes' walk up the High Street, on the corner—Jago Property Services, you can't miss it.'

I checked my watch—it was a quarter before five, so I should have time. My stomach chose that moment to grumble about the lack of food it had seen since this morning, and I gave Best a rueful smile.

'Excuse me, I haven't eaten since … God, not since breakfast on the plane. I need to get going so I can check out this Jago woman and then find somewhere to grab a bite to eat.'

'Of course, of course. Samantha will get you a good deal, I guarantee it. And the pub across the road from her office does excellent food.'

He picked up the house keys and walked around the desk, reaching over to pick up the envelope he'd left there.

'It was very nice to meet you, Miss Tregowen, and if there's anything else you need, please don't hesitate to let me know. My office can handle all the conveyance and contract matters on the house sale, so just give me a call … or I can arrange it all with Samantha—we've worked together many times.'

He smiled, handing me my inheritance, which I took, dropping the keys and envelope into my purse. He escorted me to the door, shook my hand and pointed me in the direction of the realtor.

I hurried up the road, which was lined with tourist stores, cafés and restaurants, until I came to Jago Property Services. I glanced at the display cards in the window advertising houses and apartments for sale and rent but didn't linger as I opened the door and entered.

There were four desks in the small space, three of which were occupied. Closest to me was a young woman, perhaps five years younger than myself, who looked up and smiled. On the opposite side of the room sat a much older man, with dark hair, greying at the temples, who was talking on the phone.

'Can I help you, madam?' asked the young woman brightly.

Behind her, the remaining person stood up. She was tall, her height accentuated by the coils of auburn hair piled on top of her head and the tailored pants suit she was wearing. Her pretty features radiated warmth as she smiled at me in seeming recognition.

'It's okay, Trudi, I've got this.'

She walked towards me, her hand held out.

'Hello, you must be Katherine Tregowen. I'm Samantha Jago. Please, won't you come in and take a seat?'

I took her hand, which she shook firmly and released, before leading me back to her desk.

'Well, news certainly travels fast in this town!' I exclaimed, arching an eyebrow at her as I sat down.

Her warm chuckle immediately put me at ease, and I found myself smiling back at the woman.

'Derek called me the minute you walked out the door—I've just put the phone down to him,' she explained.

I nodded in understanding just as my stomach growled loudly, once more reminding me that I needed to eat.

'Sorry, just ignore me—'

I stopped short as she held her hand up and then dipped down under the desk to pull out her purse.

'Let me buy you a late lunch—they do a fantastic steak and ale pie over at the Griffin, or the best fish and chips in Port Simon.'

She stood up and walked around the desk, motioning for me to join her. After a moment's hesitation—during which my stomach decided to answer for me—I got up as well and followed her through the office to the front.

'Alistair, can you lock up tonight, please? I'm taking Miss Tregowen across the road for a bite to eat, so I won't be back.'

We walked across the road and into the little pub opposite, where she led me straight to a quiet table at the back.

'This is very kind of you, Ms. Jago,' I said, breaking the silence for the first time since we'd left her office.

'No problem, you're a client. Besides, I'm hoping to make my money back, and then some. Oh, and call me Samantha ... or Sam, if you prefer.'

I smiled at her, liking her forthright attitude.

'Okay then, Sam. And I'm Kat.'

Before we could speak further, a tall, good-looking man with a mane of wavy reddish-brown hair approached the table, a wide grin on his face.

'Hey, Sam, how's it going?'

'Pretty good, actually. Josh, this is Kat Tregowen, a new client. Kat, this is my brother, Josh, who also happens to be the owner of this fine establishment.'

I turned and offered him my hand, which he took, shaking it as firmly as his sister had, and smiling down at me.

'It's a pleasure to meet you, Kat. And as you're an important client of my sister, and she's got a princess complex, I won't make her come to the bar to order. So, what can I get you?'

'Um, well, the fish and chips comes highly recommended.'

'Fish and chips it is ... and for you, m'lady?'

'Sod you, Josh, just bring me my usual! And we'll have two halves of Rattler to wash it down.'

'Your wish is my command, oh, precious one.'

Sam laughed, dismissing her brother with a wave of her hand.

'Um, Sam, what's Rattler?'

'It's a local cider ... you'll like it. Now, I understand you have a house you want to sell.'

'Oh, right ... yeah. Uh ... actually, Sam, I rather think I want to *buy* a house.'

Oh, fuck ... mouth, meet foot!

Chapter Two

'Let me get this straight: you want to buy Chimneys and do a complete refurb of the existing house?'

Samantha stared at me, one immaculately sculpted eyebrow raised in enquiry ... or maybe it was disbelief, I wasn't sure.

I cringed, knowing that what I was suggesting was the height of lunacy. And yet, even in the face of Sam's understandable derision, I couldn't seem to stop myself from outlining my crackpot scheme.

'Look, it's probably just a pipe dream, as I doubt I can even afford to buy the house, let alone pay for the repairs and refurbishment. The roof alone would probably cost thirty grand—'

'At least, Kat. Maybe more. And, what on earth do you want with a moldering old English pile anyway? Aren't you American?'

I sighed. It was, after all, a very reasonable question.

'Actually, I have dual nationality—my dad's English and I was born here, but my mom took me to the States when I was four. And it's true, my home is in San Francisco, and I'm not entirely sure why I want that house, I just ... do. There's a reason why I found it an hour before being handed a check for more than a quarter of a million pounds. Jesus, Sam, that's over four hundred thousand *dollars!* Plus, I've still got my grandmother's cottage, which I could live in while the work's being done on—what did you call it, Chimneys?—and then sell it for a hundred and eighty grand or so.'

'Ohh-kay.' She eyed me speculatively, probably weighing up her wish to warn me off a reckless venture against her desire to earn a substantial commission. 'Look, I hope you don't mind me saying this, and God knows the last thing I want to do is turn away a potential sale, but are you sure about this, Kat? Let's say you managed to get the house within the next month; the building work would take at least four months, probably more, considering the state the place is in. So, best case scenario, it's all done and dusted in six months. What then? Don't you have a job you need to get back to in America, or are you considering moving permanently to Cornwall? If not, what happens to the house—would you sell it, rent it? I know it's none of my business, but with the money from your grandmother, you could probably buy a really great flat, or condo, or whatever the hell you call it there. Or you could take a long, exotic holiday, buy a new car, and still have a nice little pot of money to put away for a rainy day. But that house … I hate to have to tell you this, but that house is trouble, and I wouldn't advise you to touch it with a ten-foot bargepole.'

'Trouble? What do you mean, Sam?'

She stared at me for a moment and then sighed, pushing her empty plate to one side. I'd only eaten half my food, but my appetite was gone, and I stacked my plate on top of hers.

'Look, Kat, before I go any further, you need to know that I'm not some flaky female who needs a man to change a tire, shrieks at the sight of spiders and has the screaming ab-dabs at the idea of things that go bump in the night. I don't believe in gods or ghosts, and I'm pretty sure that when you're dead, you're dead, okay?

'Having said all that, I've been in the property business long enough to know that some buildings have a tangible … atmosphere, for want of a better word. It's as if the walls absorb the life-force of the occupants, like a storage heater. I'm not a great believer in the so-called paranormal, but I'm open-minded enough to know that there's plenty of stuff in the world that is hard to explain scientifically.'

I couldn't help the small chuckle which escaped my lips, causing Sam to narrow her eyes at me.

'I'm sorry, Sam … but I get it; you're a skeptic when it comes to the afterlife. But what does that have to do with Chimneys?'

I was asking the question, but, if I was honest, I guess I already knew the answer. I'd felt it myself when I'd been there. I totally understood where Sam was coming from—we were extraordinarily like-minded in our general skepticism—but there was definitely something … *weird* going on in that house. I couldn't possibly define it in words, it was simply a … a *feeling*.

'Okay, okay, I just want to make sure you understand that what I'm going to tell you isn't coming out of superstition and fantasy.'

I nodded, gesturing for her to continue.

'Well, weird shit happens to people involved with that house. The last time anyone lived there was twenty or thirty years ago. A family called, uh, Ness or Nestor, or something. Apparently, they were only in the house for a week or two when the daughter—they had three kids, I think—fell down the stairs and wound up in hospital. Then a few days after that, the eldest boy somehow ended up with a kitchen knife through his hand, pinning him to the worktop. I can't remember the details now—I was only a kid when I first heard the story—but it was pretty damned serious, I think. There were some other unexplained accidents—which, I admit, could have been just that—but the parents also started complaining about freezing temperatures in some rooms, with ice forming inside windows and the thermometer dropping down below zero, right in the middle of a baking hot summer's day.

'The whole situation came to a head when the youngest child—a boy of four or five—fell down a well which had been sealed with a massive iron cap, weighing more than all three children put together. The father was at work, the mother was indoors with her daughter, who had a broken leg from her fall downstairs, and the boy with the cut hand was at school. There was no one else around, and by the time the mother came outside looking for the boy he had drowned in three feet of filthy, stagnant water.

'A police investigation inevitably looked at the mother, but without motive or opportunity, or viable forensics, they had no choice but to drop the case. The family left as soon as the funeral was over and were never heard of again. And no one else ever moved in."

I shook my head, drawing patterns with my finger in a small puddle of cider on the table.

'Nothing you've said so far points to any kind of conclusive evidence of … what are we talking about here, Sam? A haunting?'

She pursed her lips as I met her eyes.

'I know, you're right, but it's not just that. The big problem with the house is that it's pretty much useless as a development project. The property deeds have a number of water-tight covenants in place which prevent the house from being pulled down and replaced with multiple houses or flats. If the existing house is demolished, only another house of similar size and proportions can be built, and there's just not a big enough financial return.'

I found that hard to believe and the look on my face obviously telegraphed my thoughts to Sam.

'I know what you're thinking—a prime piece of land, just outside of popular Port Simon, with room to build a really beautiful five- or six-bedroom house—how can it not be worth doing?'

I nodded, glad that she'd been the one to state the obvious.

'You would think, wouldn't you? But land is expensive here, as it's being bought by developers who want to put up multiple dwellings—holiday flats and the like—which we've established can't be done in this case. Oh, a few have hired lawyers to try and overturn the covenants, but they've either been unsuccessful or something's happened to make them look elsewhere.'

'What do you mean, 'something's happened'?'

'Well, about fifteen years ago, some hotshot property speculator from London was buying up a lot of land across the whole of the southwest of England. It was boom time, and everyone thought they could get rich by jumping on the construction industry bandwagon— I'm guessing it was much the same in America … at least, until you guys fucked everything up with your sub-prime mortgage fiasco—'

'Oh, what, you mean the one that the British banks bought into with such enthusiasm?' I interjected, pursing my lips at her.

She waved her hand dismissively. 'Yeah, okay, whatever. Anyway, this guy gets wind of the Merrick place, which still had a roof at that time, and goes up there to take a look. Well, the agent is all over him like a cheap suit, the developer's talking about building a luxury block of flats, figures are being bandied about, and they're standing at the front of the house getting ready to shake on it.'

She paused dramatically, making me roll my eyes.

'Next thing they know, a huge piece of masonry falls from the roof, hitting the developer on the head and crushing his skull. Apparently, he was dead before he hit the ground.'

'Jesus, that's terrible … but, tragic and unfortunate as that was, it was still just an accident—'

Sam held her right index finger up.

'You say that, and maybe you're right, but when the police checked it out, they found that the lump of brickwork hadn't just been a loose piece waiting to topple, it was newly sheared off. And a very similar incident occurred not long after, but this time inside the house. A developer was looking over the property with his contractor and an agent, when a wrought-iron chandelier detached itself from the ceiling, practically impaling the guy.'

I couldn't suppress the gasp that escaped me, my hand flying up to my mouth.

'Oh my God, was he killed too?'

'No, but he was in intensive care for about a week before being transferred to a London hospital. Needless to say, no one ever saw him again. When the police looked at the chandelier, the cord was cut, not frayed. They searched the house for evidence of someone being there but found nothing. The point is, Kat, that even if you don't believe in ghosts, that house has bad karma, and everyone I know who's been there, including myself, has felt it. I'd honestly advise you just to forget about it. If you really want a house in Cornwall, I can find you something really special, something that doesn't come with a health warning.'

I shook my head. Maybe I was in denial.

'I believe you that that stuff happened, but I'm not sure I can accept what you say about karma and the supernatural. When I went inside today—'

'*What?!* You went *inside?!* What the hell, Kat?'

It was my turn to wave my hand dismissively.

'It was fine; I promise you. The back door was open, and I managed to get through the kitchen and into the foyer, although my way was blocked after that. The atrium has collapsed, which is probably what destabilized the rest of the roof and brought the whole damned thing down. But I didn't feel any of the things you describe; in fact, I have to say it was a pretty positive experience. I really like the house, Sam … there's just something about it that, oh, I don't know, calls to me, I guess. It could be so beautiful if it was restored. Obviously, it needs a detailed survey by an engineer, but from what I could see, even with the roof gone, the main structure seems pretty sound.'

Samantha stared at me as if I'd gone crazy—and maybe she was right. I decided not to mention the presence I'd felt in the house, which would definitely make her question my sanity.

'You had a positive experience, and you like the house?' She frowned, regarding me speculatively.

I could only offer a wry smile, hoping she would understand.

She sat back, and I could see the wheels turning in her head. The fact that she wasn't dismissing me and my ideas outright encouraged me to press my case.

'Look, Sam, I'm not a complete fool. I know I need to find out if I can even afford the house, and then get a survey done before I can make a final decision. If I do commit to the purchase, I'm hoping you can recommend a couple of good contractors to give me a price for the renovation. If the place is too far gone, then I'll just have to walk away. But I've got a really good feeling about it. Will you help me?'

Samantha blew out a breath, and I knew I had her.

'Okay, let's take this one step at a time. My understanding is that the house is owned by some kind of trust that was set up by the original owner. He was a local bigwig—I think the Merrick money originally came from the Cornish copper and tin mining industry, and he had the house built around the turn of the twentieth century. The whole family died during or just after the First World War and for a long time it was rented out. But there were always stories of strange goings-on, and it's been empty since the last family left—the people I told you about.

'The solicitors who administer the trust are based in Truro, so I'll give them a call and see what they say, and whether they're open to offers. The big question is, what's your bottom line? How much are you prepared to pay for that pile of trouble, Kat?'

I laughed at Sam's continued efforts to put me off. She really was unlike any realtor I'd ever met before.

'I don't really know, to be honest. I have no idea about house prices in the area—what would be your estimate of its value, based on your local knowledge?'

'Hmm, well, it's difficult to say, but if it was sympathetically restored to a reasonably high standard, I'd guess it would be around half a mil. As it stands? I reckon, at auction, you could probably get it for less than two hundred thousand.'

I mulled this over for a moment. If I could get it for, say, something in the region of a hundred and seventy-five thousand, and spend another two hundred thousand on the renovation, I would have myself a major asset. I looked up and met Sam's gaze.

'Okay, this is what I'd like you to do. Speak to the lawyers and ask them if they're still willing to sell and, if they are, find out if they have a ballpark figure. If that figure is below a hundred and seventy-five thousand, make the deal. If it's more, then offer them the hundred and seventy-five and see if they'll bite, but that's my limit, so if they play hardball, I'll just walk away.'

'Fine, I'll give them a call in the morning. I assume you'll be staying at your grandmother's cottage?'

I looked at my watch, realizing that it was too late to call anyone today, although, irrationally, I was irritated by the delay.

'Yeah, I guess. I need to have a look at it, and it will save on hotel bills. But you'll call them first thing, won't you, Sam?'

'I'll call *you* first, to make sure you haven't changed your mind. Once you've slept on it, you may well come to the conclusion that it's a really bad idea.'

There was a note of pleading in her voice, which troubled me, but I knew I wouldn't have a change of heart any time soon.

I reached across the table and put my hand over both of hers where they were clasped in front of her.

'I really do appreciate your concern, Sam, but I've made up my mind. Unless a deal can't be brokered, or there's an insurmountable structural problem, then I'm doing this, and nothing's going to stop me.'

She sighed in resignation. 'I can see you won't be dissuaded, so I'll make the call.'

'Good. Now, I need the number of a good structural engineer and a couple of reliable contractors. Then, while you're talking to the lawyers, I can start moving on everything else.'

Again, she sat back.

'The engineer's no problem. I know an excellent guy in Truro who could take a look for you. As for contractors … well, as it happens, my husband and I own a building company—he does most of the work on the properties my agency manages. I suppose I could ask him. I'm not keen on getting him involved, but he'd have my guts for garters if I didn't at least tell him about it. It's been a bit of a lean year, and a project like Chimneys would be a big deal. You will want competitive bids, of course, and there's another firm I sometimes use when Tom's busy, who I know would do a good job. Leave it with me, and I'll talk to Tom tonight. If he's interested, I'll ask him to call you—do you have a mobile number?'

'Um, well, I only have my US cell phone, so I'll need to buy one here or get a SIM card. Give me your business card, and I'll call you with the number as soon as I take care of it.'

She delved inside her purse and produced a cream-colored business card, which I slipped into my pocket.

'There's a Carphone Warehouse just up the street, and it's open until seven o'clock tonight. That way, you could call me at home on my mobile this evening. And maybe you can speak to Tom as well.'

'Great, I'll do that.'

I stood up and held out my hand.

'Thanks, Sam. I know you're a bit skeptical about this, so I appreciate your help all the more. I'll get a phone sorted and hopefully talk to you later.'

She stood and shook my hand. 'You're welcome ... I think. Besides, if this all goes through, then I'm going to be negotiating a bloody good commission from the lawyers. They've been trying to offload that house for years, so I'm hoping they'll make it worth my while.'

I laughed at her words, hoping that she would be able to get something out of this.

℘ℭℛ

'Hello ... Sam?'

'Hi, Kat. I see you got your phone sorted. I'll add this number to my contacts. Listen, I've talked to my husband and, as I predicted, he's really interested. Rather than talk on the phone, why don't we meet for a drink at the Griffin? We're just on our way out now. And, if he's not too busy, you could have a chat to my brother—he's sort of our local amateur historian and could probably tell you a lot more about the house than I can.'

'Oh, that sounds great. I was actually thinking about going to get something to eat since there's no food here and I didn't finish my meal earlier, so that'd work. If you haven't eaten, maybe you could join me?'

'Absolutely. Tom is a fiend for Josh's steak and ale pie, so we were going to have dinner there anyway.'

'Great. So, I'll see you there in, what, about half an hour?'

'Perfect, see you then.'

I ended the call and sat back in my grandmother's ancient armchair. I was more than pleased to have some company for the evening, as I was feeling inexplicably lonely, sitting here in Grandma's rather dark and dingy living room. It kind of had that old lady feel and musty smell about it, and I decided that it might be a good idea to talk to Tom about freshening this place up as well at some point. It definitely needed a new kitchen and bathroom before I could even think about selling it.

Half an hour later, I pulled into the parking lot at the rear of the pub. On the way there, I passed a used car lot, which reminded me that I needed to return the expensive rental I was driving and buy myself something to use while I was here. Of course, I first needed to see if my plans would come to fruition, but I couldn't rid myself of the idea that I was fated to buy the house which had so consumed my thoughts from the first moment I'd laid eyes on it.

Inside, the pub was moderately busy and there was a warm buzz of conversation and laughter, which immediately made me feel at home. I spotted Sam at the bar, standing next to a tall, well-built guy I assumed was her husband. As I closed the door behind me, he looked over and then nudged Sam, who turned and smiled.

'Hey, Kat, what can I get you?'

I walked over, feeling irrationally happy to see her.

'Hi, Sam! Let me get these.'

'You can get the next round. Now, let me introduce you to my husband, Tom. Tom, this is the lunatic I told you about earlier.'

I started turning toward the big guy beside her, but snapped back to look at her, wide-eyed. She simply arched an eyebrow, as if to say, 'Deny it if you can', and I couldn't help it—I burst out laughing. It was at that moment that I truly prayed I would have a reason to stay a while, as I just knew that I wanted to be friends with this woman.

Shaking my head, I turned back to Tom and held out my hand, which he completely enclosed in his large, calloused hand.

A huge grin lit up his face as he spoke in a soft Cornish burr. 'It's great to meet you, Kat, and it's a relief to discover that you're not a swivel-eyed mouth-breather who mumbles to herself and carries all her worldly possessions around in Tesco carrier bags.'

I smothered my giggles and gave him a stern look.

'Likewise, Tom. And it's a relief to *me* that you're not a hen-pecked runt who follows his wife around, drooling.'

Tom's eyebrows shot up, and he gave Sam a sharp look over my shoulder. I looked around to see her mouth fall open in shock, and winked at her.

'I never said—oh, you, you...' She pursed her lips and smacked me on the arm, making me laugh again.

Just then, I was distracted by giggles coming from the other side of the bar and glanced over to see a pretty blonde, grinning with delight. Her long, straight hair was parted in the middle and fell loose around her shoulders and down her back, and her clothes were an eclectic mix of colors and fabrics, which looked like they came straight from a thrift shop. The style she seemed to be going for was hippy chic.

'Ooh, I like you! I don't think I've ever met anyone who could render Samantha speechless. Hi, I'm Ruby.'

She thrust her hand across the bar, multiple bangles jangling, and I took it with a happy smile.

'Pleased to meet you, Ruby, I'm Kat—'

'Oh, we all know who you are—everyone's talking about you. You're the mad American who wants to buy the haunted house and go live with the heartbroken ghost of Lucien Merrick.'

'Ruby, do shut up, love, I'm trying to make some bloody money here!'

'The ghost of Lucien Merrick?' Perplexed, I looked from one to the other, but Sam just rolled her eyes at the girl.

'Don't worry, Sam, I have a feeling Kat's going to buy the house, so it's in the bag.' Ruby winked at me, and then headed off to serve another customer.

'Take no notice of her, she's an idiot who thinks she's descended from Cornish witches or something. She's always blathering on about that house and the *romance* of it all, silly cow.'

'She seemed really sweet.' I glanced back at her as she laughed at something a guy at the bar had said, but when I looked back at Sam, she was frowning.

'Don't you like her, Sam?'

Tom chose that moment to speak, before his wife could respond.

'Hey, Sammy, why don't you and Kat grab a table while I order the food?'

That seemed to put a stop to the conversation, so we chose our meals and settled ourselves down at a table near the back. After a minute's awkward silence while we waited for Tom to join us, Sam finally spoke.

'I'm sorry about that, Kat. I do like Ruby—we've been friends since school. Long story short, my brother's been in love with her since we were teenagers, and I know she's in love with him, but neither of them will do anything about it. Ruby used to say she didn't want to get tied down and spend the rest of her life in Port Simon ... she wanted to travel, see the world, she said. Well, she went to Australia, where she stayed for six months and then came back—I know it's because she missed Josh, and God knows, he was a complete drip while she was gone—but they just keep dancing around each other, seeing other people, who don't make them happy, and it drives me crazy that they won't just admit how they feel about each other.'

I nodded in understanding and sipped my drink.

'Anyway, enough of all that nonsense. Ah, here's Tom.'

I looked up as her husband walked over, tucking his wallet into his back pocket. Once again, they had refused to let me pay, citing the big profits I was going to make them.

'So, Kat, Sam tells me you've got your heart set on buying the Merrick place. She says you've been inside—which I'm here to tell you to never do again without the proper safety gear and someone accompanying you.' He looked at me sternly, and I nodded, knowing he was right.

'It *was* stupid, and I really should've known better, but I didn't go that far inside. The roof has almost completely collapsed over the central core, and I only got as far as the door from the kitchen to the stairwell.'

'Okay, I'll let you off this time. Now, I know Sam has explained about the covenants, but from what she's said, it seems you want to restore the house rather than pull it down or convert it.'

We continued to discuss my ideas, and I quickly realized that Tom knew exactly what he was talking about. Better still, he totally understood and agreed with my plans for the renovation. He made suggestions and offered ideas which were informed and useful and, as the evening wore on, I became convinced that I didn't really need to look farther than Jago Building Contractors. I was even more impressed when he insisted that I talk to the other guy Sam had recommended, just to make sure I'd be getting the best deal.

It was agreed that in the event she was able to broker a deal the following day with the lawyers, she'd see if she could obtain any plans of the house that might exist. This would enable me to start drawing up my own plans, which would allow Tom and his competitor to prepare their estimates for the job. We talked for so long that I completely lost track of time, and jumped when a loud bell rang, accompanied by Josh's shout of 'last orders.'

I looked at my watch, surprised to find that it was nearly eleven o'clock.

'You want another drink, Kat?' Tom asked.

'Not for me, thanks. I think I'm gonna get going. I want to be up early tomorrow, and it feels like I haven't slept for a week.'

I realized that I hadn't, in fact, slept for over thirty hours, what with the time difference, and I was suddenly overcome with fatigue.

Sam and Tom were leaving too, so we all left the pub together after saying our goodbyes. I was sorry that I hadn't had a chance to talk to Josh but hoped that I'd be able to speak to him the following day.

Outside, we parted ways, with promises to speak in the morning, and I gratefully climbed into the car to make the short drive back to my temporary home. I went straight to bed, thankful that I didn't even have to find the strength to climb stairs in the single-story house. It was either going to be a long and interesting day tomorrow, or a short and disappointing one. I sincerely hoped for the former, which was the last thought I had before falling into a deep, dreamless sleep.

Had I known that in the weeks and months ahead, peaceful slumber would become a rare and precious commodity, I might have been more appreciative.

Chapter Three

The following day became a blur of activity and phone conversations. While Sam made contact with the lawyers in Truro, I started the day by calling Simon Frayn, the engineer she had recommended. To my delight and relief, he couldn't have been more helpful, even when I explained that I wouldn't be able to give him a contract until I'd received confirmation from Sam that my offer had been accepted.

'No problem, Miss Tregowen. I'm free all afternoon, so why don't I meet you at Samantha's office at two o'clock? We could have a chat about what you need, talk terms, and then maybe go up to the house for an initial quick inspection. I'm familiar with the property, although I haven't seen it in years, so it will be interesting to look around.'

I readily agreed to the arrangement and ended the call.

Next on the list was the alternative contractor Sam had mentioned. Sadly, that encounter did not go as well as the first.

I called the number Sam gave me for Anstey & Son and, at first, all seemed to go well. I spoke to a Dave Anstey, apparently the 'Son' part of the deal, who was friendly and accommodating. When I told him that I was soliciting competitive bids for a major residential restoration project, he told me he was free right then, and invited me over to his office to discuss the project. I was encouraged that he wanted to meet at his place, as it meant he had no qualms about me seeing his operation, and promptly arranged to drive over right away.

Half an hour later, I was sitting across from Dave Anstey, who was staring at me as though I'd just sprouted horns and a tail.

'You wanner do up Chimneys? That shitty ol' wreck where two people was *killed* stone dead?' he asked, his voice laced with horror.

'Mr. Anstey—'

'It's 'aunted, y'know … by the ghost of Lucius Merrick, 'oo murdered the maid after 'e knocked 'er up, and then 'e murdered 'is own parents … went mad, they say … bin killing off anyone 'oo goes near ever since.'

He said it so matter-of-factly, his broad Cornish accent rendering his words faintly ridiculous, and I couldn't help it—I laughed, very loudly. If possible, his expression became even more horrified, as if there was a possibility that I, too, might be a crazy serial killer; I chose not to dwell on that. However, his ever-widening eyes were now starting to remind me of Joey from 'Friends', and just as I thought I had the laughter under control, I snorted, and it started all over again.

After watching me snigger and snort like a hyena on nitrous oxide for several minutes, his horror morphed into irritation, which finally quelled my amusement. Wiping my eyes, I shook my head at my own foolishness.

'I'm sorry, Mr. Anstey, please forgive me—I've no idea what came over me. I should tell you that I'm very aware of the history of the house, which I believe was owned by *Lucien* Merrick, but I don't believe in ghosts. I'm sure there's a very simple explanation for the various occurrences you mention, I don't know anything about any maids or murders, and I'm not particularly interested in gossip or hearsay.'

He huffed, clearly not mollified by my words.

'Call it wot yer like, all Oy's sayin' is, you should be careful … that there 'ouse, well, t'aint roight, not one bit. Plenny of other nice 'ouses you could spen' yer money on, an' Oy'd be glad o' the work. But not Chimneys. Let Tom Jago get 'is 'ead bashed in. Pro'lly won't do 'im no 'arm anyways, seein' as 'e's got shit fer brains … pard'n me French, Miss.'

His faintly hamster-like cheeks reddened slightly as he finished his little diatribe.

All I could do was shrug at his narrow-minded attitude. If that's how he felt, I couldn't force him to change his mind, and the last thing I needed was a jumpy contractor. If I was honest, it didn't really make much difference to me, as I was pretty sure I would prefer to work with Tom anyway.

'Okay, Mr. Anstey. I'm sorry you feel that way, but I appreciate your candor. Thanks for your time.'

I got up and held out my hand, which he shook without rising.

'Well, don't say yer 'aven't bin warned,' he murmured darkly.

'I won't, Mr. Anstey. Thank you.'

I left and got back in my car. As I started the engine, my phone rang and I scrabbled to retrieve it from my purse.

It was the call I'd been waiting for.

'Hey, Sam, any news?'

'I'll say! I'm pretty sure the chap I dealt with, Rupert Saxon, would have hugged me if we'd spoken face to face instead of over the phone. I've agreed a deal with him, and he's absolutely cock-a-hoop. He says he'll prepare the contract today and send it straight over to my office this afternoon.'

'Well, that's great … except you haven't told me how much yet,' I chuckled.

'Oh, shit, yeah. Well, I took a flyer and offered him a hundred and fifty thousand and asked him for a five thousand pounds finder's fee. I was sure he'd try to get me to up the offer or that he'd at least quibble about my fee, but he accepted, right off the bat.'

I was stunned. 'A hundred and fifty thousand pounds? Seriously? Wow, that's … wow. Jesus, Sam, I can't believe you got them to accept such a low offer. That's amazing.'

'I know! Am I a genius or what?'

I couldn't help laughing. 'Ha! Well, it sounds like it was more about his desperation to sell, rather than your stellar negotiation skills. But, whatever the reason, it's a damned good deal for both of us. Thanks, Sam, that's fantastic news, and I'm really glad you made some money out of it.'

'To be honest, I can't believe it was so easy. I think you're right about them being desperate.'

We spoke for several more minutes, and Dave Anstey appeared in the doorway of his shabby little builder's office, gazing at me dolefully.

'Look, Sam, I better go. I'm parked in Anstey's yard and he's just given me the brush off. Simon Frayn has asked to meet me at your office at two o'clock, before we head up to the house, and I need to get myself some safety gear first. Did he call you about it?'

'Yeah, it's fine—I've got a small meeting room you can use. Do you know where you're going to get your safety clothing?'

'Yeah, he mentioned a building supply store up on the main road, and I'm going there now. Do you think there's any chance Tom could meet us at the house, say about three o'clock?'

'I'm sure he can—I'll give him a call and I'll see you back here in a bit. Do you want to grab lunch before Simon arrives?"'

'Sure, that would be great—but this time, *I'm* paying. I'll see you at one.'

I ended the call, giving Anstey a cursory wave, and reversed out onto the road.

℘℃℞

I smiled up at Ruby as she placed two chicken Caesar salads in front of Sam and me.

'There you go, ladies. Josh is still with the accountant, but he says he should only be another fifteen minutes or so, and then he'll be happy to join you. *Bon appétit!*'

She winked at me, and went back behind the bar, leaving us to enjoy our lunch.

'So, as I was saying, the contract arrived by courier about twenty minutes before you arrived, and I've sent it straight up to Derek. He says he'll go over it as soon as he can and call you this afternoon or tomorrow morning. Rupert sent over the house plans as well, so you can look at them when you meet Simon.'

'Wow, that was damned quick, Sam! I still haven't had a chance to deposit my inheritance check into the bank yet. I don't suppose there's a branch of Citibank anywhere around here is there?'

'In Port Simon? Christ, no. I doubt there's even one in Truro … or in the whole of Cornwall, come to that. You'll probably have to go to London.'

I nodded, unsurprised. I needed to make a trip back to London to see my dad and return the rental car, so I could kill a number of birds with one stone.

Sam checked her watched and looked back up at me.

'We better get going; Simon will be arriving at my place any minute.'

Standing along with Sam, I signaled to Ruby that we were leaving, and asked her to let Josh know I'd catch up with him later.

Crossing the road, we arrived back at Sam's office just as a tall, dark-haired man approached us.

'Hello, Cousin—long time, no see. How are you?' he asked, coming to a halt in front of us.

Sam grinned and stepped forward to hug him. 'Hey, Si, I'm great. You look well.'

As we all walked in, I couldn't help looking from one to the other, seeing absolutely no resemblance. 'Are you two related?'

Sam smiled and nodded. 'Yeah, our dads are brothers, but Josh and I take after our mother. Anyway, enough of the family reunion. Simon, this is Kat Tregowen, the proud new owner of Chimneys.'

'Kat, nice to meet you. And did I hear right? You've had your offer accepted?'

I grinned up at him as I shook his hand. 'Yes, the contract is with my lawyer, Derek Best. So, it's all systems go—I need that survey done before I sign the contract, Simon.'

'Okay, let's take a look at this house of yours, then. Do you have any drawings?'

Sam walked across to her desk and picked up a small pile of folded plans, which she held up for me to see.

'Let's make ourselves comfortable in the meeting room, where we can spread these out. Trudi, could you get us some coffee, please?'

With that, Simon and I followed Sam into the small adjoining conference facility, where she immediately unfolded the plans for us to study.

Thereafter, the afternoon seemed to fly. Once we'd had a good look at the layout of the house on paper, Simon and I quickly agreed on terms, and we then set off for the house in his car. Sam stayed behind, citing pressure of work, but assured me that Tom would meet us there. True to his word, when we arrived, a dark blue pickup was already parked outside, and as we pulled up beside it, Tom climbed out to greet us both.

I followed Simon around to the trunk of his car to collect the hard-hat and safety goggles I'd bought that morning, along with my new high-visibility jacket, and tightened the laces on my new steel-toed boots, which I'd put on before we headed out. We all then trooped across to the back door and went inside.

All in all, we spent about two hours looking around. Tom had brought some hand-held, high-powered halogen lamps, and, using his brute strength, was able to push open the kitchen door a lot wider than I'd been able to achieve the day before. With the benefit of the lights, and Tom and Simon working together to clear a path through the debris, we were able to investigate much farther, although we were still confined to the first floor. Getting upstairs was out of the question according to Simon, and both Tom and I were inclined to agree.

The basement, however, proved to be far more accessible. Simon was impressed with the state of the floor at ground level and when we opened the basement door, we found a stone stairway leading down into the dark void.

I'd be a liar if I didn't say that I viewed the black maw of the entrance with some trepidation, but my companions seemed to have no such qualms, so I took a deep breath and followed them down.

Underground, the air was chilly and stagnant, but any concerns I may have harbored were quickly dispelled as Tom swept his flashlight from side to side. Excitement fluttered in my stomach as I slipped past him and twirled slowly around, letting my own lamp illuminate the far nooks and crannies of the massive room.

'Oh, wow, guys, this would make an amazing media and playroom. There would be room for a bar, a home movie theater, pool table and other games, plus I could have two or three sofas over there.'

I could barely contain my delight as I thought about all the possibilities for this fantastic space and, when my eyes met Tom's, I could see that he was on exactly the same page, making me grin widely at him.

Simon was over by one wall, casting his light up and down as he walked slowly around the room.

'How's it looking, Simon?' I asked, mentally crossing my fingers.

He stopped and walked back toward me.

'We obviously need to get proper lighting in here and the rest of the house, but I can tell you now that I'm not seeing anything serious. Let's take a look outside.'

I nodded, and he and Tom headed back up the stairs, leaving me to follow, and I fully intended to be right behind them. Taking a step towards the exit, I felt that now-familiar touch against my cheek. I became aware that the air around me had turned frigid, making my breath visible and forcing me to pull my thin jacket around me. There was an overpowering sense of something—or someone—being in the room with me, but when I swung around with my light, I could see nothing.

I turned full circle, looking up the stairs to find that Simon and Tom had already disappeared from sight through the basement door. Again, I took a step, and this time I could have *sworn* that I felt the touch of a cold finger trail across my skin.

'Kat? Are you coming?'

Was that a cool breath on my neck?

'Kat, what are you doing?'

Tom appeared at the top of the stairs, and I was finally able to move.

'Uh, yeah, I was just having a final look around. I'll be right there.'

Back upstairs, the guys gave me a quizzical look, but I just ignored them, moving past them to retrace our steps to the outside.

We spent another half an hour checking the external brickwork, but were once again stymied by the overgrown foliage, much as I'd been yesterday. We agreed that Tom would get a team out there the following day to start clearing as much of the undergrowth as possible. With that arranged, we decided to call it a day and head back to the pub to work further on our plan of action.

Climbing into Simon's car, I tried hard to push away the ridiculous notion that I'd heard something down in that dark basement—a single, whispered word.

Stay.

₭℞

DING! DING!

I jumped at the sound of the bell, as Ruby announced that it was closing time in the pub. It was late, and only a few stragglers remained as I sat with Sam, Tom and Josh. Simon had left a couple of hours ago, and I was amazed at how late it was, and how much I'd had to drink. We'd all had dinner together while discussing my ideas for the house, and Simon had offered me a workspace and drawing board at his office so that I could make a start on preparing a working set of plans.

Now, as the pub quieted and Ruby locked up, Josh smiled across at me.

'So, Sam tells me you wanted to know a little bit about the history of Chimneys, Kat.'

I nodded enthusiastically, keen to know why that beautiful house had been tarnished with such a macabre reputation.

'Well, as I think Sam has already told you, it was built by a local big-wig, Lucien Merrick, whose family struck it rich during the heyday of tin and copper mining back in the eighteenth century, although Merrick had the foresight to diversify into the import-export business when Cornish mining began to fail in the late nineteenth century. He and his wife had a son, also called Lucien, who was born in 1899, and he was apparently the apple of their eye. They had big plans for him to go to university, marry into a good family and take over the business, but then it all went a bit pear-shaped.'

I frowned at him. 'Pear-shaped?'

'Sorry, yeah, so, uh, it all started to go wrong. For a start, there was the war, which everyone had said would be over by Christmas of 1914, but we all know that didn't happen. Of course, Lucien Junior would have been too young to fight at first, and even when they brought in conscription in 1916, the Government initially promised that teenagers wouldn't be sent to the front. I imagine Lucien's parents would have felt secure in the knowledge that their son wouldn't be called up.'

'So, he didn't go to France, then?' I asked, assuming he had died at home, as Sam had indicated.

'Well, not at first, but as far as the Merricks were concerned, they had a bigger worry, because it seems their boy took a shine to one of the maids.'

Tom chuckled and slapped the table, startling me.

'Ha, a bit of upstairs-downstairs rumpy pumpy, eh, the dirty dog!'

Sam jabbed her husband with her elbow and scowled at him.

'Shut up, you perv, and let him finish. I didn't know any of this.'

Josh rolled his eyes at his brother-in-law before looking back at me.

'Anyway, it seems that young Lucien was utterly smitten, and his parents were not happy at all. In those days, it wouldn't have been such a big deal for someone like him to have a bit of a roll in the hay with the help, but quite another to fall in love—which is apparently what happened.'

I held my hand up to stop him.

'How the hell do you know all this, Josh?'

'Ah, well, I've always been fascinated with Chimneys since I was a kid, and then, when I was older, I did a lot of research into the history of the area, in which the Merrick family featured prominently because of the mining aspect. As I'm sure you know, libraries can be a rich source of information on local history, and I actually found a small volume in Port Simon Library, which was a contemporary account of the period. It was written after the war by a Port Simon resident who was acquainted with the Merricks, and because they were all dead, he obviously had no qualms about putting into print what he knew about it.

'So, from what I've read and been able to find out, the maid was sent away—all indications are that she was pregnant. I imagine Lucien's parents assumed that he'd just get over the girl—you know, out of sight, out of mind. But they underestimated his feelings for her, and he was furious. He demanded to know where she was, saying he was going to find her, so they told him she died of scarlet fever—a common enough occurrence in those days, especially for the poor. By now, it's the summer of 1918, and the next thing they know, he's enlisted in the army, apparently telling them he'll never forgive them before leaving for France.'

I felt myself become unexpectedly emotional, a lump forming in my throat as I thought about the heartbroken young man who'd fallen in love but been so thwarted by his unthinking parents.

'S-so, what happened? Did … did the girl really die?' I whispered, feeling foolish as my voice cracked. 'Did he know she was pregnant?'

'Ah, well, that's the shitty thing. Lucien survived the war but, by all accounts, he was a broken man. Just weeks before the Armistice, he'd been caught in some kind of gas attack, which left him physically and mentally scarred and with a serious respiratory condition. He was eventually shipped back from France to a military hospital in Kent, returning to Cornwall in early 1919. But his homecoming was anything but happy, because when he arrived home he found that his father had died of the flu and his mother was sick. Unfortunately, there was only the cook and a rather hopeless scullery maid left, as the butler had died, the chauffeur had been called up and killed in France, and the parlor maid had gone to work in a munitions factory in Plymouth, never to return.

'It seems it all went downhill pretty quickly, with Lucien's mother dying within days of his return. He, of course, was already hugely compromised because of what happened to him in France, and he succumbed to his injuries not long after. It's pointless to speculate whether or not he knew his girl was pregnant.'

I clapped my hand over my mouth to stifle a sob, surprising myself at the depth of my sorrow for this young man who had died more than a hundred years ago. Beside me, Tom reached over and gave my shoulder a squeeze, and I turned to give him a watery smile of gratitude for the small gesture of comfort.

Composing myself, I turned back to Josh.

'So, that was it, he never found out about her?'

He shrugged, but I could see from the sparkle in his eyes that there was more.

'I'm afraid that was all I could find out locally. But being the curious bugger that I am, I did try to delve a bit deeper, and it's amazing what you can find on the internet these days. I started looking at old census returns, parish records, and so on. I found a few possible leads, but ... well, it was only when you turned up yesterday that something clicked, and I went back to look at my research.'

'What does my arrival here have to do with anything?' I asked, giving him a quizzical look.

He smiled and held his hand up.

'Patience, Kat. Now, where was I? Oh, yeah. There was one family that was very much linked to the Merricks and so I checked back through my documentation. One girl stood out as a likely contender for Lucien's disgraced maid. She disappeared from Port Simon in 1918, but reappeared again in 1919, just after Lucien's death. I found parish records which indicated that she applied for Poor Relief for herself and her daughter, Sarah, who was apparently three months old. From the 1911 census, I discovered that her father had been the Merricks' butler—the one who died just before Merrick Senior—and that her mother was the cook, who had stayed on to look after Mrs. Merrick. After Lucien Junior died, she would have been out of a job. She also had two sons, who show up on the 1911 census as living with their grandparents, but the elder of the two was killed in the war. I don't know what happened to her after that, but it's possible she might have got another job as a cook or housekeeper.

'But then the daughter turns up, with a child, but still going by her maiden name. I had to wonder why she would come back to a place where her shame would be well known, when her father was dead and her mother had moved, presumably taking the girl's younger brother with her. What drew her back here?'

I found myself leaning across the table, hanging onto Josh's every word.

'And?' I prompted him impatiently.

'And I guess we'll never know for certain, but I like to think that she came looking for Lucien, perhaps hoping that he would take care of her and their daughter.'

I sat back, an expletive hovering on my lips.

'Fuck, Josh, I thought...' Truth be told, I had no idea what I thought, because no matter what the reason for the girl's return, there was never going to be a happy ending for her and Lucien.

'And that's it, end of story?' I asked, frustrated.

'Not quite. I did a bit more digging yesterday and found that Lucien's sweetheart died in 1930, when their daughter would have been just twelve years old.'

I gasped, amazed at the devastation I felt at the death of that poor, benighted young woman.

'What about their little girl?' I managed to ask, dreading his response.

'Ah, now that's where things start to look up a little. It seems she was taken in by her uncle and his family—the maid's younger brother. It looks like he returned to the area as an adult and married a local girl. There was a remarkably fortunate outcome for the child in the end. I kept checking through the births, deaths and marriages records, knowing that anything could have happened to her, but it looks like she got lucky. It seems she married a man called John Brodie in 1937.'

'Oh, my God ... are any of her family still here?' I asked, suddenly feeling excited.

'I don't think so—certainly not any Brodies. I'm afraid the trail goes cold after that. They must have left the area, as I can't find any other Brodies. It's not a Cornish name, so he could have been a visitor, just passing through. To find out any more, you'd need to get hold of the marriage certificate to find out where he lived and who his parents were.'

Before I could voice my disappointment, Sam smacked Josh's arm, hard.

'Ow! Fuck, Sam, what was that for?' he exclaimed.

'For leading us up the bloody garden path, you git! What the hell was all that about Kat giving you the connection?'

'Oh, yeah, well, that's the weird thing about all this. You see, the girl that Lucien Merrick fell in love with was called Catherine Tregowen.'

Chapter Four

'Kath—' I tried to speak, but the words wouldn't come … my voice just cracked and broke, rendering me mute.

In a flash—or so it seemed—Ruby was beside me, holding out a glass of water. I took it gratefully, chugging back the cool liquid, and easing my suddenly parched throat.

Sam leaned across, reaching out her hand.

'Are you okay, Kat? You've gone awfully pale. But that *was* a bit of a shocker, I have to admit.'

Taking another sip of my water, I was finally able to compose myself after Josh's startling revelation, and I now turned back to him.

'I don't know what to say, Josh … that's pretty spooky. Are you sure?"

'Absolutely. Her father was Nathaniel Tregowen and her mother was Mary. They had three children, Albert, Catherine—with a C—and Matthew.'

I swallowed, still trying to make sense of what he was saying.

'So, what does it all mean? Do you think we're related?'

'I don't know, Kat … but it probably wouldn't be that hard to find out. Do you want me to do some more digging?'

'I, uh … jeez, I don't know. This is kind of freaking me out right now. Let me think about it, okay?'

'Of course, no problem. Just let me know if you want me to keep digging—or I could show you what to do if you'd rather check it out for yourself.'

'Okay, let's leave it at that for the moment. Look, I'm pretty wiped out so I'm going to call it a night.'

Everyone nodded and we all got up to leave. As soon as I stood, though, I immediately became aware of just how much I'd had to drink and was grateful when Sam, who hadn't been drinking, offered to give me a ride home. It was agreed that Tom would pick me up the following morning and bring me back to get my car. He would then go on to start the necessary clearance works at the house, while I drove back to London to see my dad and deposit my inheritance check, which was burning a hole in my pocket.

'You bought a house? In Cornwall? What the bloody hell, Kat?'

As I had suspected, my dad was less than enthusiastic about my news—and I hadn't even told him about the state the place was in yet.

'Why wouldn't I buy a house? I thought you'd be glad I'm going to be around a bit more.'

He got up from the table, where we had just finished eating dinner, and went to the sideboard to pour himself a glass of his favorite malt whisky. I heard him sigh and watched as his shoulders slumped a little before he turned and came back to the table.

'I'm glad you're thinking about staying for a while, Kat, of course I am, but Cornwall is hardly round the corner. What possessed you to buy a property there? It's not like you're thinking of settling there … is it?'

'I don't know, Dad … maybe?'

'What? But why? It's not exactly the best place to practice architecture … hell, I don't even know if you'd get any work down there. Are you aware that it has one of the highest rates of unemployment in the country? If you've spent your inheritance on a house in Port Simon, what are you going to live on? And what about your job in San Francisco?'

I huffed out a breath, unsure how to answer him. I mean, how the hell could I explain that the house simply … called to me? And, quite honestly, I didn't need Nick Tregowen telling me I was crazy, because I already knew that.

'I'm going to ask for a leave of absence from work—I've been busting my ass for the last three years, and I need a break. Grandma's money will allow me to do that. And I didn't spend all of it on the house, nowhere near, although I will have to, well, spend quite a bit of it on the, uh, renovation.'

He arched any eyebrow at me, squinting his other eye slightly, a look I knew well from my teenage years … like he was trying hard to figure me out.

"So, how much did you pay for this house, and how much is it going to cost to *renovate* it?" I could practically see the air quotes in his tone.

'Uh, well, it was a hundred and fifty grand, and I guess I'll need to spend about the same amount to bring it back to a habitable condition.'

'A hundred and fifty thousand *pounds*? What is it, a two-bed bungalow, or something? And how the hell can it cost another hundred and fifty thousand to do it up?'

'Um, no, it's a six-bedroom, double-fronted Victorian manor house. I've been told it could be worth in excess of half a million once the work's complete.

He shook his head and knocked back the rest of his whisky.

'Shit, Kat, it sounds like a bloody money pit! If you got it so cheap, there must be a hell of a lot wrong with it—is it even structurally sound?'

I rolled my eyes—I couldn't help it.

'Please don't worry, Dad. I got it for a good price because it's been empty for so long and, yeah, it does need a lot of work, but it's nothing I can't handle. I've got a good engineer on board as well as a highly recommended contractor, and I'll still have plenty of money left over from Grandma's bequest, even before I sell her cottage. It really is a great investment, Dad, you'll see.'

He gazed at me for a moment and then shrugged.

'Okay, fair enough. I'm not trying to tell you your business, I just … well, I just don't want you to fall on your arse, that's all. I'm your father, it's my job to worry about you.'

I grinned, reaching over to grab his hand where it lay on the table.

'Thanks, Dad, your support means a lot to me. And just wait until you see it, you'll love it.'

He nodded, saying nothing, but I didn't miss the concerned look he gave me.

℘℃

I returned to Cornwall a couple of days later in my dad's Land Rover. I would probably buy a car of my own, but he said I could use his spare car until I decided whether I was definitely staying, as he mostly used cabs in London and had his Bentley if he needed a vehicle. I'd opened an account at a bank which had branches in Cornwall, depositing the check from Grandma's estate and arranging for payment to be transferred to the lawyers once it had cleared and the contract had been signed.

Everything was in place, and I once again felt the inexorable pull to return to Cornwall.

That morning, over breakfast with my dad, I had considered broaching the subject of our ancestors, to see if he could shed any light on Catherine Tregowen and her ill-fated relationship with Lucien Merrick. However, it occurred to me that if he knew about our connection to the house, he might really start questioning my ability to make sane decisions, so decided to leave well enough alone for the time being.

Back in Port Simon, the pace of activity seemed to go into overdrive, and there were times during the ensuing weeks when it felt like I was hurtling down an endless helter-skelter.

As soon as I got back, I went to see Derek Best to sign the contract before heading to Truro. Having agreed terms and appointed Simon as my engineer he set me up with a drawing board in his office, and I quickly completed the new plans for the house, together with a detailed specification of fixtures and fittings. These I handed to Tom as soon as they were ready, and he wasted no time in pricing the whole job. I wanted a high-quality result, which didn't come cheap, but his costs were fair and I was more than happy to sign him up to do the work.

With all the legal matters settled, Tom immediately erected the necessary scaffolding and made a start on clearing out the rubbish and debris from the house. He'd already cut back all the foliage from the structure, making the place look a lot bigger. He'd covered the roof with tarps and installed temporary lighting, allowing Simon to carry out a proper survey.

In the meantime, I finally had to bite the bullet and call my boss in San Francisco. Brad Robinson had taken a chance on me straight from college, and I had a lot to be grateful for. I loved working for Robinson Design, where we specialized in residential construction, with particular emphasis on remodeling vintage properties. I'd never worked on anything like Chimneys, of course, but I had been responsible for renovating a couple of houses in San Francisco that dated back to the turn of the twentieth century. The experience was going to be really useful when it came to my own project, but I was dreading breaking the news to Brad that I wouldn't be returning any time soon.

As expected, he wasn't happy, but, while I had good reason to be thankful to him for the opportunity he'd given me when I was starting out, I felt that he also owed me. I had worked my butt off for the firm, rarely taking holidays and gaining a lot of respect in the industry, both for myself and, by association, for Brad's company. Inevitably, he tried to change my mind, first by yelling and then by begging, but I was used to his M.O. and it fell on deaf ears. In the end, we compromised, as we usually did, and he granted me four months off—two months less than I had asked for—and I agreed we would review things at the end of that period. I knew this wouldn't give me time to fix up the house, but I would cross that bridge when I came to it.

Next, I called my mom. She had married my stepfather, Jose Sanchez, ten years earlier. He was a wine buyer for a national supermarket chain, and they traveled a lot. When she answered her phone, it was clear she was in a bit of a rush, and she explained that the two of them were on their way to the airport to fly to Miami. I was relieved, in a way, because it meant that I wouldn't have to go into too much detail. My mom had always been a pretty easygoing person, so I knew she wouldn't question my choices, but it was clear she was a little concerned that I might be considering moving back to the UK permanently. I couldn't make any promises, one way or the other, but I assured her that I would keep in touch and let her know what I was doing. On the other end of the line, I could hear Jose calling out to her, so I let her go, knowing that she would probably call me as soon as they arrived in Florida.

With a new sense of freedom, I plunged myself into the work at Chimneys, reveling in my role as project manager on a job which was so personal. In truth, Tom was a fantastic contractor, and his team was making great progress. Simon had come back to me with the results of the structural survey, which showed that the house was as sound as he'd originally observed. It was a miracle, really, considering the level of decay, but I was more than happy to take the results and run with them.

My goal was to make at least part of the house as habitable as possible so that I could move in before the work was complete. Tom expressed concerns about it but, as each day went by, my need to be *in* the house became ever greater. Unable to dissuade me, it was agreed that he would concentrate on getting a roof installed. This would then allow the plumbing and electrics to be done, the kitchen and a downstairs shower room installed, and one of the two main reception rooms brought to a point where I could use it as a living room/bedroom combo.

Work progressed rapidly, and when I wasn't on site, I found myself drawn into Josh's continued investigation of the Merricks and, in particular, my similarly named ancestor, Catherine Tregowen and her daughter.

I had never taken much interest in where I came from outside of my immediate family. Now, however, I discovered a hunger for knowledge about my long-lost relatives which astounded me. Josh drew up a basic family tree, to which he constantly added more information. When I wasn't at the house, I spent hours poring over old census returns, searching through parish records and wandering around local cemeteries. As Josh had explained, Lucien and Catherine's daughter, Sarah, disappeared from all the records after her marriage to John Brodie, but then he suggested I start looking through maritime passenger lists. He told me that, just like the Irish, a lot of Cornwall's poor had emigrated in the latter part of the nineteenth century and early twentieth century, either to Australia, New Zealand or, in some cases, Canada.

With renewed enthusiasm, I decided to spend an evening online checking passenger lists to the Antipodes. I knew that Sarah and John had married in 1937, so, starting from that point, I decided that if they had left Cornwall, it would have probably been sometime within the two years preceding the Second World War

I felt like a detective following a lead, and began my search with an excited, fluttery sensation in my stomach. After a couple of hours of staring at the screen, however, my eyes began to ache, and I could feel my excitement waning. Quite frankly, I was astonished at how many sailings there had been before the war, and the vast number of people who were so disenchanted with life in Britain that they were willing to risk all in a new country thousands of miles away, from which it was unlikely they would ever have the means to return.

Glancing at my watch, I noted with shock that it was nearly midnight, and I needed to be up early the next day to supervise the new roof going on. Debating on whether to just pack it in for the night, I decided to try one more search—this time for emigration to the US. Josh had said that few of those leaving Cornwall in the early part of the twentieth century had gone to America, but I decided it was worth a try. Typing "Brodie" into the search box, I watched with amazement as it flashed up "3 results". I felt my heart rate pick up as I gazed at the screen—there they were: John Brodie, Sarah Brodie and Lucien Brodie sailed from Southampton to New York on December 3, 1938.

'Oh, my God, they had a kid … and they called him Lucien!' I whispered into the semi-darkness of the room.

I couldn't help the grin that spread across my face. I felt like I'd unearthed a family treasure, and all I wanted to do was call someone—Josh, Sam, my dad … anybody. My next thought was that I needed to get Lucien Brodie's birth certificate and then start my search for the family in America. But it was late, and I had to content myself with printing the record and slipping it into the growing file on the table. Before logging off, I clicked on the website's public message board and left a note asking for any information on the Brodie family from Cornwall. It was a long shot, but worth a try, and for now, it would have to do. Tomorrow was going to be a busy day, but I would talk to Joshua and get his advice on my next move.

℘)෬

Over the ensuing days and weeks, I was at the house more often than not. I soon discovered that my favorite time was when everyone had departed and I could revel in the quiet. During the day, when the place was a hive of noisy activity, all I thought about was what was happening around me and what needed to be done. Come five o'clock, though, once the guys had packed up and left, I would wander through the first floor of the house and let that odd feeling of comfort surround me, just as it had from the very first moment I'd pushed through the broken back door.

There was, as yet, no staircase to the second floor, the old one having been torn out, and access to the upper story rooms was still confined to ladders and scaffolding. I longed to get up there but when I was alone, I couldn't afford to risk it. However, the floors were gradually being replaced, and the new staircase would be going in soon. I was impatient for the work to be completed but knew there was nothing to be gained by forcing the pace of the renovation. I wanted it to be done right—for this beautiful house to rise, like a phoenix from the ashes and, once more, be a stunning and comfortable home.

I was already nearing the end of the time allotted to me by Brad and I knew that if he insisted upon my return at the end of the four months, I would have to resign. There was just no way I could leave before the work was fully completed. Even if it could be finished in time, I had no intention of letting someone else live here—at least, not for the foreseeable future.

So, here I was, on an evening like any other, standing in the spacious foyer of my house. *My house!* I gazed up at the new glass atrium, through which the last of the evening sun streamed, illuminating the whole space and painting it gold. It had been expensive, and Tom had argued that a large skylight would work just as well and be a lot cheaper. Nevertheless, I had insisted that I wanted to replace as much of the original structure as possible, so the budget was stretched to allow for the specially made toughened glass and steel installation.

Beneath my feet, in gaps between the temporary protective boarding that had been laid, was a beautiful Victorian mosaic-tiled floor. It had only come to light when all the debris had been cleared away, and, again, I had insisted that it should be preserved and restored where necessary. This had also been outside Tom's original costs, once again hiking up the budget, but, to me, it was worth it.

Now, with the roof in place and the downstairs rooms in the process of being plastered, it wouldn't be long before I could move in. The new kitchen was arriving later in the week, and the downstairs shower room was already installed, with just the tiling to finish.

I walked across to the large room on the right, which would eventually become my library and study. It spanned the entire width of one end of the house from front to back and would have a wall of glass doors opening onto the back yard. For now, it was going to be my living space and bedroom, and I already had a bed on order.

I went over to the workbench which was used for holding lengths of wood in place for sawing and sat down. Gazing around me, I could already see how the room would look, with hand-built, oak shelving lining the walls, comfortable sofas facing the windows and a large oak desk in front of the glass doors overlooking the terrace, landscaped garden and pool at the rear.

I closed my eyes and waited.

I would rather eat my own foot than admit to anyone just why it was I felt compelled to hang around after the guys had left.

Similarly, if anyone had asked me if I believed in ghosts, I would tell them emphatically that I did not.

And yet...

Suddenly, the atmosphere in the room changed. It was subtle at first and, if I hadn't become so attuned to it over these past weeks, I might not have noticed. But I could feel my scalp tingle and the hairs on my arms and the back of my neck stand up as the temperature dropped. The house was now watertight and draft-free, but I could nevertheless feel a cool waft of air against my skin where my hair was pulled up in a high ponytail. I knew it was foolish, but it almost seemed like someone was blowing gently on my neck, and it sent a thrill of both pleasure and fear right through me. As each day had gone by the pleasure had grown and the fear had receded.

With my eyes clamped shut, I let myself be overtaken by pure sensation. I couldn't explain it any more than I could rationalize it. It was like ... oh, God, I don't know—like being touched, but not in any true sense of the word. My skin felt alive, every follicle alert. I pulled my jacket closed over my chest as the cold hit my breasts— and that's when I heard it. From somewhere behind me, a rough, almost animalistic moan punctuated the silence.

In an instant I was on my feet, swinging around to see what could have made such a noise. My heart hammered inside my chest, and I fought to control my breathing. For the first time, I noticed how much the light had faded, the corners of the room receding into shadow, as my eyes darted frantically from wall to wall.

There was nothing to see, of course, but I was shaken to the core. I couldn't explain why—it wasn't like I hadn't imagined feeling and hearing things before, but this somehow seemed more tangible, more real, and I couldn't control the dread that filled me. I started to walk backward, the fear that I had tamped down now powering through me as I tried to make sense of what had just happened. I quickly decided that discretion was the better part of valor and turned to leave. As if I needed any further inducement, a sudden cold breeze enveloped me, and I found myself practically running for the open doorway.

But before I could reach it, the breeze picked up, swirling and lifting the sawdust on the floor, and the door, which was standing open against the wall, blew shut with an almighty bang.

I screamed, the sound echoing around the empty room.

Flinging myself at the door, I grabbed the old brass knob and yanked at it, forgetting to turn it in my panic.

'Oh fuck, oh fuck, oh fuck!' I chanted.

Catherine…

I froze. The word was so soft it was barely a sound at all, but I knew what it was.

Slowly, I turned around, staring into the darkening room.

'W-what do you w-want?' I managed to stutter, my voice hardly more than a whisper.

I felt it then, just like the very first time—the sensation of cool fingers drifting across my cheek.

Catherine…

That was it. I turned back to the door, gripped the knob and turned it. It gave immediately and I wrenched the door open, running across the foyer and out the main door, adrenalin spiking through my bloodstream. I slammed it shut behind me and hurried to my car, fumbling for the keys in my pocket.

Pulling the door open I quickly climbed in, taking a moment to calm my thudding heart before starting the engine. Glancing at the house, I could see that all was quiet, all was normal, and I had to wonder at my extreme reaction. I knew I needed to get away in order to rationalize what had just happened, so made an erratic U-turn and sped up the drive to the road. I headed straight to the Griffin—there was no way I could be on my own right at that moment, so home was out of the question.

When I got to the pub, I parked the car and took a deep, somewhat tremulous breath. Once I felt a little more under control I got out and headed into the welcoming buzz of the pub, happy to be among people. Tom had told me that he and Sam had plans that evening so I was on my own, but Ruby gave me a friendly wave as I walked in and I could see Josh at the other end of the bar.

'Hi, Kat—shit, are you okay? You look like you've seen a ghost.'

I blanched at her comment, even though I knew it was innocently made.

'I'm fine, Ruby. Can I have a dry white wine, please?'

She frowned at me but turned to get my drink. When she returned, I ordered some food and went to sit down to gather my wits, not really wanting to get into a conversation right then. Lifting my glass, I noticed with alarm that my hand was shaking, and put it back down again.

'Jesus Christ, Kat, get a grip,' I chastised myself softly, before making another attempt to take a sip of my wine. This time I managed it without too much trouble and was grateful for the light burn as the wine hit my empty stomach.

For several minutes, I just sat there, willing myself to be rational about what had happened. I was tired, undoubtedly—apart from long hours on site, I'd been doing the rounds of suppliers, working on the construction budget, preparing revised specs and plans and dealing with the local authority building inspectors. On top of that, I'd spent a lot of time on the computer, often until late into the night, investigating Sarah Brodie and her family. I had to admit it was becoming a bit of an obsession and, even now, I was itching to check out some new leads I'd been thinking about.

Then there was the stress of knowing I was going to have to resign if Brad decided not to give me more time. Only the day before, I'd had to admit to my mother that I might soon be out of a job, which had then led to a long conversation about my plans and what I was going to do. Mom could be a little flaky, but she was pretty damned intuitive, and she could tell this house project was more than just an investment on my part. She knew better than to probe, but her concern was obvious.

All these things added up to a shit-ton of anxiety, and I'd be a fool if I thought that it wasn't affecting me. I'd been daydreaming in the house, letting my imagination run away with me. Clearly, there was an area that still wasn't weather-tight, and I would talk to Tom about it in the morning.

Nodding to myself, I determined there and then to stop being such an idiot. After all, it wasn't like I hadn't experienced similar odd occurrences before, and it was probably just the fact that it was getting dark and I was on my own that had caused me to get spooked. I determined that I would put a stop to the late nights, and would also give up my little periods of evening daydreaming at the house.

'Here you go, Kat ... one salmon in watercress sauce.'

I startled, letting out an embarrassing little squeak as Josh put a plate of food in front of me.

'Bloody hell, Kat, you're jumpy tonight. Ruby mentioned you were looking a bit upset. What's up?'

He sat down across from me, folded his arms in front of him on the table and gazed at me expectantly.

I looked down at my food, my appetite dissipating as I felt Josh's eyes boring a hole in the top of my head.

'Talk to me, Kat. Did something happen at the house?'

I glanced up sharply, my eyes meeting his and finding them full of concern and empathy. I took a deep breath and pushed the plate away from me.

'I honestly don't know, Josh. I … *shit!* Do … do you believe in ghosts?'

Chapter Five

I watched as Josh's face reflected a mix of conflicting emotions—surprise, speculation … and amusement.

I pursed my lips and looked away. I felt foolish enough, without Josh thinking I was losing it. I should have kept my mouth shut but had felt unable to stop myself blurting out such a stupid question.

He reached across the table and covered my hands where they were clasped in front of me on the table.

'Hey, I'm sorry, Kat. Something has obviously shaken you up, and I didn't mean to belittle that. Can you tell me what happened?'

I sighed, before meeting his eyes and finding nothing but compassion and concern. However, as I ran through the events of the past hour in my head, it all started to seem so unreal. The more I thought about it the more I started to believe that I might have been right when I'd rationalized what happened as tiredness, combined with an over-active imagination.

I withdrew my hands from Josh's touch and sat back, shaking my head.

'No, not really. I'm just being stupid. Forget I said anything.'

He regarded me silently for a moment, and then shrugged.

'For what it's worth, Kat, I don't think you're being stupid. Something up at that house has given you the heebie-jeebies, something real enough to scare you. I'm not going to push it, but if you ever want to talk about it, I'm happy to listen with an open mind. Now, can I get you another drink?'

I looked at my glass, a little surprised to see that it was empty, but shook my head.

'No, thanks, Josh. I think I'm going to head home—it's been a long day. I'll see you tomorrow, okay?'

'Absolutely. You take care now.'

We both stood, Josh picking up my untouched plate and walking back behind the bar as I made my way out to the parking lot and then home to Grandma's cottage.

That night was the first time I dreamed about Lucien Merrick.

಑ಐ

The following morning, I awoke feeling distinctly unrested, having spent a disturbed night during which I had been roused from sleep several times with the sensation that there was someone in the room with me. It was stupid, of course, and although I knew my subconscious had conjured up a faceless man, the details of the dream faded like so much ephemera as the new day brought me back to the land of the living. Shaking off the last remnants of sleep, I got up and prepared myself for another busy day, refusing to give in to any more foolish notions.

Arriving at the house, I was pleased to see that Tom was already there, and I was soon immersed in directing the work, making phone calls and meeting with suppliers. When the guys started packing up for the day, I headed to the public library to continue my research into the house and its former owners.

I was more than happy that there was no repeat of the previous day's strange occurrence, and enjoyed the time spent investigating the Merrick family history. I'd found a lot of information, and from the 1911 census I had been able to confirm Josh's discovery that Catherine was the daughter of Nathaniel Tregowen and his wife Mary, and, additionally, that she'd had two brothers, Albert and Matthew. I ordered all their birth certificates to get as much information as possible.

As the days went by, Tom and his team made fantastic progress on the house, and I was starting to see how amazing the finished result would be. In the meantime, I continued to chase down leads on the family history, my need to find out more growing each day as I slotted the information together like a jigsaw puzzle.

To my amazement, as I added to the family tree I'd created, I began to realize that there was a strong possibility that I was, indeed, directly related to the Tregowens.

This should have freaked me out, but I couldn't help but be fascinated by the connections. It seemed that Catherine's youngest brother, Matthew, had married and had a son, whom he'd named Joseph. This was a revelation to me, and later that evening I was compelled to call my dad.

'Hey, Kat, how are you?'

'I'm great, Dad. Listen, I'm sorry to call so late, but I just need to ask you something.'

'Okay. Is there a problem with the house?'

'No, nothing like that. This is to do with our family history—specifically, about Grandpa Joe.'

'Oh? Well, I'm intrigued ... what about him?'

'Well, I've been tracing the family tree of the people who built and owned my house. They were called Merrick, and it seems they were somehow connected to a family called Tregowen. A servant in the house had a younger brother called Matthew, and he had a son called Joseph, who was born around about 1930.'

There was silence on the other end of the phone, and if I hadn't been able to hear Dad breathing, I'd have thought we'd been cut off.

'Dad, are you there? Does that sound like it could be Grandpa?'

I heard him clear his throat.

'Uh, yeah, it could be ... wow, that's a little spooky, don't you think?'

I chuckled at his unknowingly apposite understatement.

'Yeah, it kind of creeped me out when I saw it in the parish baptismal records. Weird, huh?'

'Weird pretty much covers it, Kat. So, what's the connection again? My grandfather worked for these Merricks?'

'Uh, no, your grandfather's sister was a maid in the house. Their dad—your great grandfather—was the butler, and his wife was the cook—kind of a family affair.'

'Well, that's ... uh, pretty interesting. I knew my dad was born in Cornwall, but his family moved to London after the war—for work, I suppose. Mum was a Londoner, born and bred, but she fell in love with Cornwall when we used to visit for holidays, which is why she moved there after Dad died. She always used to say that there were magical forces at work there. I just thought she was being fanciful in her old age, but ... well, maybe she was onto something, eh?'

'Yeah, maybe. Oh, well, it's getting late, Dad, and I've got an early start tomorrow, so I better go.'

'Okay, sweetheart. Everything going well with the house?'

'Yeah, it's going great, Dad, I can't wait for you to see it. I should be able to move in soon, and then I'm going to get some work done on Grandma's house to spruce it up a bit before I sell it.'

'You're definitely moving in, then?'

'I think so, Dad—at least for a while. I'd hate to have done all this work and not get at least some of the benefit.'

'Yeah, I suppose I can understand that. Well, you take care ... and let me know when you want me to come down.'

'I will, Dad. Goodnight.'

When I'd hung up, I sat back and thought about what we'd talked about. It was beyond a coincidence that I was related to the Tregowens. I'd deliberately avoided telling Dad about the added connection of an illegitimate child. There was no proof that the child had been Lucien's, so I saw no point in muddying the waters at this point. The fact was, without DNA testing it was unlikely I could ever prove paternity, and, as that would involve finding the Brodies and getting permission for such a test, it was probably a dead-end.

However, it might be interesting to look into the Brodies. I'd traced Sarah as far as New York, so I might as well see if I could turn up anything more. With that thought, I shut down my laptop and went to bed.

As the days grew longer, the amount of work that could be achieved at the house grew exponentially, and before I knew it I was making plans to move. The downstairs was complete, with just decorative work now left to do upstairs. The basement had been tanked and made waterproof, the walls plastered, and the wooden flooring laid. Tom had suggested adding some borrowed light, created by installing a circular opaque glass insert in the floor of the entrance hall right under the atrium. It had a chrome rim, with concealed lighting, which made it glow, both above and below. It was an inspired idea and not only brightened the windowless room, but also made a wonderful feature when coming into the house.

I packed up the bungalow and found a charity online which took donated furniture and electrical goods to redistribute to those in need. Once he'd finished at Chimneys, I'd contracted Tom to start on Grandma's little house. He was going to put in a new kitchen and bathroom, and totally redecorate, prior to Sam coming in to value it for marketing. I'd been able to rent my condo in San Francisco very quickly to a lawyer who was paying more than enough to cover my mortgage, and my mom had gone in—albeit reluctantly—to pack up all my personal possessions and ship them over to me.

The events of the last evening I'd spent alone in my unfinished house had now taken on the qualities of a dream, and I had no qualms about moving in once the work was completed. It was an incredible house, and as each day went by, I became more and more excited about living there. Tom had eventually persuaded me not to take up residence until the work was done, saying that it would be easier to get everything finished without me being there. He also insisted that it would be better for me not to have to live with the inevitable mess caused by builders and decorators.

Now, as I supervised delivery of my new furniture, I had to admit to myself that, despite my impatience to get in, it had been a wise decision to wait. Everything was going exactly where I wanted it, and as each piece was brought in and set in place, I could see my original vision coming to life. All my belongings from San Francisco were still in boxes in the basement, but once I'd unpacked them, the house would really start to look like a home.

It was after nine o'clock when the last piece of furniture was put in place. A couple of Tom's guys, Mark and Steve, had helped me bring up the boxes from the cellar, and I was already pulling them open, excited to start unpacking my books, CDs and pictures.

'Hey, Kat, that's the last one.'

I turned to see Mark lower a box carefully to the ground and smiled at him.

'Thanks, Mark, that's great.'

I looked up to find Tom standing in the doorway, a wide grin on his face.

'Well, that's us just about done, Kat. I'll come back next week to go through the snagging items, but if you spot anything urgent, just give me a call.'

I walked over to him and held out my hand, smiling as his big paw enveloped mine.

You've done an amazing job, Tom. It's been a real pleasure working with you and your team.'

'Likewise, Kat. This has been a great job to work on, and I have to say, I'm really pleased with how it's turned out. I'll get Sam to prepare the final account and get it over to you next week, if that's okay.'

'More than okay, Tom. And I hope you and Sam, and all the guys will join me for a few celebratory drinks next Saturday evening to christen the house. I'll pop down to the pub tomorrow and invite Josh and Ruby as well.'

'Tell us what time, and we'll be here,' he chuckled.

'Seven o'clock?'

'Great, we'll see you then.'

I followed him to the door, shaking his hand again.

As he walked down the steps, he turned back to me.

'This really is a beautiful house, Kat. I hope you'll be happy here,' he said warmly.

'I'm sure I will. Thanks again, Tom—and if I don't see you in the pub tomorrow, I'll see you on Saturday.'

He gave me a quick salute and climbed into his pick-up. I watched until he'd disappeared down the drive, before closing the door and turning to lean against it.

Tom's boys had done a great job of cleaning up and the entrance hall looked spectacular. The glass floor insert glowed with golden light, and the whole space felt clean, bright and airy. I felt a satisfied grin spread across my face as I gazed around at the tangible evidence of my imagination and design skill, along with all the hard, physical effort from Tom and his team.

As I made my way back into the library, I couldn't stop myself from trailing my fingers over every surface—walls, doors, sofas, and, finally, the leather-topped oak desk which stood in front of the floor to ceiling glass doors. The sun had long since set, but there was still a trace of light in the sky, presaging the long summer evenings to come.

I turned on the small desk lamp, which effectively robbed the night sky of its remaining light, the glass now merely reflecting my own image and the room behind me.

As my focus altered, out of the corner of my eye I thought I detected movement, but when I swiveled around, the room was still, just as it had been moments before when I walked in.

I shook my head, castigating myself for being so jumpy. I would not give in to the foolish notions which had previously sent me scrambling out the door.

There are no such things as ghosts.

I headed to the kitchen to get something to eat. Tonight, some soup and French bread would suffice. Even as I sat down at the breakfast bar to eat, I felt a wave of deep fatigue wash over me and knew I wouldn't be able to stay awake much longer. I hurriedly finished my simple meal and loaded the dishes into the dishwasher. I would clean up properly in the morning, but for now I really just wanted to crawl into my new bed and sleep. With a smile, I realized that, for the first time in months, I would be able to enjoy a lie-in the following day, and, with that happy thought, made my way upstairs to bed.

Cool fingers slid up my bare thigh, raising a trail of goose bumps in their wake. At the same time, soft lips kissed a path from the hollow behind my ear down my neck and across my collar bone.

Catherine ... my love...

In that confusing limbo between sleeping and waking, I rolled onto my back, failing to suppress a soft whimper. I felt my dream lover's lips form a smile against my skin, and I gasped as his hand found the warmth between my legs. Cold fingers slipped inside my underwear, doing little to cool my heated skin. At the same time, his mouth progressed from my collarbone until I felt it capture my nipple through the thin material of my camisole. I moaned loudly as he continued his ministrations…

Suddenly, I was awake, my chest heaving as I gasped for air. Quickly, I rolled onto my side and reached over to the bedside lamp, turning it on. As the light chased the shadows from the room, I gazed around me, heart still thundering in my chest, but there was no one there.

Regaining my equilibrium, I threw off the covers and walked over to the door. Hesitating for only a moment, I gripped the knob and turned it, peeking around the door onto the dark landing. Not a sound broke the silence of the night, and I shook my head at my own timidity.

'Get a damned grip, Kat,' I muttered to myself, if only to impinge on the stillness of the house. Having spent all my life living in big cities, where there was always some sort of noise, no matter the time, I found the hush of the English countryside a little disconcerting.

I stepped out onto the landing, the energy-saving automatic lighting I'd had installed immediately illuminating the upper floor. I wandered down the stairs, peering over the banister, as more lights came on, tracking my progress.

I headed into the kitchen, grabbed a tumbler from the cupboard and filled it with water from the faucet. Chugging down half of it, I wiped my mouth with the back of my hand as I leaned against the sink. I gazed around the huge kitchen/diner, trying not to think about the extraordinarily vivid dream I'd just woken from.

Talk about an exercise in futility!

I couldn't deny that I'd been turned on; even so, something felt … *off* about it … wrong, somehow.

Realizing there was little point in trying to rationalize the workings of my subconscious, I finished my water and put my glass in the sink. I used the adjoining bathroom, and then did a circuit of the downstairs, checking all the locks, before heading back to my bedroom. It would start getting light in a few hours and I needed to get a bit more sleep before facing the morning.

I thought I might have trouble falling asleep again, but thankfully my tiredness took over, and I passed the rest of the night in a dreamless state, only waking when my alarm went off.

&)&

As soon as I'd showered and dressed, I made myself a light breakfast of toast and coffee, which I took into the library. I sat down at my desk and opened my laptop, going straight to the genealogy website I'd been using for my research. The first thing I noted was that I had a message from someone. Full of curiosity, I clicked on the little envelope icon, feeling my heart rate pick up when I saw that it was from a Helen Brodie. My excitement grew as I read.

> *Dear Ms Tregowen*
>
> *I have only just seen your message asking for information about the Brodies from Cornwall, and I can't tell you how thrilled I am to find that someone else has been looking into the Brodie family history.*
>
> *First, let me introduce myself. My name is Helen, and I'm married to Richard Brodie, whose family I believe you are researching. I have long since investigated my own family, right back to my Welsh forefathers in the 1800s. It was such fun, but when I couldn't go back any farther without visiting Wales, I decided to have a go at tracing Richard's family. We live in Sausalito in northern California, just across the Golden Gate Bridge from San Francisco, so it was incredibly interesting for me to discover that my husband's antecedents also hail from Britain – in his case, Cornwall. Is that where you live? Is it as beautiful as I've heard?*

I see from your last name that you may be related to Richard through his maternal grandmother, Sarah, whose maiden name was also Tregowen. I can't seem to find out anything about her parents, and it would be wonderful to hear from you with any information you might have.

My son, Luke, is flying to London next month on business, and I've managed to persuade him to visit both Wales and Cornwall while he's there, so if you do live in the area, would it be a huge imposition to ask you to perhaps meet with him? I promise he's very respectable and I like to think his father and I have raised him to be a gentleman, so I do hope this might be possible.

I know that, to an English person, my request may seem a little forward when we are complete strangers, but if you can forgive my American enthusiasm, I would be so grateful to find out more about you and my husband's English family.

I hope to hear from you soon.

Yours sincerely

Helen Brodie

I read the message twice, hardly able to comprehend this additional coincidence. What were the odds that Lucien Merrick's descendants would end up in my own home state of California? And, to cap it all, they had a son called Luke, which had to be an homage to his similarly named forebears. This just kept getting weirder and weirder.

Regardless of this latest development, however, there was something about Helen's note which charmed me, and, despite my initial shock at this latest twist of fate, I felt drawn to respond. I clicked out of the message and looked to see if Helen had posted a Brodie family tree online. So far, I hadn't posted mine, merely using the message board to ask for information, which I honestly believed would be a waste of time.

Perusing Helen's handiwork, I could see that she had, indeed, only been able to work back as far as Sarah and John. They had had four children—Lucien, who had been born in England and would have been just a baby when they emigrated, followed by Lydia in 1940, Anthony in 1946 and George in 1948. Lucien had married a Jane Carter, and they were the parents of Helen's husband, whose son, Luke, was clearly named after his grandfather, who, in turn, had been named for his own grandfather, Lucien Merrick.

I gazed at the chart, noting that Luke Brodie had been born in 1991—the same year as me. It was yet another coincidence, and it left me feeling a little more spooked. Referring back to the family tree I had put together, I tried to work out the relationship between myself and the youngest Brodie. I wasn't completely sure of how generational differences were calculated, but as far as I could tell, Luke and I were second cousins twice removed.

Not too close, then.

And why the hell did *that* matter?

I didn't know the answer to my own question, and decided it was irrelevant.

I went back to the message which had opened a whole new window into my family history and began composing my reply.

I didn't have to wait long for a response.

> *Dear Kat*
>
> *I cannot thank you enough for your response to my message, and for giving me your personal email address, which will hopefully make communication between us a lot easier.*
>
> *I can hardly believe the extraordinary coincidences you mention in your email. It's surely more than a fluke that you, too, are from California, and that, without even knowing it, you ended up buying the very house occupied by your English ancestors – do you believe in fate, Kat?*
>
> *The information you have provided is absolutely fantastic and tells such an amazing and incredibly poignant story. Richard and I spent the whole evening talking about what it must have been like for those poor, star-crossed lovers, and although we were both so sad to discover that young Lucien Merrick died in such tragic circumstances, especially after surviving the horrors of the First World War, we are grateful for your great-great aunt's strength and fortitude. To have suffered such a heartbreaking loss, and then go on to bring up a child out of wedlock in such times just shows what an amazing woman she was. Richard wants you to know that the child who came from Lucien and Catherine's love was a wonderful woman. Sadly, she died when he was only ten or*

eleven years old, but he remembers her with great affection. He says she was very beautiful, with a big heart and a love of life. Her family was everything to her and her death, at the ridiculously early age of 53 from breast cancer, hit them all very hard. From all that I have learned about her, I'm sure I would have loved her too.

The frustrating thing, of course, is that nobody talked about family histories when they had the chance. Richard knew nothing about Lucien Merrick or Catherine Tregowen, and with both his parents now gone it's too late to ask. I've talked to Richard's aunt and uncle, but they don't really know anything either. They said their parents never talked much about what happened before they emigrated to America, so it's always been a mystery, until now.

When I got your email, I went to see Richard's Aunt Lydia, who at least kept some of Sarah's things. She has a box of old papers and photographs, and produced a photo of a young couple, which seems to have been taken on a seaside promenade. Perhaps it's Port Simon. And that brings me to the subject of all these extraordinary coincidences you mentioned. I'd never seen this picture before, and neither had Richard. I suppose no one thought it was important until now. But here's the thing. I'm pretty sure the young man in it must be Lucien Merrick. To say that he's the spitting image of my son would be an understatement. Of course, it's in sepia tone, so you can't tell the color of his hair or eyes, but the likeness is amazing – my Luke takes after his father with his Cornish black hair and blue eyes. The girl in the picture is very pretty, and I'm wondering if it could be Catherine—from pictures I've seen of Sarah, there's certainly a family likeness. I'm asking, because her clothes don't look like those of a well-off person—more the Sunday best of a working-class girl. But more than that, although she's facing the camera, the young man is looking at her and has such an expression of devotion on his face, it's easy to see that he's in love with her. I've scanned the photo and have attached it to this email. Let me know what you think.

And now I've run on and on, probably boring you to death, for which I apologize. But I must thank you so much for your help, and for your very kind offer to meet with my *son. I am touched that you feel you can trust me with your cell phone number, which I will pass on to Luke so that he can call you when he arrives in England. I'll contact you again when he's firmed up his itinerary.*

Regardless of where our research eventually leads us, I do hope that you and I might meet one day, especially as you have such a strong connection to San Francisco. I feel that, just through this small communication, we could be friends.

Very best regards

Helen

PS: Luke's birthday is May 30th – so you're not cousin twins!

I couldn't help the smile that spread across my face as I read Helen's lovely long email. I actually found myself chuckling at her PS, feeling somewhat relieved that her son and I did not, in fact, share a birthday. Then, with an excitement bordering on the ridiculous, I clicked on the attached JPEG and watched as it opened, filling the screen.

My smile froze on my face as I gazed at the photograph that had been taken so very long ago.

My first thought was that Helen wasn't who I thought she was … that she had, in fact, decided to play a cruel trick on me.

There, in front of me, was what appeared to be a picture of a startlingly handsome young man standing next to a small, fair-haired girl—and that girl was … well, *me.*

Chapter Six

I stared and stared at the picture on my screen but could make no sense of it. On the face of it, the photograph looked genuine, but it was a scan, and I knew that photoshopping had come on in leaps and bounds in recent times. Helen Brodie was a stranger to me and I had no reason to trust her, but could she have created such a professional manipulation? And, if so, why? I would be foolish to accept this woman at face value, but my gut instinct told me that she wasn't trying to scam me. After all, what would she have to gain?

Frowning, I zoomed in on the girl's face, studying it closely. The quality wasn't great, but I could still make out some detail, and as I stared at it, I began to realize that there were subtle differences. The shape of the face was right, as were the eyes—even though I couldn't tell the color, they looked light enough to be hazel. The mouth, too, seemed to match mine, but the nose was slightly longer—whereas mine turned up a little, hers was dead straight. Finally, there was the suggestion of a dimpled chin, which I definitely did not have.

I sat back, shaking my head in disbelief. If the picture was genuine—and I was beginning to think it was—the likeness was startling, and I found it hard to get my head around it.

Unable to drag my eyes away from the image of the young couple in front of me, I was at first oblivious to the sudden chill in the air.

And then I felt it—the sensation of cool fingers trailing down my exposed neck, where I'd earlier clipped my hair in a loose twist on top of my head.

Catherine...

A loud squawk of surprise burst from my lips as I leapt up from my chair and swung around. I pressed my hand to my chest, my heart thundering in my ears, but the room was empty.

Empty or not, I knew I wasn't alone.

Feeling like an idiot, I broke the silence of the still room.

'Lucien Merrick? Is that you?'

The chill I'd first noticed behind me now seemed to envelop me, and goose bumps erupted all over my body.

Catherine...

I whipped my head from side to side, trying to pinpoint that soft, whispering sound. It seemed as if it was both inside my head and all around me, and it was freaking me the fuck out!

'What do you want?' I whispered shakily into the empty room.

You know what I want, Catherine.

I gasped, both in surprise that the … *entity* had replied to me, and from the sudden disappearance of whatever had been in that room with me. I knew that he … it … was gone because the chill had instantly dissipated, once again leaving me bathed in the warmth of the afternoon sunshine as it crept across the lawn and in through the windows.

I stumbled to the chair and slumped down at my desk, head in hands, waiting for my heart to return to a normal rhythm.

This was too incredible, too fucking unbelievable to take in. What had just happened? Was it the ghost of Lucien Merrick, or was I, indeed, going crazy? It was beyond fantastical, and I was at a loss as to how I should react.

Should I tell someone? Sam? *God, no!* Josh? Maybe, although he seemed pretty skeptical the last time I'd talked to him about the possibility of the house being haunted. Ruby, then? She and I had become quite good friends over the last few weeks, and she was, for want of a better word, quite a *spiritual* woman—not in a particularly religious way, but more new-age hippie.

I sat back and gave my situation some hard thought. If I was prepared to accept that there was a presence in the house, what did it mean? Was I in danger? Should I leave?

The answer to the latter question was pretty much dependent upon the answer to the first. Was I in any real danger? I wanted to believe that Lucien—if it were he—meant me no harm, that he was, in fact, a benign presence. Our interactions—if I could call them that—had always been friendly, affectionate. He thought I was Catherine, the love of his life, and if the photograph was anything to go by, it wasn't surprising that he should think so.

My mind went back to the dream I'd had the night before, and I immediately recalled how aroused I'd been.

Almost without realizing it, I had gone from disbelief to starting to think of Lucien as a real person.

A real person? Seriously?

But how could I think otherwise? I had felt his touch, heard his voice. Either I had succumbed to some kind of psychosis or those things had happened. He was here, in this house ... right now.

I swiveled my chair around and spoke.

'Are you here, Lucien? Can you tell me what it is you want?'

Nothing.

I shook my head. What the hell was I doing? Was I really trying to communicate with a ghost ... a frigging incorporeal being?

Of course, I'd read and heard plenty about haunted houses and the fact that ghosts hung around because of unfinished business. I hadn't believed any of it, certain that there was always a good, scientific explanation for so-called paranormal activity. Sure, Hollywood loved a good ghost story—*Amityville, Poltergeist, Blair Witch Project*. They made for scary movies which pulled in the audiences and big bucks, but I'd always considered them to be so much hokum.

If Lucien Merrick had unresolved issues, what could they be? If his spirit ... soul ... whatever you wanted to call it, lingered, what was his purpose? Did he know he was dead? Was he waiting for Catherine? Why was he still here? And was he responsible for the deaths and injuries which had occurred here, or were they just horrible accidents? Other than the normal incidents which occur on any building site, nothing at all had happened to me or Tom and his crew while they were working on the house, so I had to believe that Lucien was innocent of the charges against him.

I let out a growl of frustration and turned back to my laptop. I shifted the mouse to deactivate the screen saver, and the photograph taunted me. It offered no answers and I quickly shut the file. Helen's email once again filled the screen, so I hit 'Reply' and started typing. When I'd finished, I attached a photograph I had stored on my computer and pressed 'send'.

Closing my laptop, I got up and went into the kitchen. I'd bought a few essentials the day before, but I needed to stock the cupboards and freezer, as well as get in supplies for Saturday's party. I could order a lot online but wanted to get out for a few hours. I decided to treat myself to a late lunch at the pub, and then visit the big supermarket in town. I could issue invitations to a few more people at the same time, and maybe even talk to Ruby.

It was a pleasantly warm spring day, so I grabbed my purse and keys and went to the front door. Gripping the handle, I frowned when it wouldn't give.

Suddenly, just as before, I felt a chill surround me.

I took a deep breath as my heart stuttered. Closing my eyes, I told myself there was nothing to fear, and turned around slowly.

'Lucien ... is that you?'

My voice was shakier than I would have liked, and I felt stupid talking to an empty space.

Stay...

The word was just a whisper, without real substance, but, for all that, was absolutely clear.

'I ... I'm just going shopping. I'll be back in a couple of hours.'

Just like that, the chill receded, and, after a moment, I turned back to the door and gripped the handle. This time it depressed without effort and I was able to open the door. Stepping out, I pulled it closed behind me and walked to my car. Climbing in, I sat for several minutes, waiting until my racing heart had calmed as I gazed up at my house. My hand shook slightly as I put the key in the ignition, but when the engine roared to life, I breathed a sigh of relief. I drove slowly out onto the road and then put the power on as I headed into town.

ℰᗝᏅ

'Hi, Kat. Good to see you.'

I smiled at Ruby as she greeted me enthusiastically.

'Hey, Ruby, it's good to see you too.'

The pub was pretty quiet, just a couple of regulars at the corner of the bar and a few tourists dotted about, enjoying a late lunch or an early drink.

'The usual?' she asked, reaching up to the shelf for a wine glass, and I grinned at the thought that I was now established enough here that she knew what I drank.

'That'd be great, Ruby. Could you spare a few minutes to join me?'

She held up a finger and walked round the corner. I heard her speak to someone, and then reappear with Josh in tow.

'Hey, Kat, how are you? How's the house?'

'It's ... uh ... great, thanks.'

'You don't sound too sure. Is everything okay? Did Tom connect the sewage pipe to the water supply?'

I couldn't help laughing at his teasing tone.

'No, nothing like that. Tom's done a fantastic job and I can't wait for you guys to see it. Which brings me to the reason for my visit … well, apart from hoping you've still got some steak and ale pies left. I'm starving and have been fantasizing about tucking into one of your lovely pies all the way here.'

'Absolutely. One steak and ale pie coming up. So, what was the other reason?'

'Oh, yeah. Did Tom mention that I'm having a few people over on Saturday evening for a bit of a house-warming party? I hope you can both come.

'He did indeed, and we wouldn't miss it. I'm dying to see what you've done with the old place. We'll both be there, won't we, Ruby?' He looked down at her with a look of such warmth, I found it hard to understand why they continued to deny their feelings for one another.

'Okay, cool. I'm really looking forward to showing off the house. I'm doing a buffet and there'll be plenty to drink, so just turn up about seven. Oh, what about the pub? Will you be able to get away?'

'Don't worry about that; I've already got it covered. Wild horses wouldn't keep us away. Now, let me get you that pie before you collapse with hunger.'

He grinned and walked away towards the kitchen.

'Go grab a table, Kat, and I'll join you when Josh comes back.'

I nodded and picked up my wine, heading over to my favorite table in the bay window. When the pub was busy, it was impossible to sit there as it was usually occupied, so I took advantage of the quiet and made myself comfortable on the wide, padded window seat. It was a great spot for watching the world go by outside, and I loved to spend the odd hour or so doing just that whilst enjoying Josh's delicious food.

'So, how was your first night in Chez Tregowen, Kat?'

I looked around as Ruby dropped into the chair across from me.

'It was … interesting.'

'Ooh, that sounds ominous. Whatever do you mean?'

I looked at her, saying nothing for a moment. Before I could speak, though, her eyes widened and she leaned forward.

'Oh. My. *God!* You saw the ghost, didn't you? I *knew* it! What's it like? Is it Lucien Merrick? Ohmygod, this is brilliant!'

I laughed loudly at her excited enthusiasm, more grateful than she would ever comprehend that she had single-handedly stripped away my anxiety and trepidation about returning home. Perhaps this was something to be excited about—my very own ghost, and a pretty sexy one at that.

'Come on, Kat, quit stalling. Did it appear to you, or is it just throwing stuff around? Enquiring minds need to know!'

'Shut up, Ruby. God, you're incorrigible! No, he didn't appear, but—'

'He? So, it *is* Lucien Merrick, then? Bloody hell, that is *so* cool!'

'Well, I suppose it must be, although I'm still not convinced what happened is the work of a ghost. It could all be due to lack of sleep and—'

'That's bollocks and you know it. I can see it in your face. Everyone knows that house has been haunted since the Merricks died, and I'm betting something weird and tangible happened. But unlike all the hideous things that took place in the past, you're obviously still in one piece so it can't have been anything horrid. So, spill the beans, Kat. Did he ravish you in your sleep?'

She giggled with delight but stopped suddenly when she saw the livid blush which I could feel heating my face. Her mouth dropped open and her eyes went wide.

'Bloody hell, Kat. Seriously? Jesus wept, this is epic. Tell me everything.'

I groaned and covered my hot face with my hands, only to feel Ruby pull them away a moment later.

'Kat Tregowen, if you don't tell me what happened right now, I'll … I'll scream, so help me I will!'

'Okay, okay, calm down, you evil harpy. God, where do I start?'

'Start with the first time he made his presence known, right up to whatever spooked you today.'

I nodded and took a deep breath. Josh chose that moment to deliver my lunch and I was grateful for the interruption, allowing me a moment to gather my thoughts.

'Well, I guess the first time was when I found the house by accident and squeezed in through the back door to have a look around.'

As I ate, I told her about each incident when I'd felt and heard him, glossing over the more intimate details, and then went on to describe the correspondence with Helen, the photograph, and Lucien's "appearance" earlier in the day.

As I talked, the pub emptied out, and Josh brought us fresh drinks. He joined us just as I was explaining about the incredible coincidence of the couple in the picture bearing a striking resemblance to Helen's son and me. His eyebrows nearly met his hairline as he listened and, when I was done, he sat back and blew out a gust of air.

'Wow, Kat, that's just … *wow!* I'd really like to see that photograph.'

I nodded and told him he could look at it when he came over.

Ruby grinned, her face gleeful.

'Ooh, I can't *wait!*'

I smiled and glanced at my watch, astonished to see that it was after four o'clock.

'Shit, I need to get to the supermarket. Look, thanks for listening, you two, I really appreciate it. I've gotta run, but I'll see you both on Saturday.'

I stood and squeezed out around the table. As I did, Ruby got up and threw her arms round me, taking me by surprise. Hugging me tightly, I felt compelled to return her embrace.

'Take care, Kat, and don't let that naughty Lucien Merrick scare you. I'm sure he likes you.'

I chuckled, gently extricating myself from her arms.

'I won't, Ruby, I promise. I'm kinda getting used to him. Maybe he'll make an appearance at the party and you can meet him.'

I was joking, but her eyes went wide.

'Oh, that would be amazing. I do hope so.'

I was still chuckling to myself when I got to my car. I was grateful for Ruby's positive attitude and had to admit that it made me feel a lot better about what might be going on in my house.

'Hey, Kitty Kat, what's all this about a ghost?'

It was Saturday evening and we were gathered on the deck outside what would once have been called the drawing room, which was to the left of the front door and opposite the library. To my delight, everyone I'd invited had turned up and conversation had been flowing easily, along with the drinks. No doubt, the full attendance was as much to do with curiosity as the free food and booze.

I swiveled around at the sound of Tom's voice, which seemed to reverberate around the back yard. Cringing at his enquiry—as well as his new nickname for me—I shot mental daggers at Ruby, who had obviously spilled the beans. I didn't have time to respond, however, as he grinned mischievously and waggled his eyebrows.

'So, is he a bit saucy, Kitty? Does he fiddle about with you in your sleep?'

He guffawed loudly at his own puerile joke, causing me to roll my eyes and grimace in mock disgust. I couldn't keep it up, though, when Sam landed a hard punch on his arm, eliciting an explosive yelp from him. I laughed as he rubbed the sore spot and cast a rueful glance at his wife.

Ruby gave me an apologetic look, but I could only shake my head and smile. After all, I hadn't sworn her to secrecy and I'd also mentioned it to Josh, so I guess there was little point being coy about it now. I was just glad my father hadn't been able to make it this weekend, as I wasn't yet ready for him to know about my ghost.

'Actually, Tom, I'm developing a fondness for my ghost as he's pretty adept in the bedroom department,' I told him airily. I couldn't contain my laughter as his eyebrows shot up and his mouth dropped open.

My laughter died as I suddenly realized that I now had the attention of just about everyone there. I could feel my face heating and drained my wine, beating a hasty retreat to the kitchen to refill my glass. I caught sight of Sam approaching in my peripheral vision, her head tilted to one side to capture my gaze as her expression warred between concern and amusement.

I snorted, resigning myself to her understandable curiosity.

'Just say it, Sam. I know you're dying to ask.'

She smirked, putting her glass down on the tiled surface of the island and perching on one of the high bar chairs.

'To be honest, I'm not sure what to say. Are you seriously suggesting that you've been shagging a spectral entity?'

I barked a laugh, glad that I hadn't just taken a drink, as I would have sprayed it all over my friend. She grinned at me as I shook my head at her eloquent vulgarity.

'Don't beat about the bush, Sam. Just come right out with it', I chuckled.

'Talking about being beaten about the bush, Tregowen...'

'Oh my God, Samantha Jago, shut *up!*' I could feel my cheeks heating up, even as I fought unsuccessfully to restrain my giggles.

Sam merely regarded me levelly, one perfectly sculpted eyebrow cocked inquiringly as she waited for me to control myself.

'Okay, okay. Look, I have no idea what's going on in this house, Sam, but I swear I'm not crazy and I'm not imagining it. All I know is that there's something—or *someone* here, and although I should be shitting myself, I'm actually starting to believe that whatever it is, it means me no harm.'

Sam narrowed her eyes and shook her head disbelievingly, and I waited for her to lay into me for being a susceptible idiot. She continued to gaze at me skeptically for several long seconds, but then blew out a big breath and nodded.

'I'm sorry, Kat, I don't mean to be a Doubting Thomas—God knows, I'm aware of all the weird shit that's gone on in this house over the years, so maybe—and it's a big maybe—there's something to what you say. So, what's all this about a photograph?'

I smiled, thankful for her tacit acceptance. Picking up my refilled glass, I walked towards the door, indicating that she should follow me. Entering the library, I was surprised but pleased to find Josh and Ruby there. I'd given everyone the big tour earlier and they had both remarked on how much they liked the room.

'Hey, Kat, I hope you don't mind—'

'It's fine, Josh. I'm actually glad you're here. I was going to show Sam the photograph that Helen Brodie sent,' I told him, walking over to the desk and switching on my laptop.

Ruby drifted over, a small smile playing across her lips. I gave her a quizzical look as I typed in my password and waited for the computer to boot up. Her smile widened as she joined the others looking over my shoulder. A moment later, I glanced behind me as the door opened and Tom's head appeared.

'Ahh, this is where you all disappeared to. What's going on?' he asked, wandering across to where we were gathered around the laptop.

Ruby sighed dramatically. 'This is the room, isn't it, Kat? The one where he manifests himself. It's such a beautiful room and I think it must have been his favorite place when he was ali—oh my fucking god!'

The JPEG image was slowly appearing on the screen, and the young woman's face was now clearly visible to those assembled behind me.

'Jesus, Kat, that's fucking uncanny.' Josh's awed whisper drew my attention and I turned to him.

'I know, right? I mean, when I first saw it, I was sure it must be photoshopped, but when you look closer there are subtle differences … it's kinda creepy, though, don't you think.'

'Creepy is right,' Sam said softly, uncharacteristically subdued.

Ruby tsked behind me and I turned to see her shaking her head.

'It's not creepy, Sam, it's genetics. Don't you see? Kat's related to Catherine Tregowen, so the fact that they look alike isn't in the least bit surprising. That's obviously why Lucien's ghost brought her here, and why she's the first person he's allowed into the house who's remained unscathed. He believes she's his lost love come home to him, and maybe now he can be helped to pass over into the afterlife.' She glanced from one to the other of us, frowning as she took in our matching and plainly skeptical expressions.

'Come on, you lot, isn't it obvious? Kat, you said it yourself, your sat-nav went on the blink and directed you to a house which, completely unbeknownst to you, is inextricably connected to your family's past—how could that have happened without some kind of … of … paranormal intervention? Huh? Anyone?'

Behind me, Tom chuckled and placed a meaty hand on my shoulder.

'Maybe Shorty's right, Kitty. Maybe Casper the Horny Ghost has been sporting blue balls since 1918—which, let's face it, would put any man in a bad mood—but the chance to get his leg over has ended a nearly one-hundred-year sulk.'

Releasing me, he moved into the middle of the room, grinning widely as he turned slowly on the spot.

'Is that it, Lukey?' he called out as he revolved. 'You just needed to get your end away to stop you dropping gargoyles on people?'

For a moment, we were all as silent and still as graveyard angels, until a sudden burst of muffled laughter from across the hall broke the mood and drew my attention to the fact that I'd been neglecting my other guests. With a somewhat nervous chuckle, I turned to my friends and started shooing them out of the room.

'Come on, guys, we can analyze the shit out of this some other time. Let's go turn the music up and get drunk.'

'Now you're talking, Kitty.' Tom threw his arm around my shoulders, and we all made our way back across the hall, grabbing drinks from the kitchen on our way. Tom immediately made a beeline for my new hi-fi system, to which I had streamed all the music on my computer—nearly two thousands tracks. Finding a dance playlist, he wound up the volume, grabbed Sam and twirled her, laughing, across the room to a clear area, where they proceeded to pull some serious moves. Grinning at their antics, I was caught by surprise as Wayne grabbed my hand and dragged me over to join his boss, whereupon the whole room suddenly seemed to be dancing.

As I sang loudly along with everyone else to Pharrell Williams' "Happy", I realized that that's exactly what I was—happy. I couldn't remember the last time I'd had so much fun, or, indeed, when I'd last been in the company of such a wonderful group of people. It suddenly struck me that I hardly missed my old life in San Francisco at all. I'd been working so hard over the last ten years— pretty much since my sophomore year at college—that I hadn't made enough time to cultivate close friendships, let alone a committed romantic relationship, leaving me, on the cusp of thirty, somewhat cast adrift. No wonder I'd embraced the idea of rebuilding this house—finally doing something for myself.

'Hey, you okay?'

I turned to see Ruby looking at me with a concerned look on her face, her hand lightly resting on my upper arm.

I grinned at her, grabbing her free hand and whirling her around.

'I'm fucking awesome, Ruby,' I laughed, joining in as Florence Welch burst into the chorus of "Spectrum".

The party carried on 'til late, with Sam, Tom, Mark and his girlfriend, Susie, the last to leave. The girls had insisted on helping me clear up a little, so it was after two o'clock in the morning by the time everyone had departed and I found myself alone. Exhausted and far from sober, I locked the front door, turned off the lights and made my weary way to bed.

ഇന്റെ

Despite the alcohol I'd consumed, deep sleep eluded me, my dreams filled with thoughts of a beautiful ebony-haired boy, caught between two worlds, unable to move forward or back. My heart ached for him; he was so lost and broken as he desperately continued his endless and hopeless search for the love of his life.

Once again, I felt his cool touch, icy fingers sliding, stroking, squeezing, bringing such pleasure, as cold lips seemed to trail across my skin, leaving goose bumps in their wake. I knew I was dreaming, yet my arousal was real, as was the sensation of a presence in my bed.

And yet, and yet, it felt so wrong.

With that thought, I willed myself to wake up, but even as I clawed my way back to consciousness, it almost seemed as though the entity—Lucien?—clung ever tighter to me. I was suddenly struck with the notion that if I didn't wake up *right now,* I would be dragged down into some kind of purgatorial no man's land, my body remaining comatose and my mind unreachable in the real world. It was a ridiculous thought but, as I struggled to escape this crazy dream, I couldn't shake off the feeling of doom.

Cold lips seemed to whisper against my ear as my spectral lover enclosed me in his icy grip.

Stay ... please, Catherine, stay with me.

'Lucien, no ... please, you have to let me go!'

Did I speak aloud or only in my dream? I had no idea, but suddenly my mind and body were freed from whatever ghostly power had tethered me to sleep and I woke up with a gasp.

Chapter Seven

Desperate to avoid slipping back into the dream which had so thoroughly … *possessed* me, I dragged my tired and hungover body into the shower, in hopes that it might both wake me up and help assuage the headache which assailed me.

Emerging from the bathroom wrapped in a towel, I walked back into my bedroom with the intention of throwing on some comfortable clothes and heading downstairs to make myself a cup of much needed coffee and set about clearing up the party detritus. My plan was forestalled, however, the minute I entered my room and felt the chill which presaged only one thing.

'Lucien?' My whispered enquiry sounded shaky even to my own ears as my very breath crystalized in the air around me. Goosebumps erupted all over my skin as I felt myself enveloped by the cold. Worse still, I seemed to have been robbed of my ability to move or resist, as if I was back inside that frightening but strangely compelling dream. Frozen lips on my neck and shoulder made me shiver; although, whether that was due to the chilliness of his touch or my reluctant but tangible arousal was hard to say, and I was powerless to control the soft moan which burst, unbidden, from my throat.

My beautiful Catherine.

My hands, which had instinctively gripped my towel to my chest when I'd entered the room, now felt like lead weights, dropping heavily to my side. As I released the towel, it, too, become a victim of gravity, slipping from my body and pooling around my feet.

I was naked.

And I was freezing my ass off.

Spectral hands cupped my breasts from behind, and I felt myself being pressed back into what felt like a very *corporeal* body. One hand drifted down across my bare stomach as I felt myself being pulled back against whatever stood behind me, and it occurred to me that it would be so easy just to give in … easy but potentially dangerous, and with that thought in mind I lurched away from whatever had held me in its thrall. Breathing hard, I spun around, but the room was, of course, empty. With one arm across my chest and my free hand desperately trying to cover what remained of my modesty, I stepped forward and, with a quick glance around, swooped down to retrieve my towel and wrap it securely around me. As fast as my still trembling hands would allow, I grabbed clean underwear, a t-shirt and leggings from the chest of drawers and got dressed. It was clear from the rising temperature that Lucien had— at least, for the moment—withdrawn, but I was keen to vacate my room and head downstairs.

Away from Lucien … if that was even possible.

Away from temptation.

ༀༀ

I loaded the dishwasher, took out the trash, put away the left-over booze, and vacuumed the whole first floor. I was glad of the distraction but equally happy to finally sit at the kitchen island, a strong, hot cup of coffee beside me and my laptop open in front of me.

There was an email from Helen in my inbox.

I clicked to open it and started reading.

> *My dear Kat*
>
> *Well, what can I say? I totally understand why you might have thought I was playing a trick on you, as the similarities between the photograph of yourself and the scan of Lucien and Catherine must have been very unsettling. Please believe me when I say this just isn't something I would do, even if I had the knowledge and skills – which I really don't! After all, as you said yourself, what would I have to gain?*
>
> *Like you, I am beginning to find this whole situation ever more strange, and I can't wait for you to meet my son. He came over for dinner this evening and I showed him the photograph of Lucien and Catherine, along with the one you sent me, and I have to say I have rarely seen Luke lost for words! As a result, he is now so curious about our shared family history that he is working hard to clear his schedule so that he can leave for London earlier than planned. He is now hoping to get a flight on the 28th of this month and will travel down to Cornwall straight from the airport. Can you recommend a decent hotel in Port Simon? I do hope you will*

be able to meet with him while he's there and perhaps show him round.

Take care and I very much look forward to hearing from you soon.

Yours
Helen

Wow, it looked like my distant relative would be here in barely two weeks, and I had to admit I was just as excited about meeting him as he apparently was about meeting me.

I swiftly clicked on "Reply" and started typing.

Dear Helen

Thanks so much for your quick response to my email, and I totally believe you when you say that the scan is untouched—I know we haven't met but I feel strongly that I can trust you.

I'm very excited to hear that your son is bringing forward his trip to Europe and have a suggestion which I hope he might appreciate. My father lives in London and I need to return the car he loaned me, as my new one is being delivered next week. I could drive up to London, spend a couple of days with my dad, and then meet Luke at the airport. I assume he's intending to hire a car, so I could travel back to Port Simon with him, if he's happy to have some company. As for a hotel, I have several spare rooms, so it would be my pleasure to invite him to be my guest – after all, we are *family, and Chimneys is as much his ancestral home as mine, perhaps more so, as Lucien Merrick was his great, great, great grandfather, whereas my connection to the house is through my great, great aunt, who was only a servant!*

Anyway, he's very welcome to come and stay, although if he would prefer a hotel, I won't be offended, and will be happy to find him something – I understand that Port Simon Country House Hotel is very good. Let me know what he thinks about my plan, and, if it works for him, give me his flight details and I'll be there to meet him.

Best regards
Kat

I read through my note and hesitated for a moment with the cursor hovering over "Send". The idea of meeting Luke Brodie at the airport and driving back to Cornwall with him had popped into my head the moment I read about his change of plans. The offer for him to stay with me had come out of nowhere, and I wondered if I was being a bit pushy. Would Luke and his mom think me too forward? Would he be embarrassed by my suggestion? Might it make him feel awkward about refusing or, worse, reluctantly accepting?

And what about Lucien Merrick? Would he take umbrage at the presence of another man? He'd had no problem with Tom and his team, but none of them had stayed the night. Might he start causing trouble, as he had in the past? But this was his great, great, great grandson, so surely he would be happy to know that he lived on through younger generations.

'Oh, for fuck's sake, why am I even debating this with myself? This is my house and I'll invite who I want!'

I was aware that I sounded like an idiot—who the hell was I talking to? Shaking my head in annoyance, I quickly pressed "Send" before I could change my mind.

Returning to my inbox, I ran through the remaining messages. Most were spam, but there were a couple which needed responses. One was from Brad, asking me to reconsider my recent note to him in which I indicated that I felt it was only fair that I resign, as I had no idea when I might return. The second was from a firm of architects in Truro, to whom I'd sent my résumé. It seemed they wanted to meet me, and I sent them a reply indicating my availability. I then replied to Brad, telling him I would think about it and come back to him—I would wait to see how my job search panned out before I made a final decision. That done, I shut down my computer and stretched, glad to have dealt with everything.

Standing up, I turned and looked out over the back yard, smiling at the dawning of another beautiful day. When I'd first come downstairs the sky was only just starting to lighten, but now the sun was steadily climbing in the east and casting its golden tentacles across the lawn.

There was still much to be done to bring the garden back to what I imagined was its former glory, but the landscaper I had contracted through Tom had already made a start and I was hopeful that it would soon be complete. With that happy thought I turned and picked up the phone to call my dad, wanting to make sure he would be around for my visit in two weeks.

ℰᏏᏨ

The days that followed both dragged and sped past as Luke Brodie's arrival drew ever closer. My offer to meet him at the airport and bring him back to Chimneys to stay had been accepted with surprising alacrity by Helen, and I was already second-thinking my decision. However, it was too late to renege, and I spent much of the intervening period making all the finishing touches to Chimneys, wanting Luke to be impressed with the house. Why I should be so eager to please a complete stranger was a mystery to me, but there was no denying that I was excited to meet him.

In the meantime, my spectral Lucien was becoming ever more omnipresent and, somewhat alarmingly, a good deal more … *solid*. Whereas he had previously been a … a *sensation*, for lack of a better word, and a voice which seemed to be more inside my head than in the air around me, each new day brought a change in my perception of him. More than ever, I was convinced that I could see him, if only in terms of a fleeting glimpse of … of *something* out of the corner of my eye, and there was a definite difference in one very specific area.

Namely, my bed.

Ever since the party, Lucien had been a regular visitor, and now I was convinced that I wasn't dreaming. In fact, more and more often I was pretty sure that I was awake during our nightly encounters.

Because surely I wasn't imagining the things he did to me in the darkness.

From cool touches of lips and hands, Lucien's attentions had quickly escalated, and, just the night before, with little more than a week to go before his great, great, great grandson arrived, he had upped the ante in a way that, in the cold light of day, had me blushing just thinking about it.

Lately, I seemed to be tired all the time, having to force myself to perform all the tasks I felt were needed to get the house ready for my guest. I reasoned that my growing lethargy was understandable, considering all the work I was doing in the house and backyard, allied to the fact that my ghostly lover was keeping me awake long into the night.

Exhausted after a day of cleaning and furniture rearrangement, I had fallen into bed early, where sleep quickly claimed me. As had become the norm of late, I soon became aware of Lucien's presence—a presence I had long since ceased to fear; indeed, it seemed I now consciously sought it, welcoming his chilly embrace.

Last night, however, had been different. Lucien's touch, always gentle in the past, now became more demanding, more passionate as his icy fingers made my pulse race. I woke, like always, and waited for my breathing to calm, which generally signaled the gradual dissipation of Lucien's presence in my bed.

Over the last week, it seemed that it took longer and longer for him to fade, despite my wakeful state. I no longer leapt, fearful, from between the sheets, but instead lay still as his hands seemed to continue their exploration of my body. In the darkness, I could swear I still felt him, as real in my conscious state as he was when I slept.

This time, though, he didn't fade, his body as firm and unyielding as any man I had ever known.

'Catherine, my love.'

I inhaled sharply. This was not a voice inside my head—this was clear and distinct, and coming from the man hovering, unseen, above me.

Without thinking, I reached a hand up to where I sensed his face and gasped as my fingers made contact with smooth skin and a sharply defined jaw.

I couldn't believe this was happening. Was it possible I was still asleep, merely dreaming I was awake?

He dipped his head to brush his lips over mine, and all thoughts of what constituted my current reality flew away.

'Catherine, my angel, I've missed you so much.'

Shock robbed me of words, his weight all too real as he pinned me to the mattress.

'My darling Catherine, my dear, sweet love. Don't ever leave me again.'

His head was buried in my neck, and, tentatively, I reached up to stroke his hair. To my surprise, unlike in the photograph I'd seen, it was quite short—almost bristly—at the back and sides, but longer on top. For some reason, I expected it to be soft to the touch, but found myself grimacing at the somewhat greasy feel, only now remembering the fashion in the early part of the twentieth century for men to control their hair with bay rum and oily pomades—whatever they were!

My thoughts were cut short, however, as I was suddenly assailed by a deep, almost debilitating fatigue. Still pinned beneath Lucien's weight, I could do nothing but succumb to sleep.

ℛℬ

Consciousness came slowly, pulling me awake bit by bit until I became fully aware of my surroundings. Rolling over onto my back, I rubbed my eyes and groaned, feeling positively hungover, despite having not had a drink in days. My head ached alarmingly, and I felt disoriented and nauseous.

Reluctantly, I pushed back the comforter and swung my heavy, uncooperative legs over the side of the bed as I tried to make sense of the day.

The first thing I noticed was that the sun was obviously sitting low in the sky, evidenced by the deep shadows darkening the corners of my bedroom. At this time of year, the sun didn't set in Cornwall until nearly nine o'clock, but it seemed inconceivable that I had slept for over twenty hours. I rubbed my eyes with the heels of my hands and then picked up the digital clock beside my bed.

20:42

I stared at the numbers, uncomprehending, for what seemed like minutes, until I finally understood their meaning—that I had, indeed, been in bed for close to twenty-three hours.

What the hell?

With a groan, I forced myself to stand—then immediately sat back down as a wave of dizziness robbed me of my equilibrium.

'Whoa!'

My stomach roiled and saliva flooded my mouth as nausea gripped me. Once again, I made myself stand, pitching headlong across the room as I swayed and stumbled like a drunk to the bathroom. I barely made it, grunting in pain as I banged my arm against the door jamb before collapsing in front of the toilet and flinging the seat up. My stomach clenched and I retched, over and over, but little more than bile was expelled, last night's dinner having long been digested.

Finally, after what seemed like hours, the abdominal spasms stopped long enough for me to sit back against the cool tiled wall, and I closed my eyes, exhausted.

I was jolted awake by the sound of my phone alerting me to an incoming call.

Using the toilet as leverage, I managed to get to my feet without falling over and made my way carefully back to the bed. I dropped down heavily and picked up my phone, even though whoever had been calling had already given up. I swiped the screen and stared at the display, willing my blurry vision to clear and allow me to make out who had called. Just as Ruby's name came into focus, the phone pinged with a voicemail.

'Hey, Kat, where the hell are you? Sam and I have been calling you all day. We haven't seen you for ages, and we're getting worried. If you don't call back, I'm coming over to check on you, so ... well, just call, okay?'

I sighed when the message ended, pressing 3 to delete it. I was just too exhausted to deal with Ruby right now. I needed to shower and get something to eat before I could think about anything else. I would just lay back down for five more minutes...

I woke with a start, the ringing of the doorbell dragging me from a troubled nightmare. I lay still for a moment, one arm over my eyes, until the sound of a fist pounding on wood once more alerted me to what had awoken me. Groaning, I dragged myself into a sitting position, steadying myself with one hand on the headboard as the room spun alarmingly. As the ringing and banging from downstairs continued, my phone suddenly sprang to life, and I gazed down at where I'd obviously dropped it on the floor. I knew if I tried to pick it up I would likely fall off the bed, so decided to ignore it. It lay face down, but I suspected it was either Ruby or Sam, and they would just have to wait.

With a monumental effort, I slowly pushed myself off the bed, my legs trembling beneath me as I strove to keep my balance. I felt achy and weak and knew I had never felt so tired in my entire life, even when I'd been working fifteen-hour days. I wondered if I had caught the flu, and cursed the timing when I had so much to do.

With that thought, I took a deep breath to steady myself and, when I finally felt like my legs would support me, I let go of the bed and made my way slowly to the bathroom. With infinite care, I relieved myself and then glanced at the shower. I was desperate to rid myself of the clamminess and sweat which clung to my skin but simply couldn't muster the energy. Making my way slowly back into the bedroom, I wondered if whoever had been at the door was still outside and decided I needed to check my phone.

Fighting waves of nausea and dizziness, I slowly dropped to one knee beside the bed and picked up my phone. Unlocking it, I saw that it had been Sam calling me, and that, worryingly, I had missed a dozen calls from her and Ruby. There were several voicemails from both of them, all along a similar theme of wanting to know where I was. The last, from Sam, was the most startling, though.

'Okay, Tregowen, I am officially freaking out. Your car's in the drive and I've been ringing the doorbell and banging on the bloody door for twenty minutes. I'm calling Tom to come up here and get your front door open, because I'm coming in ... Jesus, Kat, where are you?'

Her voice dropped, cracking slightly, as she muttered her final plea, and I felt a lump form in my throat at her obvious distress. As quickly as my fuzzy brain and trembling fingers would allow, I scrolled to her name in my contacts and called her. It hardly rang before her voice, sharpened by anxiety, blared in my ear.

'Kat! Oh my God, where are you? What's happened? Why haven't you called? Wha—'

'Sam, Sam, it's okay, I'm here—.' I struggled to speak, my voice weak and scratchy from lack of use.

'Here? Where the fuck is here? What the hell, Kat?'

'I'm here ... in the house, Sam. I'm—'

'What do you mean, you're in the house? Why didn't you open the door—oh shit, have you broken your leg or something? Should I call an ambulance?'

'No, no, Sam, I'm ... I'm fine, I've just been ... I think I have the flu.'

'Tell her to go. We don't need her.'

I gasped and looked around, catching a glimpse of a tall figure standing in the shadowed corner behind me, but before I could focus, a wave of dizziness, no doubt caused by the sudden movement of my head, overtook me, and I felt my tenuous hold on consciousness start to slip.

'Kat? Kat! What the fuck is going on?'

Her voice sounded tinny as I dropped my hand, my arm too heavy to hold the phone to my ear. I could do nothing to stop myself falling forward, the floor coming up to meet me way too fast. In my last moments of clarity, I braced myself for the impact, only to feel strong arms encircle me and pull me back onto the bed, just as the darkness claimed me.

ဢၘ

'Kat, wake up! Jesus, Tom, I think we need to call an ambulance. She's bloody comatose!'

I knew that voice, but how was it so close?

With a massive effort, I forced my eyelids open.

'Sam? What are you doing here?'

I was lying on the bed and attempted to sit up. However, my leaden body refused to cooperate, and I huffed out a frustrated sigh.

'What am I doing here? Bloody hell, Kat. No one's clapped eyes on you for over a week; you don't respond to calls or messages, and when I turn up at your door, not only don't you open it, but when I call you, you sound like you're ready to push up the daisies.'

I tried again to sit up, and by some herculean effort managed to push myself up against the headboard, but the exertion required left me exhausted and even weaker. Still, the last thing I wanted was for Sam to worry or call an ambulance.

'I've just got the flu or something. I'm sure I'll be fine in a day or two.'

'Fine? Are you bloody kidding me here, Tregowen? You look like absolute shit, and you've clearly lost weight. Honest to God, I've seen healthier looking corpses. How long has this been going on and, more to the point, why haven't you been in touch with anyone?'

I was too tired for this, but I knew I needed to placate her. Besides, I couldn't be that bad—it had only been a couple of days, surely. She must be exaggerating.

Just then, I heard movement outside my bedroom, and the next thing I knew Tom was looming in the doorway.

'Hey, Kitty Kat—whew, what happened to you?'

I made to raise my hand in a dismissive gesture but could barely do more than waggle my fingers.

'It's just the flu, Tom…' I closed my eyes as exhaustion robbed me of both the ability and will to speak further. God, what was happening to me?

'Just the flu, my arse. I'm going to ring the doctor. Are you registered with a GP, Kat?'

Once again, I forced my eyes open. 'GP?'

'Doctor, Kat—have you registered with anyone? There's the Oak Hill Surgery or Dr. Henderson's practice.'

I shook my head slowly—any greater movement just made the room spin.

'Shit ... okay, I'll call Oak Hill and ask them to register you as a temporary patient and see if there's a doctor available to come out here.'

After that, I must have zoned out again. I was vaguely aware of being lifted and manhandled—Sam must have undressed me and helped me put on clean pajamas. By the time I drifted back to consciousness, I was back in bed and a man I'd never seen before was sitting on the edge of the mattress, holding my wrist and looking at his watch.

Glancing at me, he gave me a gentle smile and put my hand down, although he didn't release it.

'Ah, the patient is awake. Excellent. My name is James Laurence. I'm a doctor, and you, young lady, are rather poorly. Samantha!'

As he looked towards the door, I attempted to lift my other hand in order to push my hair off my face, only to feel something tug at it uncomfortably. I glanced down curiously and gasped when I realized an IV had been inserted. My eyes followed the narrow tube protruding from it until they came to rest on a clear plastic bag dangling from an IV pole.

'Ah, yes. I'm afraid you were seriously dehydrated, so I had to get some fluids into you as a matter of urgency. How are you feeling?'

I thought about his question and came to the conclusion that I actually felt a lot better than I had before I passed out. Before I could speak, though, Sam walked through the door carrying a tray, on which sat a steaming bowl of something hot and a glass of Coke. Setting both on the bedside table, she propped the tray against the wall and sat down on the opposite side of the bed from the doctor.

'I'm so cross with you, Kat, really I am.' She glared at me, but then picked up the bowl of soup and offered me a spoonful. 'Why didn't you call someone, or at least answer your bloody phone? Don't you know how worried we all were about you?'

I took the bowl from her with a sigh. 'I can feed myself, Sam. And I'm sorry you were worried, but I'm fine, it was just a touch of flu.'

I took a mouthful of soup and hummed in pleasure at the taste of the creamy chicken broth, suddenly realizing just how hungry I was. However, as I went to take another spoonful, my hand was jiggled by Sam's abrupt departure from my bedside. I looked up as she crossed her arms and started pacing around the bed, her eyes flickering between me and Dr. Laurence.

'Well, what do you think of that, James? Why don't you tell Kat here just how she was affected by her *'touch of flu?'*'

I frowned at Sam's rather shrill tone, surprised at how melodramatic she was being. I mean, I hadn't been hospitalized, so it couldn't be that serious, surely?

Dr. Laurence now stood and started packing his stethoscope and blood pressure equipment back into his leather medical bag. 'Samantha, I don't think now is the time for recriminations.'

I smiled at him and continued to eat my soup as he straightened up and looked at me, grim-faced.

'However, I think it's fair to point out that when I said you were seriously dehydrated, I meant it. In fact, I'd go so far as to say you were *dangerously* dehydrated and that, had Samantha and Tom not found a way in, you might well have ended up in hospital ... or worse. I can't emphasize enough just how ill you've been, Kat, and I'm going to insist you stay in bed for the rest of today and that we keep you on IV fluids until tonight. That's the remainder of this bag and another one, which I'll leave here for Samantha to hook up when that one's finished. She has kindly offered to stay with you so you won't have to be admitted to hospital, but you must follow doctor's orders. Are we clear on all that, Kat?'

I lowered the bowl to my lap and gazed up at him, a little shocked at what he'd said.

'Are you telling me I could have ... *died?*' I whispered, aghast.

He sighed but didn't respond as Sam sat back down, putting her hand on my shoulder, her anger replaced by genuine concern. She waited as the doctor said his goodbyes, with a final entreaty to call him if I started feeling unwell again, before leaving.

Once we were alone, Sam gently pushed my hair away from my face.

'That's exactly what he's saying, Kat. I'm not kidding here; you must never ignore something like this again. I don't even want to think about what might have happened if Tom hadn't been able to break the door down.'

I felt my eyes welling up and squeezed them shut to prevent an embarrassing crying jag. As I did, I was struck by something which made me forget my tears, my eyes flying open.

'You broke my front door down? What the hell, Sam! Tom said he still had a key he was going to drop off to me … couldn't he have used that?'

Sam grimaced and shook her head. 'It's okay, he's fixed it now. But that's just the point, Kat. I specifically told him to bring the key but he couldn't get it to work. It was like…'

She trailed off, glancing away from me toward the door and, much to my surprise, I noticed a slight blush bloom across her cheeks.

'It was like what, Sam?' I asked, curious as to what was making her so uncomfortable.

Her eyes narrowed as she brought them back to mine. 'I know it sounds ridiculous, but while I was downstairs getting your soup, Tom told me that there's absolutely nothing wrong with the lock, that it's working perfectly, and it just seemed … well, almost as if the house was … oh, I don't know … trying to keep us out?'

My mind immediately went to that day before the party when I couldn't open the door from the inside … at least, not until I promised Lucien I would be coming back. Sam clearly took my silence as disbelief, and before I could say anything she rushed to explain herself.

'I know it's stupid and that I said I didn't believe in all that nonsense, but I have to tell you, Kat … there's something weird about this house. I … I didn't say anything to Tom, but…'

Her voice dropped as she glanced again quickly toward the door and back to me.

'You can tell me I'm crazy, Kat, but I swear I saw someone at the guest room window. It was just for a second, and I thought it must be you, but then, when we got inside and found you comatose in here … well, I knew it couldn't have been you, but it was … Jesus, Kat, it was *someone*.'

I stared at her, warring with myself about whether I should say anything. I knew she wasn't crazy, that she had, of course, seen someone.

She had seen Lucien.

And he had tried to prevent my friends from getting into the house to help me … to stop them from saving my life.

He had wanted me to … to *die?*

Chapter Eight

I stared at my friend without really seeing her, my mind trying to make sense of what had happened.

Had Lucien *wanted* me to die? Had he, in fact, *caused* my illness? As I thought back, it suddenly seemed clear to me that the more frequent his nightly visits, the weaker I became ... and, in turn, the more *real* he appeared to get. What did it mean? Was I, through our weird family connection and my own life-force, somehow giving substance to a man who had died some four or five generations before me? I had been so convinced that Lucien was a benign presence, one who meant me no harm; was it possible that the opposite was true?

My muddled thoughts were interrupted by Sam, whose presence I had almost forgotten.

'Kat, what on earth is going on in that head of yours? Come on, I didn't mean to scare you, but this whole thing has me rattled. You've been out of circulation for days, and ... what is it?'

The mention of how long I'd been ill finally penetrated my muddled thoughts, and my look of horror had got her attention.

'Sam, what day is it?' I demanded sharply.

'What? Oh, uh, it's Thursday ... the twenty-fifth. Why?'

'The twenty-fifth? Dammit!'

I thrust the half-empty bowl of soup at Sam and went to throw back the covers. My friend, however, was having none of it. Ignoring the bowl, she put her hands on my shoulders and glared at me.

'Stop right there, Kat Tregowen. What the hell do you think you're doing? If you think I'm going to let you get out of this bed, you've got another think coming. Apart from anything else, you're going nowhere until you've eaten that soup and drunk your Coke.'

'But Sam—'

'But nothing. Eat your bloody soup!'

I sighed, knowing it was useless to argue. It didn't help, of course, that I was more than a little restricted by the IV in the back of my hand, so I dutifully began spooning soup into my mouth under Sam's watchful eye. It was growing a little tepid, but I had to admit that I was hungry enough to keep eating until I'd consumed it all.

As I dropped the spoon into the bowl, Sam took it from me and held out the glass of Coke. Despite the fluids now flowing into my system, I realized that I had what felt like an unquenchable thirst and drank deeply, only stopping when the glass was empty. The sweet, fizzy soda caused me to belch loudly, just as Tom walked back in the room.

'Whoa, nice one, Kitty Kat!" he exclaimed in surprise, as Sam beamed at me like a proud momma whose infant had just been burped after feeding.

'Pardon *me!*' I could feel my face heating with embarrassment, much to their obvious amusement.

'Better out than in, I always say. Anyway, I've fixed your door, and even though I couldn't find a damn thing wrong with the old lock, I've fitted a new one, just to be on the safe side, and left you a couple of sets of keys in the kitchen.'

'Thanks, Tom. I really appreciate it. I'm just sorry you were put to all that trouble—'

He held his hand up to forestall any further comment, an unfamiliar frown marring his usually open and guileless features.

'None of that, Kat. I don't know what kind of friends you've got in America, but 'round here, your mates pull together to help you out when you need it.'

'He's right, Kat. It's what friends do, and we're both just happy we were able to help.'

Tom nodded and the smile that was never far from his face broke out once again.

'Good, glad we got that straight. I've got to shoot off now, but I'm guessing you're gonna hang around for a bit, Sammy.'

'Yeah, I don't want to leave Kat on her own tonight—'

'Sam, you can't—'

'I bloody can, and I will, so you can shut right up, Tregowen. I promised the doc I would stay with you, and that's exactly what I'm gonna do. Tom, can you put my toothbrush, make-up, clean underwear and a change of clothes in a bag for me and drop it off when you finish work, please? You don't mind getting yourself something to eat, do you?'

'No problem, my lover. I'll go to the pub. Want me to bring you anything to eat when I drop off your bag?'

'Yeah, that's a thought. Kat's got bugger all in the fridge, so can you pick us up a few things. How about fish and chips for tea, Kat?'

At my silent nod of acquiescence, she smiled and turned back to Tom.

'Yeah, so if you could nip to the shop on your way over, we need bread, milk, bacon and eggs … oh, and chocolate. And cod and chips twice … is that okay for you, Kat?'

I smiled, feeling a little overwhelmed. In that moment, I realized that in just a few months, I had grown closer to these two people and my other friends here in Port Simon, than in a lifetime in San Francisco. It was a sobering thought, and one I really didn't know how to deal with right now. Instead, I just nodded again to Sam and smiled up at Tom.

'Good. You get off, Tom, and we'll see you later. As for you, Kat, I'm going to run you a nice bath, and while you're having a soak I'll change your sheets, as they're absolutely minging. Honest to God, Kat, you must have sweated, like, *gallons* while you were ill. Once we've got you cleaned up, I can tidy up downstairs while you take a nap … no arguments, okay? Then, when you wake up, we can get ourselves cozy and watch a film or something on the telly. Okay?'

I wasn't going to bother arguing anymore and had to admit that a bath and a nap, followed by a girly night in front of the TV sounded pretty good right now.

We said our goodbyes to Tom, and, as promised, Sam went into the bathroom to fill the tub. Under my direction, she dug out some comfy clothes for me to change into, then helped me out of bed, carefully maneuvering my IV pole as she helped me undress and lower myself into the blessedly hot water.

It was a long time since I'd been naked in front of anyone—well, anyone *alive*—and I hadn't taken my clothes off in front of another female since gym class in high school, when all my insecurities about my starkly androgynous body had made me cringe with embarrassment. It seemed to me that puberty had caused every girl I knew to suddenly blossom into womanly curves, while I remained steadfastly flat of chest and skinny of hip. Those insecurities, incubated in the high school changing room, had remained with me, even when I did finally start to fill out in my late teens, and the few romantic liaisons I had allowed time for had invariably involved sex with the lights off.

None of this, however, even crossed my mind under Sam's gentle and caring hands, and I couldn't have been more relaxed as I slid beneath the hot, foamy water and laid my head back on the towel Sam had thoughtfully folded over the lip of the tub and rested my cannulated hand on the edge. For the first time in what felt like weeks, I let my worries slip away, just for a short while. Lucien Merrick was an enigma—possibly a dangerous and malignant entity—and Luke Brodie would be arriving in England in just two days, a visit I felt wholly unprepared for. But right now, there wasn't a damn thing I could do about either problem, so I forced myself to empty my mind and let the gentle lap of the hot water lull me into a state of tranquility.

ഔൽ

I was floating in a calm, translucent ocean, my arms spread wide as a generous sun warmed my skin. Here, there was nothing to fear and I could feel all my worries leech out of me in a kind of mind detox. My fears subsiding, I let the gentle swell rock me, the warm water lapping and pulling at me. But as I floated, the swell grew, and the sea spray which had at first cooled my overheated skin now began to splash more vigorously. Even as I contemplated turning over and swimming back to shore, I was struck by the rather surprising fact that my lips tasted more soapy than salty, but as this thought took hold, a particularly large wave broke over me, filling my mouth with water.

I knew I needed to start swimming, but I couldn't seem to get my arms to cooperate as I sank further beneath the waves. I could no longer feel the warmth of the sun, and a deep chill began to seep into my very bones.

Come, be with me, Catherine.

The soft words echoed inside my head … compelling, seductive. I felt an overwhelming desire to just let myself sink to the bottom of the ocean, to open up my lungs and invite the sea in. I'd read that drowning was a peaceful way to die … and, really, what was the point of struggling?

'*KAT!* Oh my God, Kat …'

My eyes snapped open as strong arms enveloped me, pulling me back to the surface of the … tub? I took a huge breath and immediately started coughing, water violently expelling itself from both my mouth and nose, burning my throat and nasal passages.

'What the hell, Kat? Jeez, I'm beginning to think you've got a death wish. How on earth did you manage to slip under the water? What happened to the towel I left for you to cushion your head? God, Kate, you nearly gave me a heart attack, you silly bint.'

I watched Sam sit back on her heels, my mind in turmoil. Even if I had been able to speak, I had no answers for her. I scrubbed my face with my free hand, my coughing fit finally subsiding, and drew my knees up to my chest.

Pushing herself back up onto her knees, Sam reached over and pushed my wet hair away from my face, her expression both tender and concerned.

'I'm sorry I yelled, Kat, but you gave me such a scare. Are you okay?'

I nodded, as yet unwilling to explain what had happened until I had made sense of it myself.

She stood, grabbing a towel from the rail behind her, and for the first time I noticed that her front was completely soaked.

'Oh, Sam, I'm so sorry … your clothes…' I really didn't know what to say to her, gratitude and embarrassment warring equally within me.

'Oh, shut up, you daft trollop. Now, delightful as your tits are, I think it's time you covered them up, so let's be having you,' she smirked, holding the towel up.

I gave her a small smile to show my appreciation for her attempt at levity and, gripping the sides of the tub, I pushed myself up with an effort and stepped out onto the wet floor. Turning my back to Sam, I let her wrap me in the soft, warm towel.

'I'm going to put the kettle on and make us both a nice cup of tea. You dry yourself off, and I'll go rummage in your drawers for a t-shirt so I can change out of this wet shirt. Will you be okay on your own, or do I need to search the house for sharp objects you can fall on?'

I gave her a rueful look. 'No, I'm fine, Sam. I think I can manage to stay alive while you make tea. And help yourself to whatever you find clothes-wise. I am so sor—'

'I told you to pack it in, Tregowen. I've left some clothes out for you, so sort yourself out and I'll be back in two shakes of a lamb's tail.'

ဢჿଓ

I woke from a deep, dreamless sleep feeling more refreshed and more ... *alive* than I had in what felt like a very long time. With the sun chasing the shadows from my room and a soft breeze gently moving the drapes, I quickly came to full consciousness, only to discover that I was not alone. I glanced down at the hand attached to the arm wrapped lightly around my waist, which, in turn, was presumably attached to the body lying flush against my back. It was an elegant hand, long-fingered, with beautifully manicured, pearly-pink varnished nails. A diamond and sapphire engagement ring and gold wedding band adorned the third finger of said hand.

I was being spooned by Samantha Jago.

My first thought was that I should be weirded out by the very intimate embrace I found myself in, but, oddly, I had to admit to feeling comforted and protected and somewhat reluctant to disturb our new-found ... whatever this was ... *womance?* Clearly, we'd both fallen asleep last night, and she hadn't made it to the guest room.

I was so comfortable I was reluctant to move, but my bladder had other ideas. Carefully lifting Sam's hand, I managed to extricate myself from her grip and slide out of bed. Tentatively, I pushed myself to my feet, relieved to discover that there was no dizziness. At the same time, I realized I'd been unimpeded by the IV line, and a glance at my hand showed that the cannula had been removed, a small Band-Aid the only evidence of it ever being there. Behind me I heard Sam stir and I turned to see her sit up, her gaze immediately drifting to where I held my arm aloft.

'Oh yeah, I took it out last night. The bag was empty, and I thought it would be more comfortable for you to sleep. I can't believe you didn't wake up when I pulled the cannula out, but you were absolutely dead to the world. How are you feeling? You look a hell of a lot better today, and the shadows under your eyes have almost gone.'

I smiled at her, thinking about what a fantastic friend she'd turned out to be.

'I feel really good, Sam.' I looked down at the back of my hand and rubbed it absently. 'I ... I don't really know how to thank you— Tom too—for what you've done for me. I've got a feeling you may have saved my life...'

I couldn't continue, unable to speak around the sudden lump in my throat.

'Twice, you minger. You owe me big time. In fact, the next time Tom's sick, I'm gonna get you to look after him, as he's the biggest, whiniest baby when he's ill. And because you owe me so much, you won't be allowed to smack, punch, stab, or otherwise damage him. Do we have a deal?'

My tears retreated as I giggled, loving Sam even more for distracting me from my wayward emotions and removing the drama from what we both knew had been a pretty serious situation for me.

I nodded and reached across to give her shoulder a quick squeeze, knowing that anything more demonstrative would likely challenge her British *sangfroid*.

'Okay, Tregowen, let's shower and get some breakfast. You need feeding up, and the twenty pounds of chocolate you ate last night doesn't count. Then we can talk about what you're going to do about Luke Brodie.'

I gasped, recalling that the previous night I had explained my plans to drive up to London, pick up Luke and bring him back.

'Come on, no point worrying about it until you've got some good food inside you and you can decide how you're feeling.'

With that, she climbed off the bed and headed to the guest room she'd failed to use the night before, and I made my way to the bathroom.

$\wp \supset \wp$

Three hours later found me on the road, heading to the capital. Sam had, at first, been reluctant to let me go until I had managed to persuade her that I really did feel a hundred percent better and was more than capable of driving a few hours to London. Even then, she had, at first, wanted me to wait, to see if maybe Ruby could take time off to accompany me, but I assured her it was unnecessary.

'At least the spare room sheets don't need changing, seeing as I didn't make it out of your bed, you temptress … ha, maybe Mr. Brodie will be equally seduced, and you'll still have clean sheets … well, on the spare bed anyway.'

She smirked at me, waggling her eyebrows suggestively in a gesture I swore she inherited from Tom.

'Shut up, Sam, you're so not funny!" I harrumphed. I couldn't be mad at her, though, especially not in the face of all her kindness.

In the end, I managed to convince her that I could drive to my dad's without mishap, and now, as I exited the freeway—or, as I kept reminding myself, the motorway—and headed toward central London, I let myself get excited about showing Nick the photos and videos of the house, so he could see for himself how beautiful it was and what a great investment it had turned out to be.

None of that, of course, had prevented me from sending out a plea to Lucien before I left, begging him to behave and telling him I would be away for a few days visiting my father, but would be back.

I didn't mention that I would have someone with me.

I had felt a little foolish as I twirled slowly around in the entrance hall while Sam was taking my bag out to the car. There had been no further 'incidents' since my unfortunate experience in the tub, and I couldn't help wondering if it was just an accident or if Lucien had, in fact, been responsible—and, if that were the case, had his actions somehow drained his energy, causing him to withdraw to wherever it was he spent his time when he wasn't spooking me? After all, he hadn't got his 'fix' last night either!

I shook my head at my own ridiculous thoughts and headed out the door. But I swore I heard a soft sigh behind me as I left.

ഇറ

'So, Kat, let me get this straight. This Brodie bloke you're meeting tomorrow, he's come all the way from San Francisco to visit Cornwall and your house, after you were contacted by his mother to say we're related … all because you posted a message online. Do I have that right?'

'Yes, Dad, but he hasn't come here just for that; he was flying to the UK anyway for business, and his mom asked him to take time out to visit his ancestral home. It's just a quick visit, and he's come a few days earlier than planned so he can fit it in.'

'Hmmph, so you're going to drive to Cornwall with this man you've never met, and you've invited this complete stranger to stay at your place … I don't like it, Kat, it sounds like a rum do to me.'

He frowned, giving me the stink-eye I was all too familiar with when disapproval was on the table. I knew things were bad by the way he started compulsively rubbing his chin with his forefinger and thumb. He only did that when he was really worried.

And I hadn't even told him about the ghost!

'Dad, I'm pretty sure he's not a serial murderer, and besides, he's family—'

'Family, my arse! How do you know we're related? This Brodie woman could be having you on … it might be some elaborate scam; you just don't know.'

'Oh, Dad, don't be ridiculous—apart from anything else, you've seen the photograph she sent me. You can't deny the girl in it is the spitting image of me, and she says the boy is her son's double, too. And her name's Helen.'

His eyes narrowed but I knew he had no valid response to what I'd told him. His antipathy undoubtedly came from a good place, but I didn't have the energy to fight with him about this and hoped he would let it go.

'Come on, Dad, aren't you at least a little bit curious about our family history? Luke's father is, like, your second cousin or something, and Catherine's is such an amazing story of survival in a time when a baby born in such circumstances rarely had a happy ending. And just look at all the coincidences—the similarity of our names, the fact that our families both ended up in California … jeez, me buying the house where little Sarah was conceived. Don't you want to know more? I know I do. Look, Dad, I do understand your concerns, and I know you're just looking out for me, but I've got a good feeling about all this … like we were meant to connect with family we didn't even know we had. Be a little excited, eh?'

He shook his head in resignation, another gesture I knew well from all the times I dug my heels in with him as a truculent teenager.

'Okay, okay, I can see you've got the bit between your teeth and nothing I say is going to make you change your plans. I should bloody know better by know, shouldn't I? Just promise me you'll be careful, and that you'll call me from the road and when you get back to Port Simon.'

I grinned at him and stood up. We were sitting at the dining table, where I'd set up my laptop after dinner to show him the photos of the house. Walking around the table, I bent and wrapped my arms around his shoulders from behind, kissing his cheek and reveling in the familiar scent of his cologne.

'Thanks, Dad, and I promise I'll keep in touch if you promise to make time to come visit me soon.'

He chuckled, covering my hands with one of his and looking up at me.

'It's a deal, daughter of mine. I'll check my diary tomorrow and let you have a date. Now, how about a game of backgammon?'

I nodded happily, pleased to have won that particular battle. I knew Nick was even less enthusiastic about me applying for a local job, insisting that I'd be wasting my talents at some provincial architectural practice, designing house extensions. I tried to reassure him that one interview wouldn't necessarily add up to either a job offer or a firm decision on my part to stay in Cornwall, but I could tell he was concerned that I was potentially making some bad choices. In all honesty, I wasn't entirely sure I wanted to work in Truro or anywhere else in Cornwall, but I at least wanted to attend the interview and get an idea of what might or might not be possible. I would then be able to make an informed decision about my future.

80C3

The following morning, I stood at the barrier in Heathrow's Terminal 5 Arrivals hall, my heart beating wildly as I waited for Luke Brodie to appear. I held a sign I'd printed off the previous evening at my dad's, with Luke's name in large capital letters, just in case he didn't look as much like Lucien Merrick as his mother seemed to think or, indeed, the photo she had emailed to me—and also in case he didn't recognize me.

I needn't have worried.

Watching the first passengers emerge from baggage claim, my eyes were immediately and inexorably drawn to a mop of unruly black hair and my first sight of Luke Brodie affected me in ways I was totally and utterly unfamiliar with.

Helen was right—he was the image of his three times great grandfather.

Fast on the heels of that thought was the undeniable fact that he was possibly the handsomest man I'd ever seen. As he drew closer, I found myself captivated by his eyes, which were an extraordinary shade of blue—what I could only describe as the color of vibrant African violets.

So enthralled was I, that I hardly noticed when he stopped right in front of me on the other side of the barrier. He was so close and so damned tall that in order to maintain eye contact I practically had to crick my neck into a very uncomfortable position.

It was then that I noticed the languid smile which lit his face, as his hand came up to take from me the sign I was still uselessly holding up.

'I hardly think we need this—I'm pretty sure I could pick you out of a crowd at a Giants ballgame. You look even more like her than I look like him.'

Desperately struggling to recall the power of speech, I nodded and thrust out my hand.

'Um, yeah, absolutely, I'm Kat Tregowen and you're Luke Brodie—'

Smirking, he took my hand before I could prod him in the stomach and was gracious enough to ignore my ridiculous introduction—why I felt it necessary to state the obvious was beyond me.

Face ablaze, I really hoped he hadn't already formed the opinion that I was a simple-minded moron.

I blamed it on those eyes.

Chapter Nine

I huffed loudly as I reclaimed my hand. 'Can we start again, do you think? Maybe you could go back to baggage claim and come out again so we can pretend we've never met, and I can hopefully avoid acting like a complete dork.'

He laughed loudly and unselfconsciously in a way which told me he laughed often, and the sound was rich and infectious; so much so, I couldn't help but laugh at my own foolishness.

'Oh, Kat Tregowen, I think I'm going to like you!'

His grin was friendly and totally without judgment or irony, and I knew that the feeling was mutual.

I held my hand out again and, with just the merest amused arch of an eyebrow, he enveloped it within his own, much larger hand.

'Hello, Luke Brodie, I'm delighted to make your acquaintance.'

'Ditto, Kat. Now, I need to go to Hertz to pick up my rental, and then, as a fellow American, would you please take me somewhere we can get a decent cup of coffee!'

I laughed at his look of faux desperation, but recognized and understood his need, turning to lead him to the Hertz desk so that we could get out of there and find a Starbucks.

ᎦᏋ

The first part of the drive back to Port Simon passed quickly as Luke and I chatted amiably, like two old friends who hadn't seen each other for a while. It was odd how comfortable I felt in his company, especially after our slightly awkward first meeting, but I really did feel like I knew him. When we came to the motorway turnoff and started driving on the four- and two-lane highways of Cornwall I offered to take over the driving, but it was obvious he'd driven on the left before and was happy to stay behind the wheel.

'I'll have to get used to it again, as I'll be driving back on my own, and it's not the first time I've driven in the UK … I think this is my third or fourth trip. Plus, I've spent time in Australia and Japan, where they drive on the left, so it's not a problem.'

He glanced over at me, a smile on his face, and I was struck yet again by just how good-looking he was. Annoyingly, I found myself wondering about a significant other and inwardly cursed myself. He wasn't wearing a wedding ring, but a guy as attractive as Luke Brodie would surely have a girlfriend ... or, worse, a boyfriend! He did live in San Francisco, after all.

I forced myself to stop thinking about such matters, instead focusing on more prosaic concerns.

'Hey, why don't we stop for lunch in Launceston? It's the next big town, and we can stretch our legs before we head down the coast.'

He nodded enthusiastically, and I directed him to the turnoff.

ഇരു

'So, was it work or pleasure that took you to Australia and Japan?' I asked, cutting into the ridiculously large piece of battered fish on my plate.

'Uh, both really. I spent my gap year travelling around South Asia, Australia, New Zealand and Japan. And then, a few years back I spent about a year working on a building project in Osaka in southern Japan. It's an incredible country—have you ever been?'

'Sadly not. Much to my shame I'm not very well-traveled, even in the States. I'm so jealous right now. I feel like all I've ever done is study and work, and with my thirtieth birthday looming, I'm beginning to wonder what I've done with my life.'

I looked down at my plate, suddenly weighed down by the sheer absence of ... well, *living* I'd done. It occurred to me that my obsession with Chimneys and my family history was a direct result of the absence of any kind of adventure or excitement in my life up to this point. As I absently pushed food around my plate and contemplated my dreary existence, I became aware of the silence and lack of movement across the table. Looking up, I found two glittering eyes of cobalt blue staring back at me.

'Sorry, didn't mean to sound so pathetic. My life's been pretty good; I just wish I'd made time to do more ... stuff.'

He dropped his silverware loudly onto his plate and pushed it away. Putting his elbows on the table, he clasped his hands in front of his chin and speared me with a look of such intensity I could do nothing but hold his gaze. It occurred to me in that moment that Lucien Merrick might not be the only member of his family who could cast a spell over me.

'Listen, Kat, I don't know you, and what you have or haven't done with your life is no business of mine. But I googled you before I flew over here, and it seems to me that you've achieved a hell of a lot. Maybe you haven't backpacked to Thailand or walked along the Great Wall of China, but you've made a bigger mark on this world than a bunch of tourists. We may not have three- and four-hundred-year-old houses in the States, but I've seen what you've done with some beautiful houses that looked like they were ready to fall apart, preserving our American history in your own way. And now, it seems like you've done something even more amazing and exciting with a house that has been a part of both our families for over a hundred years, and I, for one, can't wait to see it. Don't sell yourself short; you're a talented designer with a great future ahead of you, so don't ever let me hear you say you haven't achieved anything.'

I just stared at him, open-mouthed, too shocked by his words to speak—or even blush, it seemed.

'If you've finished eating, let's get out of here, because I'm ready to see this fine house of yours. How much farther is it anyway?'

He stood, took his wallet out and dropped two twenty-pound notes down on the table.

'Come on, Kat. We're not getting any younger.' He grinned at me and started walking away, which finally seemed to break me out of the spell I was apparently under.

'Uh, that's too much, Luke … Luke?'

But he was already out the door, and I had no choice but to grab my purse and follow him out. It looked like it would be our waitress's lucky day.

When I got outside, Luke was already in the car with the engine running and as soon as I got in next to him, we were off.

'So, how far did you say it was?'

I looked at his profile—Christ, he had a jaw you could cut yourself on—and found myself wondering what the hell he was talking about. I dragged my eyes away and fixed them on the view through the windshield, knowing that looking at him simply robbed me of any kind of coherent thought.

'Uh, not far. We need to go left here and follow the signs to Newquay and the A30. That'll take us straight to Port Simon, which is about another thirty miles or so.'

We drove in silence for a few minutes as I continued to turn over in my mind what he'd said in the restaurant. He'd *googled* me? Jeez, even I'd never done that.

'Luke?'

'Hmmm?'

'Um, thanks for what you said back there. I, uh … no one's ever said anything like that to me, not even my parents. I mean, I know there're proud of me, but … well, I'm almost thirty and, uh, I've never, you know, had a … well, any kind of long-term relationship … except, you know, with work, and I…'

A large hand reached over and captured my fidgeting fingers, holding on to them.

'I get it, Kat. I really do,' he said softly, without a trace of condescension. Withdrawing his hand, he placed it back on the steering wheel but shot me a smile full of understanding.

'Look at us, both teetering on the edge of thirty, both single, and both still wondering what the hell we're doing. What a pair we make.'

He's single?

'You're single?' I blurted, seemingly incapable of not embarrassing myself in front of this man.

He chuckled, and I looked over at him just in time to see him glance in my direction, one eyebrow cocked and a mischievous smirk playing across his lips.

'What, you think a wife or girlfriend would be happy to wave me off at the airport to come spend the night with my beautiful third cousin once or twice removed, whatever the hell we are?'

Again, I found myself staring at him open-mouthed. Jeez, this was becoming a habit, but … he thinks I'm beautiful? Wow.

'In case you were still wondering, the answer is, no, I'm pretty sure she wouldn't, if she existed, which she doesn't. Now, do you want to know my star sign?'

I snorted. 'God, no. Astrology is a crock of shit!'

He barked a laugh and smacked the steering wheel.

'Oh, thank God—finally, a girl with a brain. I'm starting to think that you and I are made for each other … maybe we're kissing cous—'

He cleared his throat and, when I turned to look at him, resolutely kept his eyes on the road ahead. The tops of his ears, though … well, they had gone a curious shade of dark pink.

Torn between asking him to finish what he'd been about to say and saving him from embarrassment, I chose to take pity on him.

'Hey, I know what I was going to ask you. You said in the restaurant that you'd gone to Japan to work on a building project. Does that mean you're an architect, too? Jesus, how many more weird coincidences are we going to discover?'

'Uh, no, not an architect. I'm a structural engineer. I work for Carlton Associates in San Francisco.'

'Oh, wow, really? You know, just the fact that we both work in the same industry is still a hell of a coincidence. I mean, I know Carlton is a huge international firm, so we probably work on very different types of project, but it's still kind of weird, don't you think?'

'Yeah, for sure. And I have a feeling there's more … is there more, Kat?'

'Oh, uh, well … oh, you need to take the next right onto the A395 and keep heading toward Newquay.'

A moment later he made the turn and we continued without speaking for a while. It wasn't that I wanted to keep him in the dark; I just needed time to work out how I was going to tell him about my supernatural lodger. God Almighty, how had my life become so weird?! I was beginning to think that Grandma was onto something—maybe there really was magic in Cornwall.

'Okay, I can practically hear the cogs whirring inside your head, Kat. Care to share?'

I huffed out a sigh, still unsure where to start and what to say without him thinking I had a screw loose.

'Sorry, I'm just wondering how to tell you everything and not come across as someone in need of immediate psychiatric intervention.'

Again, his laughter warmed something deep inside me and seemed to ease my anxiety about what I had to tell him.

'Go for it. I promise I won't drag you to the nearest mental institution.'

Smiling to myself, I glanced out the passenger window, took a deep breath, and turned back to him, watching his profile.

'First, I want you to know that up until finding Chimneys I absolutely did not believe in ghosts, okay?'

He nodded, shooting me a quizzical glance, but saying nothing as he transferred his attention back to the road.

'So, notwithstanding that caveat, I believe that my house is haunted by the spirit of Lucien Merrick, your great, great, great grandfather and lover of my great, great aunt, Catherine Tregowen.'

I dragged my eyes from his face and looked down at my hands, cringing inwardly as I waited for another bark of laughter. But this time, I imagined it would be full of disbelief and scorn. Instead, for the second time his hand reached over to cover mine.

'Hey, I'm listening, Kat. You don't strike me as a flake, so why don't you tell me what's happened to make you change your views on the afterlife.'

Unlike before, he kept his hand on mine, and I couldn't help but be encouraged by this overt gesture of support.

So, I told him about Lucien Merrick. About how I found the house and the presence I sensed right from my first exploration. I told him about the voice, the touches, the way the temperature dropped when he was around, and that I believed he was becoming stronger. I told him about what had happened to the last family who lived in the house and the two property developers who tried to buy it before me.

I stopped talking for a moment, debating how much detail I wanted to give, but if Luke was going to be staying at Chimneys, he had a right to know everything. Just as I decided to give him the gist, if not the details, of what had been going on, I looked up at the road and realized we were fast approaching the turnoff for Port Simon.

'You need to turn left at the lights and head towards Goonhaven. Once we get there, you'll see the sign for Port Simon.'

'Got it. Why don't you finish telling me about the irascible Mr Merrick.'

'Oh God, this next bit is really embarrassing, so please let me just get it all out in the open before you comment … or throw me out of the car.'

'Not gonna happen—apart from anything else, I'm supposed to be staying at your place and I don't have a key to the house.'

'Hmm, well, after you hear what I have to say you may not want to stay,' I huffed.

'Just spit it out, Kat. As long as you're not sacrificing goats or babies in the back yard, I think I can handle it.'

'No child sacrifices, no.'

'So, just the goats, then?'

I laughed, looking at him in time to see him smirk in my direction.

'Okay, I'm just gonna say this real quick. Of late, Merrick hasn't just been a presence in the house, he's also been a presence in my ... uh, in my, b-bed.' I squeezed my eyes shut, waiting for him to say something.

'Go on,' was all he said, his voice soft, neutral.

'I ... shit, this is really, *really* hard to talk about.' I buried my head in my hands, but when Luke remained silent, I sat up straight and stared out the windshield.

'Right at the next set of lights,' I murmured.

He made the turn, and I knew that we would be there soon.

'Um, so it's got pretty, uh, intense in the last couple of weeks, but I always assumed he was harmless ... that he ... well, that he thinks I'm Catherine, that he loves me ... *her*, I mean, so he'd, you know, never hurt me. But things got really weird a few days ago, and now I'm not sure. Now, I'm wondering if he maybe wants me—or Catherine—whatever, to ... I don't know ... join him?'

I didn't mean to make it sound like a question, but I really had no idea what I was saying anymore. Saying this stuff out loud was a hell of a lot different to the way it sounded inside my head.

My musings were interrupted when I felt the car suddenly swerve to the left. I looked up to see that we'd pulled into a narrow rest area, and the car which had been behind us honked his horn to show his disapproval of our abrupt maneuver.

I had no time to think about that, though, because Luke was releasing his seat belt and swiveling to face me.

'What the fuck, Kat?' He was frowning and looked pretty pissed.

'What?' I asked nonsensically.

He sighed, looking up at the roof of the car with a pained expression. After what felt like minutes rather than seconds, he dropped his gaze and speared me with those laser eyes of his.

'Kat, will you please explain to me what you mean when you say Lucien Merrick wants you to join him.' His tone was sharp and unambiguous. Yeah, he was pissed all right.

'Um, well, I got sick, and Tom had to break the door down, even though he had a key, and then I nearly drowned in the bath ... shit, this just sounds dumb when I say it out loud...' I trailed off, as he wasn't looking any happier.

'Who the fuck is Tom?'

Oh, well, that wasn't the first question I was expecting.

'He's my builder … look, does it matter who he is? Oh, just forget I said anything—I'm being stupid.'

'Kat Tregowen, we are not moving from this spot until you tell me what's going on.'

Even though I barely knew the guy, I could tell from the stony expression on his face that he wasn't going to let it go. He ran an agitated hand through his hair, glancing away from me for a moment, before looking back and once more capturing my gaze.

'Look, I'm sorry, okay? I know we've only known each other a few hours and I don't have any right to make demands, but … Jesus, Kat, I … I feel like … like I *do* have a right to know. Please, can you just tell me everything?'

The look on his face was kind of desperate and I knew I couldn't deny him. So, I did exactly that—told him everything; how close I'd apparently come to dying for lack of hydration, Sam and Tom's intervention, the incident in the tub … even the intimacy and my theory that Merrick was draining my life-force in order to give himself greater substance and strength, my growing belief that he was, in fact, some kind of … of incubus. I couldn't look at him as I talked. Even though I had been vague in my description of Merrick's … *attentions*, it was still pretty humiliating to admit to being ravished by a ghost.

Once my overheated skin began to cool, I steeled myself to look at Luke. I expected to see incredulity, maybe even contempt, but his expression was pensive, like he was trying to make sense of what I had said, but I got no impression from him that he didn't believe me. After what seemed like an eternity, he turned face-front and leaned his head back against the seat. Frustratingly, he still said nothing.

When I could no longer stand the silence, I pushed the door open and got out. Up ahead was a rough wooden bench next to a trash can. There was no one around so I walked over to it and sat down, suddenly glad to be out of the claustrophobic confines of the car. With the sun warm on my back and a view across the fields which seemed to go on for miles, I felt myself become a little drowsy.

I was brought out of my reverie by the sound of a car door slamming, and moments later Luke joined me on the bench. Without looking at him, I decided that one of us, at least, needed to speak.

'I'm heartened by the fact that you didn't just dump my bag on the side of the road and drive off.'

'I'm sorry, Kat. I didn't mean to make you feel like I doubted you, but I'm struggling to understand what's happened here. Can you bear with me while I try to make sense of it?'

'Of course. Look, I totally get it if you think I'm a bit psycho … I'm not sure I'd believe me either, if I was in your shoes.'

He rubbed his hands over his face and sighed.

'Kat, like I said in the car, I'm very much aware that we've only just met, so there's absolutely no reason at all for me to take what you say at face value.' He paused, looking away for a moment before seeming to come to a decision. 'Having said that, I need you to know that I don't think you're lying. There may well be a logical explanation for what you've experienced, but I believe that *you* believe what you've told me. What I am confused about is why you're still living in that house. Whether you're having a psychotic break or there really is a sinister presence there, aren't you worried about going back?'

I smiled ruefully and shook my head, leaning forward to rest my elbows on my knees and clasp my hands in front of me.

'Well, apart from the fact that I've spent a fortune on it, I can't just cut and run. I mean, maybe I am going crazy and this is all the product of an over-active imagination, prompted by a tragic tale of star-crossed lovers. Perhaps Lucien Merrick's ghost is just something my subconscious is conjuring up in my dreams. Maybe I really did have the flu and, in my delirium, forgot to keep myself hydrated. And maybe I just dozed off in the tub and slid under the water—it's not impossible that's what happened.

'So, you're right, it really is all explainable. And, to tell you the truth, I simply don't want to leave. I put my heart and soul into bringing that house back to life, and, despite everything that's happened, I really love it. Even now, I can't wait to get back there.'

I didn't look at him, keeping my eyes fixed on the far horizon, but I could feel him watching me. I closed my eyes and just let the heat of the sun seep into my bones for a few minutes.

'Luke, I understand if you would prefer not to stay with me. I'm not sure if there'll be any hotel rooms available, as it's the height of the summer season, but I could ask Josh if his spare room is free. He runs one of the local pubs; Tom's married to his sister, Samantha.'

He snorted derisively, and I was forced to sit up and look at him.

'Oh, Kat, you have a lot to learn about me if you think I'd pass up the opportunity to spend the night in a haunted house with a beautiful woman.'

I looked away as my damned blush once more suffused my face. There he went again with the b-word; was he flirting with me?

'Hey, come on, let's get going. I'm dying to see this amazing house, and maybe even meet my great, great, great grandpa so I can tear him a new one for messing with you.'

He stood and held out his hand. I looked at it and then up at his face, which once again was sporting that sexy smile, and I could do nothing but take his hand and let him pull me to my feet. He let go once I was upright, but then, much to my surprise, he wrapped an arm around my shoulders and hugged me to his side as we walked back to the car.

'Don't worry, Kat. We'll figure this out—I promise.'

℘⃝℞

Twenty minutes later we swept into the wide paved driveway at the front of Chimneys. I had long since had the unpaved track at the rear fenced off and gated to secure the back of the property. It may have been how I found the house, but I didn't want anyone else inadvertently—or deliberately—gaining entry from that direction.

From the front, the house looked magnificent, with two-story bay windows on either side of the wide, double-leaf front door, the beautiful local bricks scrubbed clean, and all the choking undergrowth cleared away. The circular driveway enclosed a wide swathe of neatly clipped lawn, at the center of which was a two-tier marble fountain, the cascading water sparkling like diamonds in the afternoon sunshine.

I hadn't been exaggerating when I told Luke that I couldn't wait to return. As I took in the handsome façade, I experienced a familiar emotion, an overwhelming feeling of coming home. Considering what had happened to me here, I had to admit that it was probably an irrational feeling.

I was distracted from my internal musings when Luke opened his door and climbed out, prompting me to exit the car along with him.

'Wow, you weren't kidding, were you? It really is a beautiful house, Kat, and I can understand why you love it so much.'

'You should see what it looked like when I found it,' I exclaimed, smiling at him.

'I can't wait to see the pictures. So, can we go inside, or do you think Grandpa Merrick will start throwing stuff?'

'Making fun of your venerable ancestor will not endear you to him, you know,' I warned him; I was only half joking but led the way to the door as Luke collected our bags from the trunk.

Walking into the cool entrance hall, I whispered a quick plea to Lucien while Luke was still outside.

'He's your great, great, great grandson, Lucien, so please, *please* be nice.'

I wasn't really sure what I expected, but when absolutely nothing happened, I was confused to find that I was both relieved and disappointed at the lack of response. Had I imagined it all? Was it just the result of stress, fatigue and an over-active imagination? Or was he simply worn out from his recent activities—and the lack of an opportunity to re-charge his battery?

'Oh, all right, give me the silent treatment, then,' I muttered.

I swung around as Luke walked in behind me and dropped our bags on the floor.

'This entrance hall is amazing, Kat … wow, that atrium is fantastic.' Luke narrowed his eyes, crouching down to look at the floor more closely. 'Christ, is that a light-well into the basement?' I chuckled at his excitement, understanding exactly where he was coming from and grateful for his appreciation. Renovating Chimneys had been a labor of love, and it always filled me with pleasure when others expressed their admiration.

'Why don't we grab a beer while I show you the 'before' photographs. Then I'll give you a proper tour, and you can take your bag up to your room.'

Nodding happily, he waited while I retrieved my laptop and then followed me into the kitchen.

෨෬

'Well, if I'd ever had any doubts about your talents from what I found online, what you've done here would convince me that you are a truly gifted designer. I can hardly believe this is the same house as the one in those early photographs. It's stunning, Kat. And it sounds like you've found a star contractor in Tom.'

We were sitting on the couch in the library—it seemed my favorite room was fast becoming Luke's—and I was once again blushing furiously at his fulsome praise. After going through my extensive collection of photographs which marked the detailed progress of the renovations from beginning to end, I had given him the full tour, both inside and out. After a thorough—and thankfully uneventful—investigation of the property, I had prepared an early dinner, and, having now eaten, we were relaxing with a glass of wine. It had been wonderful to talk about such a personal project with someone who totally understood the process, and Luke's praise was all the more precious to me because of that.

'Thanks, Luke. That means a lot coming from a fellow professional in the field.'

I smiled, glancing in his direction just as a huge yawn overtook him. My answering yawn reminded me that it had been a really long day, especially after having only recently recovered from the flu—or whatever the hell had made me sick. And if it had been a long day for me, it had been even longer for Luke, who had gained eight hours and traveled nearly six thousand miles. It wasn't even ten o'clock, but I reckoned that an early night would benefit us both.

I just hoped my night wouldn't be interrupted.

'God, I'm sorry—you must be absolutely exhausted. Why don't we call it a night, and tomorrow I can show you around town and introduce you to our local historian and pub owner, Joshua Frayn. Then I can get you up to speed on all the research we've done so far.'

'My apologies, Kat, but I must admit I'm really tired. I left home yesterday morning, and even with a Business Class flat bed, I didn't get much sleep, so it actually feels like I've been awake for the whole thirty-eight hours. Right now, an early night sounds wonderful.'

'No problem. I'm pretty tired myself. I'll just get you some water to take upstairs.'

ℴ)(Ω

I woke with a start, the room still dark. I had no idea what had roused me from my blessedly deep, dreamless slumber, wanting only to turn over and go back to sleep. The sound of my bedroom door clicking softly shut and an overwhelming awareness of a presence in the room, alerted me that all was not right, and I scrabbled to turn on my bedside light.

The sight that greeted me caused me to gasp out loud, an expletive exploding from my lips.

Across the room, standing by the door in nothing but a pair of close-fitting black boxer-briefs, stood Luke Brodie.

Chapter Ten

'Luke? Is everything okay? What...?' My voice died in my throat as I looked at him standing immobile, like a statue, by the door. It wasn't so much his unexpected presence in my room, but more his appearance.

If I thought his hair was messy before, it was utterly chaotic now. It almost looked as if he'd been violently tugging at it and dragging his fingers through it all night so that tufts stood up in every direction. But what had really rendered me speechless were his eyes.

Those sparkling violet orbs were obsidian dark ... depthless ... *scary*. They seemed to pin me in place, like a butterfly on a display board, and I felt naked and vulnerable.

'Luke? What's going on?' I silently cursed my wavering voice and pulled the sheet up to my neck.

Still he remained motionless, and I was at a loss to know how to break this current impasse. Was it possible that Lucien had somehow ... *possessed* Luke? The very thought immediately sent a chill down my spine, even as my rational mind worked hard to dismiss the idea as fatuous—this wasn't a movie, this was real life and I badly needed to believe that such a thing was impossible.

Finally, I gathered my diminishing courage and slowly climbed out of bed. Despite the warmth of the night, I felt cold and exposed in my short silky nightgown, so I grabbed my robe from the chair in the corner, slipped it on and tied the belt tightly. Emboldened by my cloth armor, I took a couple of steps toward the almost naked man in my room. His gaze remained fixed on me, while, at the same time, seeming to look right through me.

I took another step forward, endeavoring to keep my eyes focused on his face, but, if I'm honest, the body below was a sight to behold. Broad of shoulder and slim of hip, he was all lean muscle and smooth skin, with just a smattering of dark hair sprinkled across his pecs and dissecting his abs.

I may have been scared, but I couldn't deny my attraction to this spectacular man.

I came to a halt an arm's length from my late-night visitor, wondering what I should or could do to break the spell he seemed to be under. Knowing I had to do something and praying he wouldn't react violently, I tentatively reached out a hand and placed it softly on his chest, over his heart. I was aware that it was an intimate gesture, and that I should probably have touched his arm instead, but it somehow seemed appropriate.

As contact was made, skin on skin, I saw something flicker in Luke's eyes, and he seemed to tremble slightly, like a nervous horse.

'Luke, talk to me. What are you doing here?' I asked him, keeping my voice low. In that moment, I saw his eyes refocus as the pupils contracted and those glorious sapphire irises reappeared. At the same time, the intense, slightly menacing façade that had clouded his face fell away, to be replaced by confusion and embarrassment. He looked down at me, his gaze lingering for a few seconds on my face. Then his head snapped up, his eyes darting around the room, before returning to me and my hand on his chest. I started to pull it away, but in a movement which belied how disoriented he appeared to be, his hand shot up and his fingers wrapped around my wrist, holding my arm still.

'What?' he asked, his voice hoarse and uncertain.

'I asked what you're doing here … in my room. Luke, do you remember why you came in here?'

Again, he looked around, more slowly now, seeming to fully take in where he was.

'I … no, I don't. Jesus, Kat, I have no idea how I got here.'

He looked so bewildered, and I wondered what I should do. Could he have been sleep-walking? Unfortunately, much as I wanted answers, I didn't think it was a good idea to have an a near naked Luke in my room. The warmth of his skin beneath my trapped hand was distracting, as was the whole sexy, muscly, manliness of him.

'I was dreaming … and then I was here…'

All of a sudden, he seemed to become completely aware of his surroundings and that he was gripping my wrist. Almost as if my touch was burning him, he released me and stepped away, his back hitting the wall.

'Christ, Kat, I'm sorry. I don't understand how I got here. I'm so sorry. Please believe me … I would never assume … I would never take advantage…'

'Luke, stop. It's okay, honestly.' I took a step toward him and reached out to gently rub his arm. The muscles there were tense as he flattened his hands against the wall.

'How can you say that?' he whispered.

'Look, you're exhausted. You've spent the better part of a day traveling, and you're in a strange bed in a strange house after listening to me blabber on about it being haunted. It's no wonder you're disoriented and confused. Come on, let's get you back to bed, and we can talk about it in the morning when we're both a bit more *compos mentis*.'

I leaned past him and opened the door, all the while keeping my hand on his arm. He let me guide him out of my room and down the hallway. The guest room door was open, and I could see that his bed was a mess. The nights now were so warm that I had only put a sheet on the bed, with a light, summer comforter, but these were twisted and tangled and trailing on the carpet. One pillow looked like it had been punched into submission, while the other was on the floor.

Sighing, I started straightening everything while Luke headed into the bathroom. A few seconds later, I heard the water running briefly in the basin, and as I finished making the bed, he re-emerged. He still looked a little like he might be in shock, so I sat on the end of the bed and held out my hand for him to join me. Blinking rapidly, as if trying to shake off whatever had caused him to get lost inside his head, he managed to give me a small smile as he walked across the room and sat down beside me.

'Jesus, Kat … where the hell do I begin? I am so, so sorry. Oh God, what must you think of me?'

Slumping forward, elbows on knees, he buried his face in his hands. Instinctively, I reached over and rubbed his back. As I did so, it occurred to me that, within less than twenty-four hours of meeting him for the first time, I had touched Luke's bare torso twice now. Prior to this, it had taken many weeks for me to become this intimate with someone, and I wondered why it didn't seem in the least bit inappropriate or premature with this man.

'Hey now, Luke, don't beat yourself up so much. I could tell immediately you weren't yourself. Your mom assured me that she and your dad raised you to be a gentleman, so I'm pretty sure you're not a pervert. In fact, I suspect you have some sharper moves than just turning up in a girl's bedroom in your underwear.'

He snorted and sat up, a wry smile on his face.

'You think I've got moves?'

'Oh, I don't doubt it for a moment.'

He chuckled, shaking his head, but his amusement quickly vanished, to be replaced by a frown.

'I can't explain it, Kat. I was dreaming … goddammit, why can't I remember? It was so clear, but now all I have is a vague impression of being by the sea … Shit, it's no good, it's gone. The next thing I know, I'm in your room, and you're standing in front of me with your hand … well, I guess you know the rest.'

I nodded. 'Have you ever sleep-walked before, Luke?'

Again, he leaned forward, resting his forearms on his thighs. 'Never—not even as a kid. I have no explanation for what happened, none at all.'

He dry-washed his face with his hands and sat up again, looking at me. 'I'm so tired, Kat. Can we talk about this in the morning?'

His exhaustion was written all over his face. In the low light of the bedside lamp, his eyes looked bruised and a light stubble shadowed his jaw, making his skin appear sallow and unhealthy.

'Of course. We both need to get some sleep. I'm sure an explanation will present itself when we're rested and fed.'

I stood up, my hand once again seeking contact as I reached out to squeeze his shoulder. I assumed he would either shrug it off or, at best, ignore it, but he immediately lifted his own hand to cover mine.

'Thanks, Kat. I don't know many women who would be so … sanguine about what happened tonight.'

He dropped his hand, allowing me to do the same. I gave him one last smile and turned to leave, but as I reached the door he called my name softly, causing me to look back over my shoulder.

'I'd feel a lot better if you locked your door.'

I frowned but nodded, knowing my acquiescence would help him rest easier. I pulled his door shut behind me and returned to my own room, engaging the lock as promised. For a moment, I stood with my back to the door, letting my gaze flicker from wall to wall. Feeling a little foolish, I closed my eyes and spoke in hushed tones.

'Lucien, are you here?' I waited but felt none of the familiar indicators of a ghostly presence.

'Lucien Merrick, if you can hear me, I'm begging you to leave Luke alone. This … whatever it is, is between you and me. You can't use your own flesh and blood like that, it's not fair or ... or right.'

Suddenly, the temperature plummeted, a shiver coursing through me.

'Lucien?'

Catherine.

Wrapping my arms around myself, I stepped into the middle of the room, trying to ignore the goose bumps erupting all over my skin.

'He's your great, great, great grandson. Please don't mess with him. He'll only be here for a couple—'

A small decorative trinket box sitting on my dressing table flew across the room, missing me by millimeters and hitting the opposite wall where it left a small divot in the plaster. I let out a squeak of surprise and fear, hurling myself back against the door.

'What the hell, Lucien?!'

But just as quickly as he had arrived, he was gone. The temperature returned to normal, and I knew I was alone. Slowly, I walked over to where the little box lay on the floor, picking it up and turning it over in my hands. One of the hinges was broken, and the lid was twisted and hanging off. It had contained several pairs of stud earrings, which I gathered up, carrying the box and its contents back to my dressing table. I dropped heavily into the chair there, absently matching up the earrings as I contemplated what had just occurred. Lucien's tantrum had taken me by surprise, but I couldn't help thinking that he had chosen one of my least valuable—and breakable—possessions on which to vent his ire. In the end, I couldn't decide whether I was amused or scared by my first experience with his temper. The big question was: what had sparked it? Was he angry that I was trying to spoil his fun with Luke—if fun was what he was having—or was he jealous?

A massive yawn chose that moment to overtake me, reminding me of the late hour and my own fatigue. I longed for my bed, and with Lucien having apparently departed in a spectral huff, I hoped that both Luke and I would be left in peace for what remained of this extraordinary night.

This was one wish, at least, that was fulfilled.

෨෬

I woke late, the angle of sunlight pouring through my windows telling me it was past ten o'clock. A shower partially revitalized me, but I needed coffee STAT. The house was silent, so I left Luke undisturbed while I headed to the kitchen and started breakfast.

Over the past few months, I had started to get into the habit, particularly at weekends, of eating an English style breakfast of bacon, poached eggs and toast, although I still couldn't stomach those weird English sausages. However, this morning, in honor of my visitor, I decided to make a proper American breakfast, whipping up a batch of fluffy pancakes, with a side of crisp bacon, sweet English strawberries, fat juicy blueberries and maple syrup. Just as I slid the stacked plate into the oven to keep warm, I sensed movement behind me. Straightening up, I turned to see Luke leaning against the door jamb, his arms crossed over his chest. He'd clearly just showered, his hair still damp and temporarily under control, but he looked tired. Still, he had a lazy smile plastered across his handsome face, and I could swear I saw his eyes snap up from where I had a strong suspicion they'd been focused on my butt. The thought caused my cheeks to heat and Luke's smile to turn a little sheepish. Desperate to distract us both, I turned back to the oven.

'Um, I hope you like pancakes. I've made lots, and there's bacon and fruit, and the coffee's fresh, if you want to help yourself. So, uh, yeah … there's cream in the fridge, the sugar's over there …' I pointed to the side and forced myself to stop babbling.

Luke used his shoulder to push away from the door and strolled across to where I had set a place for him at the island.

With a rueful smile and a soft 'good morning' he helped himself to coffee while I served the food. I nodded gratefully when he brought the coffee pot over to top up my drink, and then we both sat down to eat a much-needed breakfast.

We tried to make small talk as we ate—Luke complimented my cooking and told me more about his parents; I talked about the house, Cornwall, even the damned weather, surely demonstrating that I'd been in the UK too long. However, it quickly became obvious that we were simply avoiding the elephant in the room. Wiping his lips with a paper napkin, Luke pushed his empty plate aside and leaned back in his seat.

'That was great, Kat. Thanks. Now, do you want to talk about the weather some more or shall we cut to the chase?' He screwed his napkin into a ball and tossed it onto his discarded plate. I could feel his eyes on me as I watched it roll across the syrupy surface and come to rest against his fork. 'Kat?'

Reluctantly, I lifted my gaze to his, knowing we needed to talk about what had happened the night before.

'Okay, you're right. We do need to talk, but I'd rather we didn't do it here. You've heard that expression about walls having ears? Well, I think the ones in this house really might. How do you feel about taking a drive into town? We can take a walk down to the beach. It'll be busy, but there's a really pretty cove at the far end which is a lot quieter. What d'ya think?'

I really hoped he would agree, and I couldn't hide my smile when he nodded.

'Sounds great, let's do it.'

With a grin, he leapt to his feet and started collecting the dishes. Working together, we got everything cleared away and the dishwasher started in double-quick time. Once we were done, I told him I just needed to run upstairs to use the bathroom and brush my hair.

'No problem, me too—well, except the hair-brushing thing. I'll see you outside when you're ready.' He grinned, taking the stairs two at a time, leaving me to follow behind at a more leisurely pace.

Walking into my room, I was immediately aware of the plummeting temperature, just as the door slammed behind me.

Gasping, I swung around and grabbed the doorknob, but it was jammed solid. The familiar sensation of Lucien's cool touch on the back of my neck caused me to turn, pressing myself against the door.

'Lucien, what are you doing?'

I was surprised at the evenness of my tone, because it certainly didn't reflect the wild pounding of my heart. I looked frantically around the room until something in the corner caught my eye. My breath froze in my throat as, just for a moment, it seemed as though there was somebody standing by the window, almost like a dark, shimmering mirage—and then it was gone.

'Lucien, you can't keep me locked in here. Please open the door.'
Stay.

Just like before my illness, the voice seemed to be both inside my head and right behind me, as if his lips were mere millimeters from my ear. Impossible, of course, since my back was pressed hard against the door.

'I'm just going down to the beach. We—I'll be back before you know it.' I spoke as if to a fractious child, my tone gentle and placatory.

He wants you, Catherine.

'What? No! He's just visiting for a couple of days. He's part of you, Lucien—he's your great, great, great grandson—'

'NO!'

I let out a high-pitched yelp as Lucien's voice seemed to echo around the room, loud and clear. I watched in horror as he seemed to pulse into view, but this time he was a solid mass, as real as me. Dressed all in black, the very epitome of an English Edwardian gentleman, he seemed to hurtle toward me from across the room, his mouth open as he shouted his denial of Luke, and his eyes like two black holes, full of anger and enmity.

My own scream was the last thing I heard before my vision blurred and the floor rushed up to greet me.

℘⃝℞

I became aware of something pushing against my leg and reflexively yanked it away. I realized I was lying face-down on the floor, my arms trapped beneath me. Clarity returned in a flash of memory, and I was grateful that, even as I'd passed out, instinct had kicked in and I'd put my hands out to cushion my fall.

'Kat? Jesus, are you all right? Can you move your legs so I can get the door open?'

Luke's frantic voice penetrated my fuzzy thoughts, and I pushed against the floor to help me roll over. The movement sent a sharp pain through my left wrist, making me cry out.

'Ow, crap!' I managed to sit up, cupping my injured arm against my chest. My change of position finally allowed Luke to open the door wide enough to step through, and he immediately dropped to his knees beside me. Clutching my shoulders, he dipped his head to capture my attention, giving me an uncertain smile as our eyes met.

'What the hell happened, Kat? I was downstairs wondering what was taking so long. Then I came up here and knocked, but you didn't respond. Did you faint?'

'No—uh, yeah, I guess I must have. I—I'm not really sure what happened.'

I tore my eyes away from his, not really sure why I didn't tell him the truth. Maybe I wasn't ready to admit that things were getting out of control. Why that might be, I couldn't say. Was it because I didn't want to give substance to my growing fears about Lucien? Or was it because I didn't want to give Luke a reason to leave?

Perhaps it was both.

'Did you hurt your hand? Let me have a look.'

Tenderly, Luke pried my arm away from where I had it cradled against me, his long, elegant fingers gently probing and testing my injury. A large bruise was already forming, and I couldn't hide my hiss of pain.

'Can you flex it?' he asked, his eyes flickering up to mine.

I wiggled my fingers and carefully rotated my hand. It hurt, but I knew it wasn't serious.

'Doesn't look like you've broken anything. It's probably just a mild sprain, but we should get it checked out at the ER if you're in a lot of pain.'

'No, it'll be fine. I've had worse when I was in high school. Anyway, I think the nearest ER is in Truro, which is about twenty miles away, and on a holiday weekend it'll probably be packed. I really don't want to spend half the day waiting around for someone to tell me something I already know. I've got a tensor bandage I can wrap around it. It's in the medical kit I keep in the kitchen.'

After a moment's hesitation, he nodded and stood up. I pulled my legs under me, and when he offered me his hand, I took it. With seemingly no effort at all, he pulled me up, his arms encircling me as the speed of my ascent unbalanced me. He didn't immediately let go, and I found myself gazing up at him, once again spellbound by his eyes and a smile that had probably reduced more than one woman to a breathless, wanton mess. I seemed I was not immune.

'C'mon, Kat. Let's get you strapped up,' he murmured in a low, ridiculously sexy voice.

God help me, he had gone all Christian Grey on me and, just like Ana Steele, I was suddenly all 'kiss me, kiss me'.

For what felt like minutes, but was probably only seconds, we just stared at one another. His eyes seemed to change color, from violet to stormy blue-gray, and I could have sworn he really was going to kiss me. He was holding me so tightly I could feel the accelerated thump of his heart, which matched my own.

I ached for him. It was a sensation with which I was utterly unfamiliar, and yet standing here in his arms made me feel like I was right where I was meant to be. I saw his eyes flicker to my mouth and, with a will of its own, my tongue slipped out to lick my parched lips. His pupils dilated, black overtaking blue, and he dipped his head.

'Kat,' he whispered, his breath mingling with mine as my eyes fluttered closed.

The clamorous ringing of his phone was like an electric shock, and the spell was broken.

We jumped apart as if our polarities had been reversed. Crushing disappointment washed over me as I watched him pull his phone out of his pocket and look down at the screen. Glancing back at me, I saw resignation and apology flash across his face.

'I'm sorry, Kat, but I, uh, need to take this.'

'Sure. I'll just...' I waved vaguely at the door and hurried past him. He followed me out onto the landing as he answered his phone, but I continued down the stairs, practically running to the kitchen.

By the time I'd found the bandage, wound it securely around my wrist and swallowed a couple of ibuprofen pills, I could hear Luke in the foyer. He didn't sound very happy, and I delayed joining him, not wanting to interrupt. Leaning back against the wall out of sight, I didn't even bother to pretend to myself that I wasn't listening.

'I told you, Ben, there's nothing I can do until I get to London. You need to speak to Li in Shanghai. Tell him that if that rebar isn't on a fucking container ship by tomorrow morning, we're going to start invoking penalties ... I don't care, Ben, just fucking tell him. Jesus, it's lucky for you that I flew here early *on my own fucking time.* When you've spoken to Li, call Johnson in London and tell him I'll be there tomorrow and that I can meet him at three ... no, I can't get there any earlier. I need to know you can handle this, Ben, so fucking sort it out ... Okay, call me when you've talked to Johnson.'

I didn't hear him say goodbye, but from the silence I guessed that he'd finished his conversation with the unfortunate Ben. Oh boy, was he pissed, and now it seemed that instead of the three days he'd intended to stay, he would be leaving after barely two. It was stupid, but I felt robbed. It was only one day, but it felt like it might have been filled with possibilities. I knew I was probably being foolish, especially as we'd only just met the day before, but after what had almost transpired between us upstairs, I realized I wanted to spend a lot more time with Luke Brodie. I couldn't explain the pull I felt toward him, which I was pretty sure went far deeper than mere physical attraction. If I'd believed in such things, I would think that we had met in a previous life and were fated to be together. But I didn't believe in all that reincarnation bullshit ... did I?

I was jolted from my existential musings when Luke appeared in the doorway, startling us both.

'Shit, Kat—'

'Jesus, Luke—'

We both spoke at once and stopped at the same time. I put my hand up and pushed away from the wall.

'Sorry, Luke, I wasn't trying to eavesdrop—I just didn't want to interrupt you. Did I hear you say you have to be in London tomorrow?'

'Yeah, I'm so sorry, Kat. There's a problem with the steel for the project and I need to meet with the developer and the architect tomorrow afternoon. They wanted me to go today, but I've told my Project Assistant that the earliest I can be there is tomorrow.'

He looked utterly crestfallen, which was kind of comforting—at least he seemed as sad to be leaving early as I was to see him go.

'Uh, well, if you need to leave now, we could do all this some other time.' I said the words, but I didn't mean them and I prayed he would ignore me.

'What? No way. I wouldn't even be in the country if I hadn't come early to spend some time in Cornwall and meet you, so they can damn well wait. Uh, unless you want me to leave?'

Wow, I couldn't believe that this handsome, confident man was now looking at me with such uncertainty.

'No, absolutely not. Look, I know all about what it's like when there's a problem with a project and the client is bellyaching and demanding your personal attention, so I completely understand that you have to go. I'm just kinda bummed that we won't have much time to, well, get to know each other.'

I couldn't look at him, my eyes dropping to where my fingers fiddled with my bandage, blushing like a damned teenager. So intent was I on the task of checking my nursing skills that I jumped like a startled rabbit when I felt the back of his fingers lightly brush my cheek. My eyes instinctively sought his, my breath catching in my throat at the intensity of his gaze.

'Kat, please believe me when I say that I have every intention of making sure we get to know each other … *really* well.'

He leaned into me and, just for a moment, I thought he was actually going to kiss me this time. But then his mouth was right by my ear, so close I could feel his breath cool my skin.

'Breathe, Kat,' he whispered, and without even looking at him I knew he was smiling that cocky smile.

I smacked his chest, pushing him away.

'Come on, let's go. If you're going to desert me, you owe me an ice-cream on the beach, Mr. Brodie.'

He laughed as he stepped back. 'You're on, Ms Tregowen.'

He grabbed my good hand and led me out of the kitchen to the front door. As he reached out to open the front door, I had a momentary thought that it wouldn't open, but the handle worked perfectly and the next thing I knew we were out in the blazing mid-day sun. I let go of Luke's hand, letting him walk to the car while I pulled the door closed to lock it. Just before it shut, through the narrow gap I thought I heard the distant sound of something smashing in an upstairs room. Turning the key, I laid my hand against the wood and sighed. I would just have to deal with Lucien later.

Chapter Eleven

I leaned back, locking my arms behind me and tipping my face up to the heavens. After almost a lifetime of San Francisco's often tenuous relationship with the sun, I couldn't help but revel in Cornwall's seemingly endless summer days and how good it felt to bask in that glorious heat under clear, azure skies. Beneath me, the sand was soft and warm, and, with my eyes closed, my senses were filled with the sound and scent of the ocean. It occurred to me that if I stepped off this beach into the sea and swam directly west, the next landfall would be Newfoundland. Yeah, I probably wouldn't make it.

That spectacularly random thought made me giggle—which turned to a shriek when I felt something icy cold slide across my collarbone. I sat up with a gasp, only to find Luke looming over me, laughing his stupid, gorgeous head off. Shading my eyes with one hand, I scowled up at him.

'Har-de-har-har! Where's my ice-cream, Butthead?'

He grinned widely and dropped to his knees, holding out a popsicle.

'I decided I'd never get ice-cream back here before it melted, so I bought these. They're strawberry and apparently have ice-cream in the middle, so I thought it would be a good compromise.'

I took the proffered confection, quickly stripped the paper off and wrapped my eager lips around the bright red popsicle. I quickly worked out that no strawberries had likely been harmed in its manufacture but hummed in pleasure at its icy sweetness. Biting into it, I discovered that Luke was right—underneath the flavored outer layer was a filling of creamy, deep-yellow Cornish ice-cream.

'Ummmm,' I moaned, my eyes fluttering closed. A long-forgotten memory of sitting on a beach as a child, eating this exact same thing, suddenly popped into my head, causing me to suck in a breath and open my eyes, only to find Luke's even gaze focused on me. No sooner had our eyes met than he blinked and shook his head, looking away from me to the surfers riding the waves. Frowning, I forced my eyes away from his profile to follow his gaze, and we both watched as a guy in a black and orange wetsuit seemed to fly as he rode the crest of a particularly big wave. My eyes flickered back to Luke.

'Do you surf?' I asked, just for something to say.

For a moment, I thought he wasn't going to reply as his gaze remained fixed on the guy out at sea, but then he scooted in front of me on the sand, mirroring my cross-legged position and smiled.

'I used to, back in my teens and early twenties. Spring break in Hawaii … what a blast—beer, babes and barrels, nothing better.' He grinned and then winked—*winked!*—at me.

'Barrels?'

'Uh … you know, like the inside of a wave?'

'Oh,' I murmured blankly. 'So, uh, why did you stop?'

He shrugged, his eyes drifting back to the guy we'd been watching earlier, who was now paddling back out to catch another wave.

'Oh, you know … work, life, stuff. Plus, it's a young man's game. You need to be really fit to do it well, and if you're not prepared to do it well, I don't see the point.'

'You look pretty fit to me,' I said, recalling in sharp detail his broad shoulders and well-muscled body from the previous night. He wasn't ripped in that contrived, gym-jockey way, it was more that he was naturally toned from working hard.

Luke's chuckle broke me out of my delightful reverie, and I suddenly realized what I'd said. Cue violent blush. Oh, for the love of … I must have blushed more in the last twenty-four hours than in the entire previous twenty-four years!

'You think I'm fit, huh?' His grin was wide, his eyes full of mischief.

I put my popsicle stick in my mouth and sucked the last of the ice-cream from it, drawing it out slowly and then languorously licking my lips. All the while, my eyes were fixed on Luke's, and I watched with satisfaction as his pupils dilated. His mouth dropped open slightly and his Adam's apple bobbed as he swallowed.

'You know you are, Butthead,' I told him, giving his foot a soft kick. It was fun to gain the upper hand for a change, especially as I was constantly a hair's breadth away from being a drooling mess in his company.

'Hey, if you keep calling me Butthead, I'm gonna have to call you Beaver.'

'It's Beavis, Butthead!' I snorted, hardly able to contain my laughter.

'Uh-uh, Beavis is a boy, and you are most definitely a *girl.*' He smirked at his own cleverness, waggling his eyebrows like some kind of silent movie villain.

I could no longer keep it in, flopping back and giggling uncontrollably, eyes closed against the bright sunlight and my arms flung up above my head.

Suddenly, I was in shadow, and my eyes flew open to find Luke straddling my hips. My laughter died in my throat as I looked up at him. With the sun behind him, his expression was hard to read, but I could almost feel the intensity of his gaze.

'What are you doing?' I whispered, unable to speak louder for fear my voice would tremble and crack.

He leaned forward, planting his hands on either side of my head.

'I have no fucking idea, Kat. All I know is that we've just met, we hardly know one another, we live six thousand miles apart, and … God help me, if I don't kiss you right now, I think I might actually, seriously explode.'

I swallowed. This was absolutely crazy—we were moving way too fast. We could count the time we'd spent together in hours, and I had never kissed a man so soon after meeting him. But I *had* seen him nearly naked.

Oh, fuck it. If I'd learned nothing else from the tragic tale of our long dead ancestors, I surely understood that life was too short to waste time worrying about moral ambiguities and so-called social norms.

'So, what's stopping you?'

Before I had time to change my mind, he dipped his head and brushed his lips against mine. Without a second thought, I reached up and slipped my hand around the back of his neck, letting my fingers bury themselves in the thick hair at his nape. For just a fleeting moment, my mind flashed to several days ago when I had touched Lucien's hair—or, at least, had imagined touching it—and been slightly repulsed at the oily feel of it. No such thoughts assailed me now. Despite looking like it was artfully gelled, Luke's hair was softer and silkier than I would ever have believed. Instinctively, I tugged at it, pulling him down to me so that this time our mouths collided in unambiguous passion. My lips parted and his tongue immediately sought mine. There was nothing tentative about it—no awkwardness or hesitation. It was a kiss like none I'd ever experienced before. I never wanted to stop.

I pulled in oxygen through my nose, desperate to keep this man's mouth on mine, and his body pressed against me.

'Oy, get a room, you pervs ... there are kids on this beach!'

The shout came from several yards away, and whoever it was may as well have thrown a bucket of cold water over us.

'Fuck!' Luke quickly rolled off me and sat up, as I, too, pushed myself into a sitting position. I snorted a strangled giggle, too amused to even be embarrassed and glanced up through my eyelashes at Luke's strained expression.

'I'm delighted you find me so entertaining,' he murmured through gritted teeth, but he couldn't disguise the sparkle in his eyes and the almost imperceptible curl of his lip.

After several seconds of smirking at one another, Luke stood up and held out his hand for me to take. Once again, I was pulled into his arms, but this time he kissed me softly on the forehead and let me go. I stooped to pick up my purse, smiling at Luke when he grabbed my hand as I straightened up.

'Come on, let's go get a drink. Somewhere we can talk without getting sidetracked, because you, Ms. Tregowen, are one major distraction.'

'Speak for yourself, Mr. Brodie.'

Our matching grins spoke volumes as we headed back to the promenade, our hands tightly clasped.

ஐலை

'I need you to know up front, Kat, that I have never—and I mean *never*—made a move on a woman this fast.'

We were sitting in a small pub a short walk from the beach, two sodas sitting on the table in front of us.

Despite the fact that the streets and cafés with tables outside were busy, the pub we chose was practically empty, having just opened. We could have sat in the pretty little beer garden at the back, but opted for the cool, slightly dim interior, which seemed to suit our purpose better. We had sipped our drinks in silence for a few minutes, neither of us seemingly willing to start the conversation we needed to have. Finally, Luke sighed, and I looked up from my Coke to meet his eyes.

'Not even in college?' I asked with a smirk. It was inconceivable to me that a guy as attractive as Luke Brodie wouldn't have been getting laid on a regular basis when he was a hot young student.

He chuckled ruefully, shaking his head. 'Not even in college. Come on, Kat, you know how hard we had to work in our line. College was brutal, and I had neither the interest nor the energy for that whole frat house party scene. You probably got more action than me.'

I snorted, struggling to swallow the mouthful of soda I'd just taken. 'No way! Like you said, it was damned hard work, and I was always either studying or sleeping. I think I went to maybe three parties the whole time I was there, and I can honestly say I left them all early, sober and alone.'

'Oh, come on! You're not going to sit there and tell me a girl as beautiful as you didn't get hit on all the time in college.'

He looked so aghast at that notion that I laughed out loud. I didn't miss that he'd used the b-word yet again.

'That's not what I said. I just wasn't into drunken hook-ups at parties. Sure, I dated a couple of guys, one who I shared some classes with and one who was a friend of my roommate. But we weren't talking about me.' I arched my eyebrow at him, challenging him to get back on track.

'No, well, it seems we have a lot more in common than a shared heritage, because what you've just told me pretty much matches my own experience. I went to a few parties I was dragged to under duress, where drunk girls wearing too much make-up and too few clothes made fools of themselves. I just found it so boring. I preferred to meet girls who shared at least some of my interests and who had some self-respect. I had a girlfriend in high school who I'd been with for two years. We tried to do the long-distance thing, but I went to MIT and she went to UCLA, so we barely made it past our first semester. I kind of threw myself into my studies after that and didn't really date for a long time. There were a couple of girls on the surfing scene, when I could find the time, but then I met Louise, who worked in the library where I did most of my studying. We were together for nearly two years and it was great, but she was a year older than me, and when she graduated she got a really great offer to work in Hong Kong which she would have been a fool to turn down. I'm pretty sure I loved her at the time, and I was really sad when she had to leave, but I think we both knew that we'd maybe come to the end of the road and that there was no point even trying to keep it going long-distance.

'It's all good, though. Louise and I still keep in touch, and she's met a really great guy. I met up with them both when I was in Hong Kong last year, and it was nice to see her. We'd been good friends in college who became more for a while, and all the things that made us friends were still there, so we had a really good time.'

I could only nod uncertainly. I had never stayed friends with any of my exes, preferring to avoid them at all costs after we'd split up, so I had no concept of what it would be like to even see one of them again, let alone hang out with them.

'Okay, I believe that you're not a player, but what exactly *are* you saying, Luke?'

He sighed and set his drink down. 'I'm not sure, Kat. I have no idea what's going on here. I … look, I know this sounds bizarre and a little crazy, but I feel a … jeez, I don't even know how to put it into words. Some kind of … of a *pull* toward you that I just can't fight … oh, God, that sounds like such a line when I say it out loud.'

He swept an agitated hand through his hair, and when his eyes met mine I could see that he was practically pleading with me to understand. I reached over and put my hand on his where it lay on the table.

'Believe me, Luke, I totally get it. I feel the same way. In fact, I felt it the moment I saw you emerge from baggage claim at the airport.'

I smiled at him as a look of relief flashed across his face. He pulled his hand free, but only so that he could clasp mine fully, his thumb gently stroking my knuckles. For a moment, we just sat there in our new-found solidarity, eyes fixed on our conjoined hands, until Luke lifted his gaze, a frown painting his features.

'Trouble is, I'm not sure if our connection, for want of a better word, is entirely organic. I mean, I'm glad to hear you say you felt it at the airport because I did too, but it's escalated very, very fast, which isn't something I've experienced before, and after what happened last night … I'm wondering if, well … there are other forces at work here.'

Letting go of me, he sat back in his chair, raking both hands through his hair in what I was starting to notice was a nervous tic of his.

'Jesus, Kat, I can't believe I'm even saying the words out loud. I'm a practical man, a problem-solver; I don't believe in ghosts and ghouls and things that go bump in the night. I'm way out of my comfort zone with this, but I can't overlook the fact that, without conscious thought, and totally against my instincts and upbringing, I made my way into your bedroom last night and...'

'And?'

He leaned forward again, resting his forearms on the table, and stared at his clasped hands.

'I ... I didn't tell you this ... *fuck*...' He glanced up to meet my gaze, a look I could only describe as agony in his own dark blue eyes. 'I honestly have no memory of how I got to your room, Kat, but I do have an overwhelming feeling of what I wanted when I got there.'

He stopped again, lifting his hands to cover his face.

'What, Luke? What did you want?' I asked, also leaning forward.

Dropping his hands, he speared me with a look so intense it just about took my breath away.

'To utterly possess you, body and soul, to ... to take you over and over again.' He leaned closer and dropped his voice. 'If you'll forgive the vulgarity, to fuck your beautiful brains out. That's what I wanted.'

My heart seemed to stutter inside my chest, and I inhaled sharply.

'Oh.' The word was little more than an exhale as we continued to stare at one another, seemingly unable to look away.

Our silence seemed to stretch on *ad infinitum*; although, inside my head my thoughts were far from quiet. The roar of blood through my veins, and the wild thump of my heart drowned out all other sound, so much so that I became convinced Luke would hear it.

After what felt like an eternity, I forced myself to take a deep breath and let it out slowly. Just as I gained control over my wayward heart, Luke sat back and closed his eyes for a moment. When he opened them again, he seemed a lot more composed.

'So, what are we going to do?' he asked wearily.

'Do? About what?'

'About ... this,' he qualified, waving a hand vaguely between us.

'I ... I don't know.' I was lying, because I did know. The thought alone was sending blood rushing to my poor, benighted cheeks.

That lazy, sexy smirk spread across Luke's face, and I just *knew* he knew what I was thinking. I waited for him to call me out, but he said nothing—whether that was to save my embarrassment or his, I couldn't tell. Whichever it was, it was clear to me that a change of subject was urgently needed.

'Do you believe in God?' I blurted.

His eyebrows shot up, and he looked at me askance. 'Um ... wow—that's kind of out of left field, isn't it?'

'Yeah, sorry. It's just that I don't. I mean, sometimes I kind of wish I did, especially when I think about losing people I love, but I just can't make myself believe. Anyway, before I get into a whole theological treatise, what I mean is that I don't believe in heaven and hell or an afterlife, and so I don't know how to explain or understand what may or may not be going on in my house. I ... I want to believe that you and I have made a genuine connection, one that means something more than some kind of spirit possession, but I can't ignore the fact that something truly weird is going on. If I believed in God, maybe I would consider exorcism, but as I don't believe, does that mean it wouldn't work? Is that even a sensible question, or am I just talking out of my ass?'

I shrugged, knowing I sounded irrational and unable to keep the pained expression off my face. Despite his contention that he didn't believe in ghosts, I had no idea whether Luke would be offended by my lack of religious conviction; all I knew was that he seemed as confused as I about what was happening to us.

He leaned forward again across the small circular pub table, resting his forearms on the surface, his hands clasped in front of him. The smirk was gone, and his expression was serious, so I was pretty sure that he wasn't going to mock me.

'Okay, let's start with your first question. Do I believe in God? In all honesty, I've never given it a great deal of thought. My family isn't religious, and neither am I. My dad is Chief of Surgery at SF County Hospital and believes in science and his skill as a surgeon to save people. My mom's first husband was some kind of Christian fundamentalist, who was an asshole. He treated her like a chattel, and she finally left him when he nearly beat her to death. Dad was the one who put her back together in every conceivable way. You won't be surprised to learn that she's eschewed religion ever since. I think she believes in God—hell, I think I probably do—but not enough to get worked up about. Does that mean I believe in an afterlife? I just don't know—maybe, maybe not. Do I want to believe that when my parents die, they'll still be looking down on me from somewhere? I guess so … although preferably not when I'm getting shit-faced with friends, or I'm in bed with a beautiful woman.'

I'd been hanging on his every word, but when he stopped speaking and winked at me—again!—I was once more rendered breathless. While I fought to keep my equilibrium, he carried on without missing a beat.

'I tend toward the idea that we live on in our children, grandchildren and so on down the generations. Just look at us, for instance. We've both been brought together by a house which was once occupied by my three times great grandfather and your two times great aunt, who, we discover, we resemble physically to an uncanny degree. Which, by the way, freaked me the fuck out, because even though I get my hair and eye color from my dad, I always thought I looked more like my mom. Who do you look like?'

I shook my head, my thoughts thrown into confusion by the sudden change of subject. 'Oh, uh, well, I guess the Tregowen genes have been a little more consistent. I look a lot like my dad—same boring hazel eyes and mousy hair.'

A small 'v' appeared between Luke's eyes, and he reached across to lift my chin with his forefinger and thumb.

'Boring? Christ, Kat, nothing could be further from the truth. You have the warmest, most beautiful eyes I've ever seen—they put me in mind of warm summer days, and I just want to drown in them. As for your hair, it's like molten gold, and I can't stop wondering what it would be like to bury my face in all that sweet-smelling softness. You are … perfect.'

He'd spoken softly, the last words little more than a whisper, but it was if he'd tattooed them on my skin. I could hardly breathe, and my heart thrummed like a hummingbird's wings. It felt like it was going to beat right out of my chest, and I had the fleeting thought that this man might well be the death of me.

The next thing I knew, Luke had pulled his hand back and, almost in the same movement, had stood up. I gasped in surprise, wondering what I could possibly have done wrong. Looking up, I met his dark stare.

'Let's go, Kat. We need to be … not here.' His voice was a little husky, and I finally realized he was waiting for me to take his hand.

Swallowing hard, I let him pull me to my feet and into the welcome circle of his muscular arms. I gripped his biceps as he held me close; so close, in fact, that I had to tilt my head back to look at him. When I did, his eyes were fixed on my mouth, and I instinctively licked my lips. Much to my disappointment, he squeezed his eyes shut and let his head fall back. Thinking that I'd maybe misinterpreted his motive for wanting to leave, I tried to extricate myself from his embrace, but he only held me tighter, his head coming down until I felt his lips brush my ear.

'I want you, Kat; don't ever doubt that. Just not here. Let's go … please.'

His husky, commanding tone made me weak at the knees, and I knew that any arguments about it being too soon or ill-judged meant nothing. He and I were going to make love—it was as inevitable as the sun rising in the east, and I had neither the strength nor the will to fight it. It was just a question of when and where.

It was at that moment that I knew I had to tell him about the events of that morning. Sighing, I pulled away and sat back down. He looked at me quizzically, but then followed my lead.

'What's wrong, Kat? Am I … God, I'm going too fast, aren't I?'

I smiled ruefully and shook my head, thinking we were way beyond such mundane concerns. Reaching across the table, I took one of his hands in mine.

'Luke, listen … about this morning. I didn't faint—well, I guess I did, but there's more to it than that. Before we go any farther—and believe me, I want that—I need to tell you what happened.'

He frowned, but said nothing, allowing me to continue at my own pace. Haltingly, I stumbled through an explanation of what had taken place in my bedroom earlier, and, just like yesterday, he let me talk, without judgment or censure. It was only when I got to the part where Lucien had made the trinket box fly across the room that he suddenly pulled away, muttering an expletive. I paused, watching as his mouth clamped shut and then opened, his eyes reflecting the war raging within.

'Jesus, Kat, why didn't you say something? Don't … don't you trust me?'

He ran an agitated hand through his hair and speared me with a look of such anguish that I was overcome with guilt. Immediately, I reached across the table, hoping against hope that he would take my hand. When he did, I exhaled a breath I didn't even know I'd been holding.

'I'm so sorry, Luke. I do trust you, I swear. I just … didn't want to give you another reason to question my sanity. Please forgive me.'

He stared intently at me for what seemed like a really long time until, to my profound and utter relief, he lifted my hand to his mouth and pressed his lips to my knuckles. Lowering our joined hands back to the table, he smiled at me.

'Nothing to forgive, Kat. I have no right to demand your trust after such a short acquaintance, but I will prove to you that you're right to give it to me.'

As I nodded gratefully, he stood up again, pulling me to my feet.

'Now, I hope you meant it about trusting me, because I want us to go back to Chimneys so I can get my stuff and you can pack a bag. I'm sorry, Kat, but you are not spending another night in that house until we can figure out what's going on and do something about it. Agreed?' He bent his knees so that we were at eye level, waiting for my response.

I swallowed but couldn't look away. The pull of that house was as strong as ever, affecting me on an elemental level. A big part of me wanted to tell Luke to go to hell, that there was no way I was going to be driven out of my home.

'Kat, please.' He straightened, releasing my hand and gripping my upper arms. 'Look, Kat, I'm not going to try and force you to do something you don't want to do … but I am asking you, please, let's find somewhere else to stay tonight.'

I took in the desperation in his eyes and knew I couldn't refuse him—because he was right. Regardless of my irrational need to return, I knew it wasn't safe, that I could no longer make excuses for what was happening.

'I'll call Joshua at the pub and see if he can put us up. If not, I'll ask Sam. Come on, let's go.'

஀௧

The drive back to the house was quiet, with just the radio playing softly to break the silence. It wasn't uncomfortable, though. As soon as we left the parking lot, Luke's hand reached across the console and found mine, clasping it against his thigh all the way home. He only relinquished his hold when he pulled up in front of the house, allowing us both to get out of the car.

Searching through my purse for my keys, out of the corner of my eye I thought I caught movement at an upstairs window. When I glanced up, however, there was nothing there, and I had to wonder if it had, indeed, been Lucien watching us or just my feverish imagination.

Strong arms wrapped around me from behind, and I leaned back against Luke's solid chest with a sigh.

'You okay?'

'Yeah, sorry. I thought I saw something...'

I felt him tense and knew he, too, was now surveying the upper story windows.

Shaking my head, I pulled away from him and walked to the door.

'Come on, let's just run in, grab our things and head over to the pub.'

I retrieved my keys from my purse and opened the door. As it swung open, I stepped across the threshold, smiling over my shoulder at Luke. Before he could follow me in, his phone rang, and he paused to answer it. I kept going, assuming it was his colleague again and wanting to give him some privacy this time.

'Ben, what's up?'

It was all I heard before the door slammed shut behind me ... with Luke on the other side.

Chapter Twelve

With a gasp, I rushed back to the door and tried to open it. It was futile. With a sense of inevitability, I realized that I was wasting my time.

'Kat? What's going on? Open the door.' Luke's voice was muffled, but I could hear him furiously banging his fist against the thick wood.

Looking anxiously around me, I realized the best way for him to get in was through either the library or sitting room window. Dropping to my knees I pulled open the letterbox flap. A second later the external flap opened and a pair of worried blue eyes met mine through the narrow slot—thank God for the British postal service which meant that mail was delivered directly into every house.

'Kat, are you okay? What happened?'

'I'm fine, but the door's jammed. I'm going to open the window in the library so you can cli—'

Before I could finish what I was going to say, the library door slammed shut, the sound reverberating through the house like a shotgun going off.

'What the fuck was that?' Luke's voice was frantic, but I couldn't take the time to answer him.

Scrambling to my feet, I ignored the closed door, guessing that any attempt to open it would fail. Instead, I ran towards the sitting room door on the other side, desperate to reach it before it, too, barred my way. It stood ajar and I almost wanted to pump my fist when I got there in time. Slapping both hands against the smooth oak, I started to push, only to come up against an immovable force. I leaned my shoulder against the wood and pushed harder, but the next thing I knew I was violently thrust back when this door also slammed, causing me to stumble and fall on my ass.

'Goddammit,' I yelled as pain shot up my injured wrist to my elbow.

'Kat! Jesus Christ, what the fuck is happening in there?'

I slowly got to my knees and shuffled over to where Luke was still peering through the letterbox, his eyes wild as they settled on me.

'I'm okay, but I can't access the downstairs rooms.'

'You don't look okay. Did you hurt your wrist again?'

'Yeah, a bit. I thought I could get into the sitting room, but when he shut the door, it kind of jarred my arm. I've got some ibuprofen in the kitchen—'

'He?'

I sighed and glanced around me surreptitiously—a pointless gesture, I knew, but I couldn't help it.

'You know who I'm talking about, Luke. Don't make me say his name.'

He stared at me for a moment and then, reluctantly, nodded his head. 'I guess … Jesus, this is fucked up!'

He pushed his hand through the slot, and I immediately grabbed it, ridiculously comforted by the skin-to-skin contact.

'Okay. I need you to go find me something I can break a window with—a hammer or something. Do you have any tools in there?"

'Uh, yeah, in the kitchen … but it won't do any good. I had toughened glass fitted in all the first-floor windows for security. You'd need a jack-hammer to break it.'

Releasing my hand, he sat back on his heels, gazing up at the house and from side to side, before leaning forward again to speak to me.

'What about at the back of the house? The kitchen's got a sliding door, hasn't it? Maybe we'd be able to get that open.'

Even as he said the words, we both heard the kitchen door slam shut, and I knew gaining access that way was no longer an option.

'Fuck! Was that the kitchen door?'

'Yeah, but I doubt that would have worked anyway. The only way through to the back from there is via a solid oak door set in a ten-foot wall. Without a key or a ladder to get over the wall, there's no way for you to get around there.'

My shoulders slumped in defeat as I realized there was nowhere for me to go except upstairs or into the basement—and that windowless space was definitely not a viable choice. As I contemplated our diminishing options, Luke's fingers poked back through the letterbox and I gripped them like a lifeline.

'Hey, don't worry, we'll work something out. Can you call your contractor guy? You said he and his wife got in here before when you were sick.'

Tom! Of course. I let go of Luke's fingers and gathered up my purse from where I'd dropped it earlier. Delving inside, I felt a groundswell of relief when my fingers closed around my phone. My relief turned to despair when the screen failed to light up.

'Kat, what's wrong?'

'My phone ... the battery's dead. It was fully charged this morning and now it's completely dead. Oh, Jesus, Luke, what are we going to do?'

'Kat, baby. It's going to be all right. Here, give it to me.'

I passed the phone to him and watched with a sinking feeling as he withdrew his hand and the letterbox clanged shut. It was stupid, I knew, but I could barely control the panic which took hold when our one point of contact closed, and I scrabbled desperately to open it again. The internal draft-proof flap was easy, but Luke needed to push the spring-loaded, brass outer flap from his side, and I could feel a scream building up in me at our loss of connection.

'Luke, open the letterbox ... please, open it now ... *Luke!*'

Suddenly, his fingers appeared, and I could see his beautiful eyes.

'Kat, shhh. It's okay—I'm here.'

I grabbed his hand, lowering my head and pressing my cheek to his fingers. A loud sob broke free and I knew I was close to losing it, which would help no one.

'Kat ... Sweetheart, listen to me. Do you have a landline you can get to? You need to call your friend ... sorry, I can't remember his name.'

I lifted my head and sucked in a deep breath. His calm voice and practical suggestion helped to ground me, and I could feel the panic receding somewhat.

'You mean Tom? Yeah—dammit, his number's in my phone. And I only have landline phones in the library, sitting room, kitchen and my bedroom. I can't get in any of the first-floor rooms and I'm not going upstairs, Luke. I-I just can't.'

'No, stay there. Look, I'm going to use your phone to prop open the letterbox so I can call Tom on my phone. What's the name of his company?'

Feeling a little more in control, I gave him Tom's details and waited while Luke searched for his number. My knees were beginning to ache but if I sat down, it would be really difficult to keep the flap open, and there was no way I could face giving up my view of Luke. Luckily, my phone was just the right width to prop open his side, but the one on the inside swung loose on a rigid metal wire which was fixed on either side of the letterbox with small screws. It would have to go.

I searched through my purse for the small Swiss Army knife I kept in there for emergencies and set about dismantling the internal brass flap. A few minutes later it was off, and I slumped against the door in relief. It was short-lived.

'Kat? I can't get a decent signal so I'm going to walk to the top of the drive to see if it will improve—'

'No! Luke, you can't leave me.' I glanced around, expecting to see Lucien materialize at any moment.

'Listen to me, Kat. You'll be fine—I'm just going to move away from the house a little so I can get a signal. You'll still be able to see me. I promise I won't leave you ... okay?'

I took a deep breath, trying hard to find the inner strength I'd relied on all my adult life as a woman working in what was still very much a man's world.

'Okay. I'm sorry. I just...'

'Hey, I know, okay? You don't have to explain anything to me. You're doing great, love. I don't know any other woman who wouldn't have completely fallen apart in your situation. But you—Christ, Kat, you're amazing. Did you just produce a tool from your purse and calmly take apart the letterbox? My God, but you are one strong—and very cool—woman. You have no idea how fucking turned on I am right now.'

He slid his hand back through the open slot and I took it gratefully. I knew he was just trying to bolster my spirits, but it was working. His words were like balm to my soul.

'Thanks, Luke. You're right—I'll be fine, I'm sure. I mean, all that's happened is a bunch of door-slamming. Even if it's really Lucien doing it, he's not actually here; I would feel it if he was, and there's nothing. No drop in temperature, no flying ornaments, no ice-cold touches, nada.'

'That's good. Maybe he wore himself out with all that door banging, eh?'

'Yeah, maybe.' I wasn't completely convinced of that, but I needed to believe it if I was going to let Luke walk away from the house.

'Okay, I'm gonna head across the drive, Kat. I'll make sure to stay in your eye-line, and if anything happens or you get scared, just shout and I'll be back. I'm gonna get you out of there, I promise.'

He pulled his hand back, pressed two fingers to his lips and then reached in to touch my mouth. I leaned into the gentle pressure, steeling myself against the tears which threatened at his simple, yet overwhelming gesture.

'Hang in there, love.'

I nodded, afraid to speak in case my voice broke and gave away the fact that I wasn't anywhere near as strong as he seemed to think I was.

I watched as he slowly got to his feet and started backing away. His eyes flickered between me and his phone, and I prayed he would get a signal before he had to go too far. He kept moving, holding his phone up. He began to swivel around with his phone in the air, and I could feel my panic starting to return as he moved farther away, breaking eye contact.

And then I felt it.

As if he'd just been waiting for Luke to leave me, I knew Lucien was now here. The temperature dropped like a stone, and, dressed only in a tank-top and shorts, my exposed skin quickly broke out in goosebumps. My eyes were still glued to Luke, who was now a good fifty yards from the house, and I was terrified to turn around.

'Catherine.'

The softly spoken name was immediately followed by the all too familiar touch of those icy fingers on the back of my neck, and I instinctively twisted away and onto my bottom.

There, right in front of me, just a few feet away, stood Lucien Merrick, just as I'd seen him this morning in my bedroom. Pressing my back against the door, I looked up into his eyes of deepest black, seeing, for the first time, a world of pain and anger. It scared the shit out of me.

'Lucien! Wh-what … what do you want?'

'Catherine, my love, why do you hurt me so?'

'Lucien, please, I'm not Catherine—I'm Kat. Catherine died eighty-five years ago. She had a—'

'NOOO!'

His screamed denial caused me to try and throw myself backwards, pedaling furiously across the tiled floor, but all I managed to do was crack my head painfully against the wooden barrier behind me.

'Catherine, you're breaking my heart. Why are you doing this? Is it my parents? Are they making you betray our love with these cruel lies?'

He moved closer and I tried my best to push myself through the door.

'Luke, help me,' I cried, but my voice was little more than a strangled whisper.

'I'm here, my love.'

Something in me snapped then.

'I'm not talking to you,' I screamed, suddenly furious. 'You're fucking dead!' I could feel my anger escalating and used it to fire myself up. Pushing against the floor, I stood and took a step toward Lucien.

'You died in 1919, Lucien,' I barked, my voice rising, getting stronger. "Catherine had a baby—your daughter—but Catherine died in 1930 ... Catherine died, Lucien, but your daughter, Sarah, lived on.'

As I spoke, I chanced another step forward, hoping he would back off. I didn't know what I'd do if he didn't, but I was fueled by my fury. Much to my relief, he seemed to fade a little, appearing to move away from me. I followed him.

'Your daughter married and went to America, Lucien. She had a son, who she named after you, and he had a son, who called his own son Lucien; your great, great, great grandson, Luke Brodie. That's him outside, and he's scared shitless right now because you've trapped me in here with you. But I'm not Catherine, Lucien. I'm Kat Tregowen. My great grandfather was Catherine's brother, Matthew. Are you listening to me, Lucien? I am not Catherine, she's dead and so are you. I need you to leave this house, go be with Catherine, and leave me be.'

'You lie!'

'No, Lucien—I'm telling the truth. Go! Get out of my house.'

I was stalking him now as he seemed to float across the floor, fading in and out of view.

'Noooooo!'

My anger dissipated at the sheer agony in that long, drawn out denial, and I stopped moving. Sadness overwhelmed me at the depth of his pain, and I knew I couldn't continue to lash out at him. Speaking softly, I held out my hand in a conciliatory gesture.

'I know you loved Catherine very much, and she loved you. She came back for you with her daughter after the war, but she was too late. I am so, so sorry, Lucien. But there's nothing here for you anymore. You have to let go. You need to find peace.'

'Catherine.'

'She's gone, Lucien. You need to look for her elsewhere. Maybe if you can let go of this place, she'll be able to find you and lead you home. Please. Your life here on Earth is done, it's over. You have to go.'

My final words were barely a whisper, as Lucien's image simply faded to nothing. I knew he was gone, just as I always did, when the temperature suddenly shot up, warming my skin.

For a moment, I just stood stock still, my heart thundering in my chest. Excess adrenaline still spiked through my blood, and I had to take several deep breaths to calm and center myself. It was at this point that I realized someone was pounding on the door.

'Kat? For fuck's sake, what's happening in there. *Kat!*'

With a gasp, I turned and ran to the door, dropping to my knees to find a very agitated Luke gazing back at me.

'Oh, thank fuck. Are you okay? Jesus, I heard you shouting but when I ran back, you'd moved out of sight, and I could hear you shouting, and then I couldn't hear you … and then, I swear to God, Kat, I heard another voice. Fuck, Kat, what the hell just happened in there?'

I reached through the opening and let my fingers graze his jaw before pulling my hand back so I could see him.

'I'm okay, Luke, honestly. Lucien was here—he appeared as soon as you walked away, but...' I sucked in a breath and glanced back over my shoulder before continuing. "I think maybe he's gone.'

That quizzical 'v' appeared between Luke's eyes. 'Gone?'

'Yeah, gone … like, for good, I think. Maybe. I'm not sure, but, yeah, I really think it's over.'

I jumped as Luke banged his hand against the door again. 'Fuck this, I need to get in there.' He grabbed the door handle and jiggled it in frustration. We both gasped when the door started to open, smacking me in the face.

'Ow—fuck!'

I sat back on my heels and rubbed my forehead where it had made contact with solid wood. It didn't really hurt—I'd been too close for the door to gain any momentum—I was more shocked than anything else. I had no time, though, to dwell on it, as Luke's hand appeared, gripping the edge of the door, and his insistent voice shook me out of my momentary ennui.

'Kat, come on. You've got to get out of there.'

Galvanized into action by his urgent tone, I clambered to my feet, allowing Luke to get in. Immediately, I was enveloped in his warm, safe embrace, and all my residual fear melted away. I could have stayed in his arms for hours, but all too soon he was pulling back, his hands gripping my shoulders.

'God, Kat, you scared the shit out of me. Are you okay? Are you hurt?' His concerned gaze flickered over my face and down my body.

'I'm fine, Luke. Honestly.' I leaned into him, pressing my cheek to his chest and hoping he would once again hold me close as I really needed that contact. He didn't disappoint, wrapping his arms tightly around me and kissing the top of my head. I reveled in the tender gesture, squeezing him hard to let him know I appreciated it.

At last, by some kind of mutual but unspoken agreement, we both parted. Luke lifted one hand to cup my face, brushing his thumb gently across my cheekbone.

'We should get out of here, Kat. I don't know if what you say about Merrick being gone is true or not, but I don't think we should take any chances until we know for sure.'

I stepped away from him, turning slowly as I cast my eyes around the entrance hall. I felt nothing, sensed nothing. Of course, Lucien may have just withdrawn to whatever dark recess he occupied when he wasn't trying to give me a heart attack, as he had in the past; maybe he was merely 'recharging his batteries', but I really wanted to believe he was truly gone.

'Kat?'

I swung around to face Luke. 'He's gone, I'm sure of it. But I think it's probably a good idea to stick with our plan and get out of here for a while. Did you manage to get hold of Tom?'

'No. I just couldn't get a signal... He pulled out his phone and frowned. 'Son of a *bitch*!'

'What?'

He held his phone up, showing me the screen. 'Five fucking bars.' He shook his head in disbelief.

I shrugged, unsurprised. If Lucien could affect the GPS system in my rental car, then he could certainly block a phone signal. 'Oh well, at least he's not going to come roaring up the drive, only to find us standing here like a pair of idiots.'

As Luke continued to stare at his phone in consternation, I grabbed my own from where it was still propping open the letterbox. Pressing the power button, I was relieved to discover that it, too, was now working.

'Come on, let's grab your bag and some overnight things for me and look for a hotel. We'll probably struggle to find anything decent, but I don't think I've got the energy right now to deal with the inquisition if we ask about a room over the pub.'

Luke glanced up and my breath hitched when I saw that the sparkle was back in his eyes.

'I couldn't care less where we stay as long as we're together.'

℠⌘

As it turned out, the place we found was beyond anything I had hoped for. The Cedars Hotel was absolutely beautiful. It was the fifth place we called, and I was beginning to think I'd have to call Josh or Sam after all. It was actually in a village about ten miles from Port Simon, but they had a room available because the couple who'd been using it had had to leave early due to a family emergency. It was their best room and the receptionist apologized that they would have to charge us £250 for one night. I couldn't believe our luck and I think the woman on the other end of the phone was a little taken aback by my enthusiastic confirmation that we'd take it.

I packed the bare minimum for an overnight stay, while Luke sat on my bed and waited; we had decided it was best not to separate, so I then joined him in his room and watched while he gathered his stuff together. By the time we got to the hotel it was early evening, and we were both hungry and exhausted. Lacking the will or the energy to find somewhere to eat, we ordered room service and collapsed onto the large, comfortable couch opposite the bed.

Tiredness washed over me like one of those huge waves we'd seen earlier at the beach. The sensation of being pulled under was almost a tangible thing, and I barely noticed as Luke gathered me in his arms and laid us both down. I was asleep mere seconds after my head settled on his chest.

A loud knocking on the door roused us, seemingly only minutes later, and I groaned as Luke rolled away from me and stood up. He let the waiter in with our food and we ate at the small dining table in the window nook, through which we had a stunning view across the landscaped gardens at the rear of the hotel. We mostly ate in silence, both of us too wrapped up in our thoughts to make idle conversation. Less hungry than I ought to have been, having eaten nothing but a popsicle since breakfast—or perhaps just too tired to give justice to the fine food in front of me—I pushed my half-eaten meal away.

'Is that all you're going to eat, Kat? Do you want me to order you something else?'

'I really can't eat anymore, Luke. It was lovely, but I guess I'm just not that hungry.'

He nodded and reached across the table to pick up my hand and give it a gentle squeeze. 'Hey, it's okay. Do you want to go for a walk? It looks beautiful out there.'

I shook my head. 'You know what? I think I just want to go to bed.'

I watched as his shoulders slumped a little, an odd expression I didn't quite understand flickering across his face. Was that … *disappointment?* Before I could process it, he gave me a smile which didn't reach his eyes.

'No problem. I'll, uh, take the couch.' He looked away and started to extricate his hand from mine. Reflexively, I gripped it tighter.

'No!' I blurted. He'd clearly misinterpreted my statement, thinking I wanted to go to bed alone, but I needed our physical connection right now and wasn't prepared for him to sleep anywhere other than right next to me. Whether he still wanted me physically after the clusterfuck of earlier I had no idea, but at this precise moment in time it seemed of little importance.

'No?' He turned puzzled eyes on me.

'No … I mean, I understand if you don't want anything more to do with me after today, but I need you right now, Luke. Could you just hold me, at least until I fall asleep … please?'

Suddenly, he was standing and pulling me to my feet. The next thing I knew, he was holding me tight, one hand spread across my lower back, the other buried in my hair, pressing my head to his chest. I slipped my arms around his waist and clung to him as though my life depended on it.

'Oh, Kat, haven't you figured it out yet? I don't just want to hold you 'til you fall asleep—I want to keep holding you. I don't think I ever want to let you go.'

I lifted my head to look up at him.

Thirty-six hours … was that long enough to fall in love? Maybe thirty-six minutes … or thirty-six seconds was long enough. I'd never believed in love at first sight or the whole idea of people having soulmates. Indeed, I had begun to doubt whether I was even capable of falling in love, wondering whether my parents' broken marriage might somehow have blighted my ability to commit myself to anyone. But now, looking into the impossibly blue eyes of this incredible man, I had to question everything I'd ever believed. We'd been brought together by the most extraordinary set of coincidences, and it seemed to me that even the most cynical and world-weary skeptic would have to concede that Luke and I might just belong together.

'Okay,' I whispered.

'Okay?'

'Don't ever let me go.'

The words were barely spoken before his mouth was on mine, robbing me of both breath and reason. His tongue sought mine in a kiss which seared my heart like a branding iron. Just when I began to crave oxygen, he broke away, only to scoop me into his arms and turn toward the huge four-poster bed across the room.

In the past, I had always found this part of first being with a man an awkward and somewhat embarrassing event—all that fumbling out of clothes, trying to work out what we liked and didn't like (and rarely succeeding), getting my hair trapped or catching the guy in his most sensitive area with a flailing hand or knee. No such trepidation assailed me now. Like a well-rehearsed dance, our clothes seemed to fall away, and our bodies aligned and moved in a sensual choreography that defied logic. We worshipped one another with our hands and mouths, our pleasure given voice in moans and gasps. When at last Luke paused, questioning me with his eyes, even had I not been able to confirm my acquiescence, I would never have been able to deny him.

Sliding into me, our simultaneous groans were muffled by a kiss that was so much more than a mere exchange of breath. The connection I felt wasn't just sexual; it was bone-deep, a Vulcan mind-meld. It was as if we had been lovers for years, knowing every nuance of what made our bodies sing. Nothing I had ever previously experienced could prepare me for the depth and breadth of the bond I knew was being forged between us.

My orgasm rolled and crashed through me like a Florida storm, taking me to a place I had never been. With my arms and legs wrapped tightly around Luke, I reveled in the muttered curse which fell from his lips as his own climax steamrollered through him. He buried his head in the crook of my neck and we clung to each other as if we feared that some force outside our control would tear us apart. At last, our breathing returned to normal and Luke rolled onto his back, bringing me with him. Settling into his side and with my head on his chest, it seemed neither of us felt the need to speak, and it wasn't long before the steady beat of his heart lulled me into a mercifully peaceful slumber.

Chapter Thirteen

An insistent beeping dragged me reluctantly from the best night's sleep I'd had in months. As consciousness invaded, I became aware of two things almost simultaneously. The first was that the annoying beeping noise was some kind of alarm going off on the nightstand nearest me. The second was that I seemed to be completely enveloped in man, from the top of my head right down to my toes. A muscular arm held me so close I doubted you could even slip a sheet of paper between us, and the hand attached to said arm was gently cupping my left breast. A long, slightly hairy leg was hitched over my thigh and wound around my own leg, and his face seemed to be buried in my hair.

A slow smile spread across my face as our night together filled my mind, making me wonder how soon we could have a repeat performance. Just then, the arm which had been holding me so close unwound itself from my body, and I felt Luke lean over me as he reached across for his phone, where it was still beeping and skittering across the tabletop. Grabbing it, he silenced the alarm and dropped it back on the nightstand. I waited for him to roll away from me and get out of bed, but all he did was return his hand to its former position, giving my breast a gentle squeeze before sweeping my hair from my neck and trailing soft kisses across my exposed skin.

What followed was the sweetest assault, which left us both breathless and sated, hearts pounding in tandem as sweat dried on our naked bodies. Lying in Luke's arms, knowing that our time together was coming to an end all too soon, I knew that the future was full of uncertainties. Of one thing, however, I had no doubt—I was falling in love with him.

ഔര

'Will you call me while you're in London?'
'Of course I will, you silly girl.'
Luke had me pinned against his car outside the hotel, our arms around one another's waists, as we said our goodbyes. He was

driving straight to London, and I was waiting for a taxi to take me to the pub, where I'd promised to stay until we were sure it was safe to return to the house. I'd called Josh earlier, and not only had he offered me a room, but he'd done so with no questions asked, for which I was truly grateful. I knew I would have to give him—and, more importantly, Ruby—some kind of explanation, but I didn't want to have that conversation over the phone.

'I wish you were coming with me, love.'

'Me too, but you know I've got that interview tomorrow, and I would feel bad about cancelling at short notice. Plus, I also have to pick up my new car this afternoon. I promise that as soon as I'm done in Truro, I'll be in my car and tearing up the road to join you. And I really want you to meet my dad.'

'Oh, you do, do you?' He smirked down at me, eyes twinkling. 'I guess this is the real deal then.'

'You better believe it, mister. I'm pretty sure you're stuck with me.'

'I can't think of anyone I'd rather be stuck with.' His smile faded and his eyes grew serious. 'You better not take that job, Kat, because when you get to London, we really need to talk about what happens next. I'm going to call my boss about extending my trip for a week or two, but after that I'll have to get back to SF. I need to know that you'll at least think about coming with me.'

I sighed and leaned my forehead against his chest for a moment, before looking back up to meet his beseeching gaze.

'I can't sort everything out in just a couple of weeks, Luke, especially if I spend most of it in London with you. I've made a home and good friends here and, despite what's happened, I feel kind of tied to this place.'

I watched as his handsome face darkened into a frown, and I lifted a hand to cup his cheek. 'Hey, I'm not saying I won't ever go back to San Francisco. I just need a little time to work things out, okay?'

I slipped my hands around the back of his neck and stretched up on tiptoes to press my lips to his. Luke met me halfway, pulling me closer as he slid his tongue into my mouth. The kiss was full of passion, need and desperation, and I wished with all my heart that we had more time.

The sound of others leaving the hotel brought us back to reality, and Luke pulled back just enough to rest his forehead against mine.

'God, Kat, I hate leaving you like this.' Lifting his head, he brought his hand up and gently rubbed the back of his fingers across my cheek. 'Promise me you'll join me in London as soon as possible.'

'I promise, Luke. I won't be able to stay away.' I tried to smile but felt my bottom lip tremble as I thought about him leaving me.

'And promise you won't go to the house. I'm not kidding, Kat— I'm really not convinced it's safe, and I can't bear the thought of you going back there alone.'

'Look, I'll have to go home at some point to get more clothes—'

'No, Kat—please. Tell me you won't go back there, or I'm gonna go out of my mind with worry.'

I placed a hand on his chest. 'I was going to say that I'll have to pick up some stuff for my interview and pack for London, but I'll ask Josh or Tom to go with me. Honestly, Luke, I'll just run in, grab some things, and run out again. I doubt I'll be inside for more than twenty minutes, and I *promise* I'll have someone with me the whole time.'

He frowned, but I could tell he was conceding the argument— albeit reluctantly. 'Okay, but make sure whoever you take literally stays right there with you in whatever room you're in … and don't let them walk out of the house ahead of you.'

'Okay, okay, I promise.'

'Good. And call me as soon as you finish your interview to let me know you're on the road.'

'I will.' Glancing down at my hand, which still rested against his heart, I noticed the time on my watch and grimaced. 'Shit, you better go, or you'll be late for your meeting.'

He sighed, a pained expression on his face. 'Yeah, I know. Dammit, Kat, I really hate this.'

'Hey, come on, it'll be fine. We'll talk later and again in the morning, and before you know it, I'll be there.' I wasn't sure who I was trying to convince with my upbeat spiel, but I doubted I was fooling either of us.

We kissed again—long and deep and heartfelt—and I tried hard to persuade myself that this wasn't goodbye, merely *adieu*.

At last, Luke got in his car, and I watched as he drove slowly away. Even after he had disappeared from view, I continued to stand there in the parking lot, staring at the last place I'd seen him. I was only broken out of my reverie when a taxi turned in through the gate and swung around in front of the hotel. My ride to the pub had arrived.

ᔍᄭ

It was almost noon when I got to the Griffin, and as soon as I walked through the door Ruby flew around the bar and practically threw herself at me. For such a little thing, she sure could hug up a storm, and despite being in danger of having the breath squeezed right out of me, I couldn't help but feel comforted by her embrace. Just as I was beginning to think I'd have to cry 'uncle', she stepped back, her hands gripping my forearms.

'Oh, Kat, we've been so worried about you. How are you? You look so pale. Did something happen in the house? Are you hurt?' Barely pausing for breath, she flicked her eyes up and down me, as if checking for damage, and then looked over my shoulder toward the door.

'Ruby, I'm fi—'

'And where's your spooky relative?'

"What?"

For a moment, I thought she was talking about Lucien, even though he wasn't related to me, and I mentally quaked at the notion that he could leave the house and follow me.

She sighed, releasing me and crossing her arms over her chest. I could almost sense her metaphorically tapping her foot.

'Yes, Kat. The bloke who's a dead ringer for your ghost, who you picked up from the airport and took home with you—what's his name ... Luke Brodie?'

'Oh, yeah, he, uh, had to get back to London for a client meeting; he left this morning.'

'But I thought—'

I held my hand up. 'Ruby, I promise I'll tell you all about it, but right now I really could use a nap. Yesterday was exhausting, and I, uh, didn't get a lot of sleep last night.'

Tired as I was, I couldn't help the shiver of pleasure that coursed through my body at the reminder of what had happened with Luke the night before and this morning. Of course, Ruby, being the annoyingly observant little witch that she was, totally caught it. She dropped her arms and grabbed my hand, squeezing it.

'Oh my God, Kat—you and Luke Brodie? Bloody hell, that was quick!'

Blushing furiously at how it must seem to Ruby, I felt compelled to explain somehow. 'It wasn't like that, Ruby, we just—'

'Kat, please. You don't have to justify yourself to me. It was inevitable that you and Luke would get together. It's fate—don't you see? Whether it was last night or next year doesn't matter. I mean, it's been more than a century in the making, hasn't it?'

I just stared at her, wide-eyed. 'You really believe that, don't you, Ruby?'

She shrugged, finally releasing my hands. 'Of course I do. How could I not?'

After a moment, I just nodded. Who was I to argue with Ruby's logic when I had no better explanation myself?

'Oh, bugger, I've got to go. Josh is giving me the evil eye—the lunchtime rush is starting. I'll just take you upstairs and leave you to it. Okay?'

'That's fine, Ruby. I'm just really grateful for the room.'

She waved her hand dismissively. 'Don't mention it, Kat—that's what friends are for.'

She led me past the end of the bar, giving Josh a massive eye-roll as she went. He just shook his head, clearly resigned to Ruby's insubordination. Pausing in front of him, I put my hand on his forearm.

'I'm sorry, Josh. I promise I'll send her right down. And thanks for the room, I really appreciate it.'

He smiled down at me. 'You're more than welcome, Kat. I'm just glad we could help you out. And don't worry about Ruby—we both know she does whatever the hell she wants.' He chuckled, and with a gentle squeeze of my shoulder, he turned away to serve the growing crowd at the bar.

Upstairs, I followed Ruby to a room at the end of a long passage. I couldn't wait to just fall on the bed and close my eyes for a few hours, but when she opened the door and I crossed the threshold, I came to an abrupt halt. Looking around me, it was immediately obvious that this wasn't a 'spare' room.

'Ruby, is this … your room?' I asked, peering at the framed photographs on the chest-of-drawers.

'It is … well, it was.'

'Oh, Ruby, I can't take your room. I'll go back to the hotel—'

'You'll do nothing of the sort, Kat Tregowen.' She crossed her arms and gave me that determined look I had come to recognize.

'But Ruby…'

She dropped her arms and sighed. 'Kat, the room is yours for as long as you want it. I … well, I don't really use it anymore. I just haven't got around to … moving my stuff into Josh's room.'

She arched an eyebrow at me and just stared at me for a moment, clearly waiting for the penny to drop through my tired mind. When it finally did, I gasped, my hand flying up to my mouth.

'Oh my God! You're … you and Josh … you … oh my God, Ruby!'

A radiant smile spread across her face as she watched me figure it out.

'Ruby Ellacott, you sly dog, you!' I laughed, before throwing my arms around her. Pulling back, I held her at arm's length. 'How long?' I demanded.

'Since the night of your party. We'd had a lot to drink, and … well, you know how it is. I mean, I've been in love with Josh since I was fifteen years old—'

'Ruby, will you please get that gorgeous arse of yours down here NOW!'

Josh's voice was loud and clear all the way from the bottom of the stairs, making me grimace. Ruby merely sighed and rolled her eyes. 'I better go, or he's gonna have a conniption, and you and I will end up sharing a room after all!'

I laughed and waved my hand to shoo her out. The last thing I wanted was for Josh to regret his hospitality. Besides, I really did need to rest before I could face explaining to my friends why I needed it in the first place.

As soon as Ruby was gone, I sat on the bed and pulled my phone out of my purse. I briefly contemplated calling the people in Truro to cancel my interview. I hadn't completely made up my mind about returning to San Francisco—I needed more time to think and committing myself to a job wouldn't help that process. However, I was still curious, and, having agreed to meet with them, I really did feel compelled to honor the arrangement. Instead, I called the car dealership to check whether my new car was ready to pick up. When they confirmed that it was, I made an appointment to pick it up later that afternoon, as I would need it for the drive to Truro in the morning.

Next, I called Sam. I wanted to ask if she or Tom could give me a ride to get my car and then go to the house with me to get the rest of my stuff. She was curious when I told her I was staying at the pub, but thankfully chose not to interrogate me over the phone, instead agreeing to meet me later.

Finally, I sent a text to Luke to tell him I was safe and sound at the Griffin, knowing he would still be on the road and not wanting to distract him with a call. That done, I used the bathroom, then stripped down to my underwear and crawled beneath the thin summer comforter. I was beyond exhausted and was barely aware of putting my head on the pillow before I was out for the count.

ᏕᏋᏇ

I slept for a couple of hours, but weird, dark dreams forced me awake in the middle of the afternoon. Getting up, I took a shower and then headed down to the bar, where I found Ruby shooing the last of the lunchtime stragglers out the door. Locking it behind them, she turned and grinned at me.

'Okay, we're closed now until five-thirty, Josh is getting us drinks and Sam is on her way over. You,' she said, jabbing a finger in my direction, 'sit yourself down and prepare to tell all.'

I nodded, resigned, knowing there would be no way to avoid this and feeling oddly relieved to talk about it with someone other than Luke. Just as I took a seat at the table she was pointing to, Sam swept into the bar, all red-headed energy and cool poise, and came over to where I was sitting with Ruby in the bar.

'How goes it, my little Yankee Doodle Dandy?' she enquired, making me laugh. 'And don't tell me you're fine, because Ruby called me this morning after you rang her, to say you'd asked for a room, so I know something's up … and you look like shit.'

'Why, thank you, sweet Samantha. I'm all the better for your kind compliment.' I pouted, but she just shrugged.

'You know me, Kat. I just call 'em as I see 'em. Now, what the hell happened that Josh has felt compelled to close the pub during the day? He hasn't done that since Ruby buggered off to Australia and he fell into a blue funk.'

I frowned over at her brother, who was bringing drinks over to the table. "Josh, you really didn't need to close the pub. How much is that going to cost you?'

Expertly setting down the four drinks, he straightened and gave my shoulder a squeeze.

'Don't worry about it, Kat. It's only for a couple of hours, and, despite what my dear sister says, I do occasionally close the bar if I need a few hours off and there's no one to cover. I just put up a sign saying the water's been turned off or there's been a flood in the toilets. At this time of day, any losses are minimal, even in the summer, as most people are on the beach, shopping or taking a siesta.'

He pulled out the chair next to Ruby and sat down across me. We were all silent for a moment as we tasted our drinks, and then I was acutely aware of three pairs of eyes focusing intently on me.

Unable to delay the inevitable any longer, I took a deep breath and launched into my story, right from before I got sick. They obviously knew some of what had happened during Sam and Tom's rescue operation but were clearly shocked when I explained the details of what I could no longer deny—that Lucien Merrick was haunting my house and may well have tried to … well, *kill me*. When I finished describing the events of the previous day, all three of my friends wore expressions which ran the gamut of shock, horror and wide-eyed amazement. On none of their faces, however, did I detect any hint of disbelief or mockery. Apart from the odd brief request for clarification, and the occasional gasp of surprise, they had all listened without interruption and, when I finally stopped talking, I looked from one to the other, awaiting their reactions.

An extended silence followed, as it seemed they were all struggling to make sense of what I'd told them. It was Josh who broke it, pushing his chair back and standing up. 'Anyone want another drink?'

I asked for a Coke, knowing I'd be driving later, as did Sam, while Ruby just held up her empty cider glass.

We watched him walk over to the bar, until Sam's hand slapping down on the table made Ruby and me both jump, immediately getting our attention.

'I bloody *knew* there was more to the bath incident than you falling asleep. That *bastard*! I still feel sick every time I think about how different things could have been if I hadn't come back upstairs when I did. Jesus, Kat, you have to get rid of that house.'

I reached across and rubbed my hand up and down her arm, smiling at her. 'But you did get to me in time and everything's fine, Sam. And I understand your concern, but I'm sure he's gone now.'

She frowned, but it was Ruby who spoke. 'If you're so sure he's gone, Kat, why are you sleeping in my old room?'

It seemed her romantic notions of a spectral love affair had dissipated somewhat.

'Well, I promised Luke I wouldn't go back there on my own until we can be completely sure it's safe.'

'But how will you know?'

I sighed. In truth, I had no idea how to prove my theory, other than to go back to the house on my own, and I was pretty sure my friends would baulk at that idea—and Luke would likely read me the riot act if he found out.

'I guess I won't, Ruby,' I conceded, as Josh returned with our drinks. 'But there was something about the way he left this time, when I shouted at him—I don't quite know how to put it into words, but when he went I just … felt his absence in a way I never had before. Since the first moment I found that house I've *felt* Lucien, even if it was just a vague sense of, of … *something* … shit, I don't know how to explain it, except to say that the house seems empty now. *It's never* felt like that before. That's why I'm convinced he's gone for good.'

'So, what's the plan, Kat?' Josh asked, taking his seat opposite me.

'Um, well, Sam is giving me a ride to Truro to pick up my new car, and then I need to go home to pack some more clothes for my interview in the morning and for London. I'm gonna join Luke there and spend some time with him before he has to fly back to the States.'

The whole 'Luke development' was, of course, news to two of my friends, although, predictably, it was Sam who showed the greater interest.

'Hmm, so when you told me on the phone earlier that you'd spent the night at a hotel, I'm guessing it wasn't in separate rooms?'

I frowned, unwilling for the moment to share details of what had transpired between us the day—and night—before.

'Uh, well, they only had one room…'

Josh reached across the table to grip my forearm. 'It's none of our business, Kat,' he said, throwing his sister a stern look.

Releasing me, he sat back and gazed pointedly from one to the other of us. 'The priority here is that Kat doesn't spend any time in that house on her own. Sam, is Tom working today?'

'Uh, well, he was finishing off at the Morgans' house this afternoon, but—' She glanced at her watch. 'He should be done by now. Why?'

'I don't like the idea of the two of you going back to Kat's alone.' He held up his hand to forestall Sam's objection. 'I know you're a tough old bint, but I'd feel a lot happier if Tom went with you, and I'm betting he would too.'

Sam pouted, but I could see that she agreed with his assessment. 'Okay, I'll ring him and ask him to meet us there.'

With that, she grabbed her purse and pulled out her phone. As she dialed her husband, I stood and made my excuses to freshen up in my room before leaving. I wanted to call Luke and preferred to do so in private. Upstairs, I quickly checked my phone, seeing that I had a missed call from him and a message. I'd muted it earlier when I'd taken a nap and had forgotten to turn it back up, but he'd only just called, so I immediately pressed redial without even bothering to listen to the message. It rang only once before he answered.

'Kat, thank God. I was so worried when you didn't pick up. Are you okay?'

'Hey, calm down, I'm fine. I just forgot that I put my phone on vibrate while I took a nap, and then I was talking to my friends in the bar, so I've only just checked. How'd your meeting go—are you done?'

He sighed, and I could just imagine him running his hand through his hair. 'Yeah, we finished about fifteen minutes ago. The client is being an idiot, but I think the fact that I was here to deal with his concerns in person has made all the difference, so I guess I'm thankful I flew in early.' His voice dropped, his next words making me shiver. 'And I'm not just talking about today.'

Swallowing, all I could manage was a slightly croaky 'oh', eliciting a faintly salacious chuckle on the other end of the line.

'So, anyway, the reason I called was to say I'm on my way back to the car, and I'll drive back to Cornwall this evening—I don't want to wait until tomorrow to see you, Kat.'

'Oh, Luke, you can't do that.'

'Why the hell not?'

'Well, it's too long a drive to do twice in one day. This isn't the States, and you know what the roads here are like. It'll be dark before you get here, and you shouldn't drive at night when you're tired.'

'It's less than five hours, Kat. I can be there by ... ten-ish if I get going right away.'

'Luke, it's five o'clock already, and it'll take you at least two hours to get out of London in the rush hour. Please, I'll worry about you the whole time. I don't really want to wait either, but it's only one night and if I finish my interview by ten, I can be with you by early afternoon. I'd feel much better knowing that you're tucked up safe and sound in a hotel room. I can call you tonight, once we're both settled, and we can chat for as long as we want. Okay?'

He was silent for so long that I had to check the phone screen to make sure we were still connected.

'Luke?'

I heard him sigh loudly. 'I don't like it, Kat. I know it's what we agreed, but I hate the idea of spending the night away from you. I know we've only just met, but ... I don't know...it just feels wrong.'

'I'll be fine, Luke. Sam and Tom are coming with me to the house after I get my new car; they'll stay with me while I pack a bag and then we're out of there and heading back to the pub. I'll be with friends all evening, and you and I will talk later. It'll all work out for the best—trust me.'

'Okay, okay, I guess you're right. I'll find a hotel and let you know where I am—I usually stay at the Park Lane Sheraton when I'm here, so I'll try there first. Listen, Kat, are you sure you don't want me—'

'I'm sure, Luke. Now go find yourself somewhere to stay, and I'll call you later.'

'Okay. I'll miss you tonight. And I know that sounds stupid when we only met a couple of days ago, but I really will. I mean, I miss you right now ... Jesus, Kat, please tell me it's not just me that feels this way because I'm kinda freaking out right now. I feel like I'm on a runaway express train that's gathering speed, and I'm terrified and ... and excited, all at the same time.'

I squeezed my eyes shut and drew in a tremulous breath in a vain effort to keep my voice steady. 'It's not just you, Luke. I ... I'm pretty confused right now, but one thing I know for certain is that I really want to ... take this as far as it can go. *God*, I can't wait to see you again, but maybe being apart tonight will give us both a chance to give some serious thought to what we want and what we do next … you know?'

'I guess—but it doesn't make it any easier.'

'You're right, but we'll see each other in less than twenty-four hours, so I'm sure we'll survive. Look, I've got to go, but I'll call you later, or you call me, okay?'

'Okay. You take care now, sweet girl. I need you healthy and rested when you get here, because I've got plans for you which involve room service and a kingsize hotel bed.'

Oh, God! 'Shit, Luke, you can't say stuff like that when you're five hours' drive away and Sam is downstairs bellowing at me to get my ass into gear.'

He chuckled, but finally let me go with more promises that we would talk later. I knew he wasn't happy about staying in London, but I couldn't bear the thought of him having an accident because he was driving tired on twisty, narrow Cornish roads in the dark.

I headed down to the bar where Sam was waiting impatiently, and we finally set off on our short trip to Truro.

℘)℃

It felt strange pulling into my drive an hour or so later, despite the fact that I had only been away for one night. Sam's Mercedes and Tom's pickup were already parked outside the house, and they were both leaning side by side against her car. Turning off the engine of my new SUV, I watched the grin spread across Tom's face as he walked over and opened my door.

'A Volvo, Kat? Seriously?'

Scowling, I climbed out of the car. 'Yes, Tom, a Volvo. What's your point?'

He chuckled and patted the hood. 'Well, you know what they say, don't you?'

Crossing my arms over my chest, I narrowed my eyes. 'No, Tom, what *do* they say?'

'What's the difference between a Volvo and a sex shop?' He paused for a beat, flashing his dimpled grin. 'It's less embarrassing being seen leaving a sex shop.' He laughed loudly at his own joke, but it was cut abruptly short when Sam walked up behind him and smacked him across the back of the head.

'Ow! Dammit, Sammy, that hurt,' he whined, rubbing the sore spot.

I smirked at him. 'Now, *that's* funny,' I said, brushing past him and giving Sam a wink as I headed to the front door. I pulled my key out of my purse, only to have Tom pluck it from my fingers and unlock the door.

'I'll go in first and Sam will follow you.' All trace of the joker was gone, and I could see that he was deadly serious.

I shrugged. 'Lead on, McDuff,' I told him, indicating with my hand for him to proceed.

Inside, the hallway offered a cool respite from the heat of the day. Gazing around, all was as I'd left it the day before, including the letterbox flap, which still lay on the ground where I dropped it. Tom followed my eyes and bent to pick it up, turning it over in his hands.

'I did that—I, uh, needed to keep the slot open so I could see Luke. Just leave it, Em. I'll run upstairs and pack a bag quickly, and then we can leave.'

Sam put her hand on my arm to stop me. 'Not without us, Kat. Tom, you go ahead again and we'll keep Kat between us. We'll stay with you while you get your stuff and then we'll all leave together. Okay?'

I blew out a breath and shrugged. Everything was quiet and I had no sense at all of anyone—or anything—being there. Lucien was gone. Of that, I was becoming more and more convinced. However, I was acutely aware that my friends' actions were indicative of their trust and belief in what I'd told them, so I once again gestured for Tom to lead the way.

Twenty minutes later, I locked up and we all left the house without mishap. Tom and Sam insisted I get in my car and set off up the drive before they did the same, and in no time at all we were all pulling into the pub parking lot.

₭)ℛ

It wasn't that late when I decided to turn in for the night. I'd had a laughter-filled dinner with my friends, during which Ruby and Tom were relentless in their pursuit of details about both Lucien's activities and what had happened between me and Luke. I was happy to tell them what I could about the paranormal events at the house but remained tight-lipped about everything else. The more they probed, the more intransigent I became, much to their annoyance and my amusement. In the end, it was as much about escaping the third degree as needing a decent night's sleep which sent me to my room.

I decided to get my clothes and papers together for my interview and then get ready for bed before calling Luke, as promised. With that in mind, I took out my phone, only to find that the battery was dead. Cursing, I set it to charge and busied myself with preparing my stuff for the morning. I took my suit out of its protective bag, hanging it on the closet door, and then picked up my briefcase. As I did, I realized with a sinking feeling that I had forgotten to collect my portfolio from the library at Chimneys. Cursing, I sat down heavily on the bed. I couldn't go to an interview for a job as an architect without having the means to show them what I was capable of. I knew, of course, that it was unlikely I would accept an offer, should it be made, but the professional in me just couldn't turn up empty-handed. And, if I was honest, I was proud of my achievements and wanted to show off a little.

Sighing, I stood up and grabbed my purse from the chair by the window. I really didn't want to leave it until the morning, as I wasn't sure how long it would take to get to Truro in the city rush-hour—if such a thing existed in Cornwall—and I didn't want to risk being late. It would take less than half an hour to drive over to the house, grab my portfolio and get back to the pub. The decision made, I went downstairs to see if anyone would go with me. I didn't think it was necessary, but the promise I'd made to Luke was ringing in my head, and I didn't want to go back on my word. However, when I went through the door which connected the private areas to the pub itself, I immediately realized that Sam and Tom must have already left, and Josh and Ruby were both busy serving customers who were three deep at the bar. Even if I were able to catch their attention, there was no way either of them could leave until closing time. I didn't want to wait that long, as I really wanted time to talk to Luke and still get to bed at a reasonable time. So, with that in mind, I retreated back the way I had come and slipped out through the back door to where my car was parked nearby.

There was little traffic, so I quickly reached the house, pulling up right outside the door. It was twilight and the last of the day's light was almost gone; however, a rising full moon cast a bright, silvery glow across the landscape, throwing the building and grounds into sharp relief. Getting out, I glanced around but just like earlier in the afternoon, all was quiet, and I didn't hesitate to unlock the door and step inside.

I really had few qualms about being back here alone, but even so, I had a moment of uncertainty on first entering the house. Something sharp and brittle crunched under my foot; I looked down but could see nothing in the darkness. Frowning, I reached over to switch the hall lights on, and the gasp which escaped me echoed loudly in the cavernous space.

In the dim glow cast by a single remaining light bulb my shocked gaze fell on a scene of such devastation that I could barely process what I was seeing.

My first thought was that there had been a gas explosion.

The beautiful mosaic floor was smashed and ripped up, the handrail and bannisters of my custom-made, solid wood staircase were splintered and broken, the maple doors on either side of the foyer were similarly damaged, and a massive crack radiated through the six-inch glass lightwell in the floor like a monstrous cobweb. Shards of glass from the chandelier and wall uplighters littered the floor, along with the pulverized remains of the pretty little yew side tables that had been placed against the walls and the vases that had sat on them.

My hands came up to cover my mouth as I tried, and failed, to stop the cry which escaped me. As rational thought began to return, I realized that this had been no accident, nor was it any kind of act of God.

My house … my beautiful house.

Without thinking, I dropped my hands and screamed, 'WHAT HAVE YOU *DONE?*'

As the echo of my despair faded, there was only silence.

And then I heard it.

It started as a dull drone, and I fought to pinpoint its source. But very quickly the sound grew and swelled to a head-pounding roar which seemed to fill the house from basement to rafters. Covering my ears with my hands, I took a step back, intent on leaving, but instead of the open doorway, I came up against solid wood.

The door was shut.

I tried to turn around, but it was if I was caught in a maelstrom, the noise like a living, breathing entity surrounding me, and my movements were sluggish. With more hope than expectation, I reached behind me for the door handle, but my hand simply flailed impotently as I became more and more disoriented.

'*Lucien,*' I cried, but I couldn't even hear myself inside the hellish vortex of sound.

Except that it was no longer just a noise.

Like some kind of freakish tornado trapped indoors, I felt like all the air was being sucked out of the space as a cold wind whipped and whirled around me, picking up shards and splinters of glass, wood and ceramic tiles, swirling them around in a spiral of lethal debris.

'Lucien, *please…*'

Again, my desperate plea was snatched from my lips, dissipating like smoke in a hurricane.

And then, above the tumultuous uproar, I heard him.

'*I will NEVER let you leave me again … you're mine, Catherine … MINE!*'

Below me—for real this time—a dull explosion made the floor seem to undulate, followed by an ear-shattering crash as the lightwell disintegrated and a huge plume of black smoke and orange flames shot up from the basement.

I screamed, my legs no longer able to support me. I sank to the floor, covering my face in a futile attempt to protect it from flying debris. I cried out for my love—but not the warped, hateful specter who demanded my life; my heart broke in that moment, knowing that I would never see Luke Brodie again.

Because that's when I knew I was going to die.

Chapter Fourteen

'Sir? Would you like the room?'

Across the reception desk of the Park Lane Sheraton in Mayfair, the well-groomed blonde cocked her head at me, frowning slightly. No doubt she was confused by my lack of response, but she had no idea of the war that waged inside my head. While I stood in the beautifully appointed art deco marble and teak foyer, my mind remained in Cornwall, preoccupied as I was with the stunning woman who had undoubtedly captured my heart from the moment she fumbled her way through that seemingly inauspicious first meeting at the airport.

God, but she'd taken my breath away, and nothing that had happened since—not that terrible nightmare, my inexplicable sleepwalking, nor the shitstorm of weirdness which had occurred the day before—could diminish the extraordinary attraction I felt for Kat Tregowen.

I wanted her. And after sharing a bed with her, I knew I had to have her in my life. Permanently.

'Sir? Is everything all right?'

Jarred out of my muddled thoughts, I focused on the girl in front of me. 'Uh, yeah, I'm fine, thanks.'

'And the room, sir?'

'Oh, yes, right.' I found myself gazing at her, unable to process what it was she wanted.

'You'll take it?' A slight note of frustration had crept into voice, and I realized she must be wondering if I should be allowed out on my own.

Shaking my head to clear it, I managed to crack a smile. 'Sorry, yes, I'll, uh, take it.'

As soon as the words left of my mouth, I started wondering if I was making a huge mistake. Ever since leaving Kat at the hotel that morning, I had been assailed by a growing sense of unease. Nevertheless, I handed over my credit card and watched in silence as the receptionist checked me in and handed over a keycard.

Once inside my room, I left my bag next to the bed and went to the window. I stood there for a few minutes, just gazing out over

Green Park, which reached all the way from the front of the hotel to Buckingham Palace. It was a stunning vista, but right now it was a poor substitute for the raw beauty of Cornwall, where my heart undoubtedly languished.

I pulled my phone out and speed-dialed Kat. If I could just talk to her, I was sure I'd feel a lot better. I listened anxiously as it rang … and rang, finally going to voicemail. Cursing, I wondered if she'd remembered to turn the volume up after we last spoke.

I sat down heavily on the bed, my thoughts in turmoil as I dropped the phone next to me. Minute by minute, that sense of unease I'd been feeling had grown in direct proportion to the distance I'd put between myself and Kat. Sitting in this London hotel room, my heart seemed to be hammering inside my ribcage, and I felt sick to my stomach. A sense of impending doom crept over me, swamping and surrounding me like a toxic miasma. Burying my head in my hands, I fought to calm my steadily rising heart rate, to no avail. I picked up my phone and pressed redial, but once again it just rang until it diverted to voicemail. All I could do was leave a message asking her to call me back, which did little to settle me.

At last, I stood up. I knew now that my escalating anxiety wouldn't dissipate until I saw Kat again and could see for myself that she was safe.

I looked around me. Apart from the slight imprint of my ass on the bed, there was no evidence of my occupation so, with a renewed determination, I grabbed my case and left the room. Returning to the lobby, I told the same woman who'd checked me in that a sudden emergency had called me away, and she kindly told me there would be no charge. Quite honestly, I couldn't give a shit whether they made me pay or not—all I knew was that I had to get back to Cornwall … back to Kat.

I headed straight to the hotel parking lot, found my rental and threw my bag in the trunk. Moments later, I was exiting onto Piccadilly—and straight into the London rush-hour. Kat had been right about the traffic, which was heavy and slow moving, but I told myself that it didn't matter what time I got to Port Simon as long as I was on my way and would reach her tonight. As the line of cars stopped and started, I grabbed my phone and tried her again. This time it didn't even ring, going straight to voicemail—which meant she'd either deliberately turned it off or the battery was dead. Either way, it didn't help my blood pressure as I stewed in my stationary vehicle.

Just like Kat had predicted, it took me nearly two hours to get onto the motorway, and traffic leaving town was dense. Still, at least it was relatively fast-moving, allowing me to keep to a pretty steady seventy miles an hour. Whenever possible, I cranked up the speed, mindless of getting a ticket when I was so desperate to make up time in order to get me closer to the woman I was now sure I could no longer live without.

It had been less than three days since we'd met, but I had no doubt she was the one for me. Never in my life had I felt such a strong connection to another person, and it terrified and thrilled me in equal measure. There would be those, of course, who would put it down to our shared ancestry, and maybe they might be right, in part; but I knew it went deeper and was more profound than simple genetics.

I wanted a chance to explore what that meant, to find out if Kat felt the same way and whether whatever was happening between us had the potential to be much, much more. But first I had to get her away from that house. She might be convinced that the entity which filled every room with its malignant presence was gone, but I wasn't so sure.

When Kat had first told me about what had been going on, I didn't question that what she said was true—at least, in her own mind. There were so many explanations for what she'd experienced, and a ghost wouldn't have been my first thought. However, after what had happened to me on my first night there, I was starting to believe that some kind of paranormal incursion lay at the heart of all that was wrong in Kat's home. If that hadn't been enough to convince me, the events of yesterday had left me in no doubt that the house was a dangerous place to be, *especially* for Kat.

Up ahead, the traffic slowed as a line formed to take the exit for Heathrow Airport, so I plucked my phone from the passenger seat and pressed redial. Once again, it went straight to voicemail. I knew Kat had gone with Sam and Tom to pick up a car and then go to the house, but she should surely have been back at the pub by now. Tossing it back down, I cursed that I hadn't taken a number for at least one of her friends—I didn't even know any of their last names. I thought hard, trying to recall the name of the pub, but I wasn't even sure Kat had mentioned it. All I could do was keep going, knowing that at least I was shortening the distance between us with every mile I covered.

By the time I transferred from the motorway out of London to the one which would take me down into Devon, traffic had lightened considerably and I was able to pick up speed. If I got a speeding ticket, so be it—all that mattered was getting to Kat. Even as I got closer, my anxiety continued to escalate. I kept trying her number, but she never answered, and I could no longer placate myself with the thought that all was well. As the time when she was supposed to call me came and went, I knew—I absolutely *knew* in my heart—that something was very, very wrong.

℘⃝

I sat on the floor, my knees pulled up to my chest and my arms covering my head as smoke and debris swirled around me. I could feel the heat of the flames belching out of the light-well, which now resembled nothing less than the very mouth of Hell.

I knew I needed to at least try and get myself out of there, but my body seemed to have become detached from my brain. Fear was my only companion, and I was beginning to think that there was no point fighting. Merrick would never let me leave, and he wielded all the power here. In his warped mind, the only way he could be reunited with the love of his life was for me to die, and no amount of insisting that I wasn't Catherine would dissuade him from his destructive and murderous course.

Something smashed against the wall beside me, making me scream, and I chanced a quick look around me. My only thought was that I had descended into a truly Stygian underworld. Red hot embers littered the floor, smoldering and gradually igniting the piles of splintered wood. Flames licked along the edges of the doors and up the stairs, and I could see black, oily smoke seeping and curling like dark, sinuous fingers from the kitchen. The floor on which I sat had bulged from the basement explosion and a fissure had opened, dissecting the entrance hall from one side to the other. My eye followed it to a massive crack which now snaked up the wall like the branches of a lifeless tree.

I had time to consider the fact that the damage to my house was now far worse than when I had first seen it after being abandoned for sixty years. What a bitter irony.

Even as the thought crossed my mind, another dull explosion ripped through the house, emanating from the kitchen. This time, I was pretty sure it was caused by the gas line being severed, and it was only a matter of time before the whole place went up in smoke. A loud sob escaped me—whether for my house or myself, I was uncertain. All I knew was that I had run out of time.

As if he could read my thoughts, that other-worldly voice cut through the chaos around me, filling my head.

'Catherine, it's time. Come to me. We'll be together for eternity, my love.'

He was close, his words at once both comforting and abhorrent to me.

Raising my head from where it had been buried in my hands, I gazed at the creature before me, little more than five or six feet away. To think that I had welcomed his caress, had sought his touch. The whole notion of how I'd allowed myself to be seduced by something that wasn't even … *human* filled me with horror, and I finally felt myself overwhelmed by something other than fear.

I was fucking *furious*.

Unlike yesterday, however, my anger wasn't tempered by sympathy or compassion. It was white-hot and all-consuming. Adrenalin spiked my blood, and I no longer felt tethered in place. Pushing myself up, I stood with my feet braced against the uneven floor.

'We are not…' I coughed, my voice hoarse from crying and the dehydrating effect of the smoke and dust. Swallowing hard, I tried again. 'We are not going to be together, Lucien.' I tried to inject some volume and defiance into my voice, but I could barely get the words out as I started coughing again.

'Fuck!'

Without seeming to move, I was taken aback when I realized that Merrick was now right in front of me, no more than a couple of feet away—indeed, had I lifted my arm I could have reached out and touched him. He looked so real—more real than ever before, and I vaguely wondered if that was because I was about to die. I may not have reached for Merrick, but as I stared up at him in his high collar and black frock coat, he raised his hand to cup my cheek.

I wanted to turn my face away but felt powerless to move as his black eyes bored into mine. My skin tingled where his hand lay, and it seemed as if someone had turned the volume down on the cacophonous maelstrom which filled the house.

He looked so much like Luke ... my beautiful, sexy, blue-eyed, *flesh and blood* Luke.

'You have been away from me too long, little Catherine. You have fallen in with common folk and riffraff, and such language cannot be borne. When we are married you must overcome your low birth and try to be a lady worthy of being my wife. Now, come. I will tolerate your prevarication no longer.'

I was transfixed, his voice seeming to ... *inhabit* me. I could feel my will slipping as he once again held me in his thrall. It would be so easy to just let go, I knew.

Sucking in a huge breath, I summoned up my last ounce of resolve. 'No, Lucien. I can't go with you. You must leave.' I closed my eyes for a moment, trying to break the hold he had over me. 'Dear God, Lucien, you've hurt so many people ... killed people ... killed a *child* for fuck's sake. This must end.'

His eyes, blacker than midnight, nevertheless seemed to blaze.

'The child was never supposed to die ... his mother should have come sooner.'

'But she didn't, and he died. That was so wrong of you, Lucien. Why—'

'ENOUGH! Stop defying me. We must go. I have waited too long already. Come.'

His hand dropped from my face to my upper arm, enclosing it in an iron grip. With a herculean effort, I resisted, but when he turned that soulless glare on me again, I felt my self-control dissipate, like smoke on the wind. My mind screamed at me to fight, but my body was apparently incapable of resisting. Slowly but surely, he pulled me towards the stairs, which were now well and truly alight. Flames licked and swirled around the bannisters as the carpet smoldered and burned. Once I was dragged up that blazing stairway, there would be no way back down.

I wanted to weep for all that I was losing, for my beautiful Luke and the life that we could have had. I prayed that he would stay away from Chimneys. If there was a God, he had long ago abandoned this dreadful place. My tears remained unshed, however, the heat drying them before they could fall.

As we approached the first step, I could almost feel my last hope ebb away and a bone-deep fatigue overtook me. My knees buckled and I would have hit the floor, had I not been kept aloft by Merrick's unbreakable hold on me. My smoke-filled lungs protested, causing another round of hacking coughs to escape me. My vision blurred as I failed to draw in any clean air, and everything started to grow dim. The last thing I heard was an ear-splitting crash behind me, like the sound of a great tree falling.

Then everything went black.

ℒℴℛ

My foot was practically to the floor as I tried to coax more speed out of the straining engine of my rented Ford. The dark, twisting road threatened to put an end to my headlong progress, but I refused to let up, wrestling with the steering wheel as I desperately attempted to close the distance between myself and Kat. I had thought that the closer I got, the calmer I would become, but it seemed the reverse was true—for every mile I covered, my anxiety grew, rendering me almost incoherent with fear.

I had no explanation for why I should be so worried. Yes, I'd failed consistently to get hold of Kat on the phone and she hadn't called me as promised, but those two things alone could not account for this level of panic. I knew—on an elemental level—that something really bad was going down, and that thought kept my foot welded to the pedal, heedless of speed limits and traffic cameras.

Finally—*finally*—the sign that welcomed visitors to Port Simon loomed in front of me and the road straightened, allowing me to step hard on the accelerator. I knew that I was close now and that once I rounded the next shallow bend, I would begin the long, gentle climb to where I would have the house almost within sight. In fact, mere moments later I crested the hill, only to discover what should have been a dark horizon lit up by an orange glow.

Stamping on the brakes, I fought the steering as the car fishtailed alarmingly across the thankfully empty road. Coming to a slithering halt, I stared in shock at what my brain refused to process.

Getting out of the car, I quickly vaulted up onto the hood and then onto the roof, gazing in growing comprehension and horror at the flickering light in the distance. Something was on fire.

Yes, it could have been any number of houses or buildings in Port Simon, but I knew—I fucking *knew*—it was Chimneys.

Jumping down, I got back into the idling car and, without even bothering with the seat belt, I slammed it into drive and crashed my foot to the floor, making the car shoot forward with a squeal and the stench of burning rubber.

Careering down the road, I almost missed the turn and had to brake hard and yank the steering wheel to make it through the gates. Thankfully, they stood open, but it didn't stop me clipping the post hard as I skidded through.

The sight that greeted me caused me to pull up sharply, right behind a black SUV.

The house appeared to be engulfed in flames. Black smoke poured out of the chimneys as the fire flickered and danced behind every window. Even as I looked on, the sound of glass smashing drew my eye upwards, where I realized the atrium must have collapsed. Flames now erupted through the roof, along with an oily, toxic-looking cloud of smoke.

Grabbing my phone, I quickly dialed 911, cursing loudly when I recalled that the emergency number here was 999. Again, I dialed, climbing out of the car as I waited for a response.

'*Emergency—which service?*'

'Fire—there's a fire at Chimneys in Port Simon. You need to get here now!'

'*Yes, sir. Can you tell me the address, please?*'

'Oh, Jesus, I don't know. It's the house called Chimneys … on the road from, uh, Newquay to Port Simon. The old Merrick house. Fuck, someone must know—'

'*Sir, you need to keep calm so we can help you. Are you at the property at this moment?*'

'Yes, I'm standing right in front of it. Please, you have to get here—'

'*It's all right, sir, we can get your location from your phone signal; just keep it switched on. The fire service has been alerted and a fire engine is on its way. Sir, can you tell me, is anyone in the house?*'

I looked at the black car, guessing it had to be Kat's, and squeezed my eyes shut.

'Uh, yeah, I think my girlfriend is in there.'

'*You think, sir, or you're sure?*'

'I'm sure, goddammit!' Because I knew she was in there. Stupid girl. Why couldn't she have just stayed away?

'Okay. I understand you're concerned, sir, but I need you to move a safe distance from the house and wait for the fire service to get there. Can you give me your name?'

But I wasn't listening anymore. I knew Kat was running out of time, and if I didn't do something, it was going to be too late.

Pushing my phone into my back pocket, I ran to the front door and placed my hands flat against the wood. It was warm but not unduly so. Knowing Kat, I guessed it would meet, if not exceed, building regulations, which meant it would hold out against all but the fiercest fire for at least an hour. Unfortunately, it also meant that the chances of breaking it down were pretty slim; I'd be more likely to break me.

Desperately, I looked around and my gaze fell on what I had assumed was Kat's new car. It was a Volvo and was therefore built like a tank.

Would she have left the keys in the ignition? If she'd just come here to grab something she'd forgotten, maybe she hadn't bothered taking them into the house with her ... would she keep them separate from her house keys?

Hurrying over to the vehicle, I tried the door and sent a swift 'thank you' to the heavens when it opened. There on the passenger seat was Kat's purse, and dangling from the steering column was a set of keys.

I didn't waste any more time, climbing behind the wheel and firing up the engine. I hoped she'd forgive me for fucking up her new car, but as far as I was concerned, what I was about to do was well and truly a case of *'force majeure'*.

I maneuvered the Volvo around so that it was more or less head on to the house and secured my seatbelt. Then, without giving myself too much time to think twice, I revved the engine, thrust the gear lever into drive and covered my face with my hands—then I floored the accelerator.

The car leapt forward like a greyhound out of a trap, hitting the front door with an almighty bang, followed by the airbag exploding in my face and the engine stalling.

Momentarily blinded, I flailed at the swiftly deflating bag and looked up through the windshield to find out if my wild plan had worked.

To say that it had was an understatement.

The double doors had shattered spectacularly, and the Volvo's front wheels now rested on top of them, halfway across the threshold. A huge crack zigzagged diagonally through the glass of the windshield, and I could see that the hood was massively crumpled. Yet the interior was undamaged, and I quickly released my seatbelt and attempted to open the door.

Unfortunately, I hadn't taken into account that the width of the vehicle was only inches narrower than the opening.

'Fuck!'

I stared ahead, and the sight which met my eyes made the blood freeze in my veins. My doppelganger, dressed like an Edwardian gentleman, was kneeling on the ground, bent over the woman I was pretty sure I loved, who lay prone on the ground at the bottom of the stairs. Her eyes appeared to be closed, her skin ashen … and she looked like she might be dead.

My nemesis slowly raised his head, and the blackest, most soulless eyes I had ever seen stared back at me. It was like looking into the eyes of Beelzebub.

'Fuck this!' I shouted, reaching forward to turn the key in the ignition.

God bless Volvo and the automotive geniuses who build their cars. Without even a hiccup, the engine roared to life, sending me hurtling right inside the house. At the last moment, I braked, narrowly avoiding the light-well, from which bright orange flames shot high into the air. The car skidded and struggled to gain purchase on the tiled floor, but eventually came to a stop facing the staircase, about five yards from where Kat badly needed my help.

I kept my eyes fixed on Merrick, who was now glaring at me with such enmity that the saying about 'if looks could kill' seemed like it might actually be possible.

The house was full of noise, which I could hear even from within the relatively protected confines of the car. Dirt and debris flew around in swirling eddies, and I could see small cuts on Kat's face and arms. The sight of her blood made me clench my fists in fury, and I hurled myself out of the Volvo.

'Get the fuck away from her, you bastard!' I shouted, only to be met with a grim smile of pure malevolence. This ghost, specter— call it what you will—may have been a decent man once, but a century of grief, bitterness and anger had clearly warped him into something utterly evil and self-serving. My own anger wasn't enough to temper the fear that slithered through me like a living thing, and I hesitated.

Before I even understood what was happening, I was lifted off my feet by unseen forces and tossed aside like a rag doll. I flew through the air and hit the floor just inches from where smoke and flames seemed to spew from the bowels of the earth. Seriously winded by the impact and feeling like I'd been kicked by a horse, it was all I could do to roll to one side in order to avoid being swallowed up by that hellhole. I fought to draw breath in the increasingly hot, airless space, coughing and wincing as I inhaled the filth which danced and hung in the fetid atmosphere. Air from the open doorway was clearly feeding the fire, which, in turn was sucking all the oxygen out of the room. With difficulty, I propped myself up to look back across the hallway, and my heart faltered inside my chest.

Merrick was now hovering over Kat's unmoving form, and at first I thought he was kissing her. That thought alone was enough to nauseate me, but then I gasped as I finally understood what he was doing. Transfixed with horror, I saw his mouth lift from hers and a bright, silvery vapor seemed to flow between them. If I hadn't seen it, I simply wouldn't have believed it—it seemed he was literally *sucking* the life out of her.

Galvanized into action, despite what I suspected were bruised ribs, I pushed myself to my feet and hurled myself at the macabre tableau before me. I had no time to form a plan or consider whether I would achieve anything. All I knew was that I had to at least try to save Kat, and I acted on pure instinct.

Before I could give tangible thought to whether I would actually be able to touch the entity or simply pass right through him, I was there, my arms reaching out to pull him off Kat and break their grotesque connection. So intent was he on draining my beautiful girl of her lifeforce, he hardly seemed aware of my presence. My forward impetus took me straight into him, and I wrapped him in a crushing bear hug from behind that my high school wrestling coach would have been proud of. It was like hugging a statue.

I'd been worried it would be like trying to grab vapor, but my great, great, great grandfather was a good deal more corporeal than I had bargained for.

Right now, though, I didn't give a flying fuck, because he was no longer on top of Kat, and I'd successfully broken their connection. I couldn't take time out to check on her because I was about to learn a swift lesson in what happens when you grab a tiger by its tail. I leaned back, pulling him with me, forcing myself to hang on tight and ignore the excruciating pain in my side as I frantically back-pedaled, praying I wouldn't slip or stumble. With an inhuman shriek of surprise and fury, Merrick tried to twist away from me, but I hung on for all I was worth. I knew he had powers against which I had no defense—probably more so since he had 'fed' on my girl like a fucking vampire—but I knew I would rather die than let go.

Screaming like a banshee, he wriggled and hissed in my grip, but just like Coach Springer had taught me, I let his superior strength work in my favor, forcing our momentum to carry us ever closer to the fiery pit into which he had so recently tried to cast me. A spectral entity he might be, but it seemed that by absorbing Kat's essence he had trapped himself inside a solid—yet vulnerable—human form, thus giving me something to fight against.

'I will kill you for this ... for touching what's mine, you filthy cur!' he spat, grabbing at where I'd locked my fisted hands in front of him. I felt long, sharp fingernails bite into my skin, making me hiss with pain, but still I refused to let go.

'Fuck you, asshole!' I could barely afford the agonizing breath I needed to force the words out, but I wasn't going to let him get away with calling me out for touching Kat.

He was like a fucking octopus, writhing in my arms and kicking out, all the while making an ear-splitting, unearthly sound which made my brain feel like it was being ripped apart. A couple of blows caught me in the shins, and it hurt like a motherfucker. My ribs felt like they weren't just bruised but cracked, and I knew I was swiftly reaching the limit of my endurance.

The heat now was unbearably intense, and I chanced a quick look over my shoulder to see that we were almost on top of what had once been a stunning feature of this beautifully restored house. My anger at what Merrick had done lent power to my voice as I yelled in his ear.

'You could have looked out for her, let her live in this house that she poured so much love into, but you had to ruin it all, you worthless piece of shit!'

He stilled in my arms and, just for a second, I thought that maybe I had struck a nerve.

My howl of agony broke the momentary silence as he embedded his nails into my arm, ripping the skin away in bloody gouges.

With the last of my waning strength, I spun us across the floor, knowing that, even if I could dispatch Merrick, I would probably be unable to save myself from following right behind him, but better that than leave Kat to be dragged into a hell of his making. I had no idea whether she was alive or dead, but at least this way, even if she didn't survive, I could hope that she wouldn't be with Merrick, forever damned.

Suddenly, we seemed to be surrounded by flames. A shrill, mind-numbing scream erupted from Merrick as I finally released him, letting him fall away from me into the pit as I abruptly twisted to one side. I hit the floor and forced myself to roll, despite the breath-taking pain which shot through me, threatening to render me unconscious. It was like being kicked repeatedly in the ribs with a steel-toed boot, and my flesh felt as if it was being flayed from my body as my shirt smoldered and burned.

I cried out as I fell against the Volvo's front wheel and then, moaning loudly, pushed myself to my feet and kept moving. There was no time to rest and count my injuries, my focus was on where Kat lay as still as a corpse at the bottom of the stairs.

Oh, please, if there's a God, let her be alive.

I stumbled toward her, holding my left arm to my side in a vain attempt to mitigate the pain in my ribs and stem the blood which oozed from the wounds inflicted by Merrick. But before I could reach her, a massive explosion erupted under foot, and the crack which snaked across the floor opened up like the entrance to the Underworld.

Without pause or thought, I took a step back and then leapt across the ever-widening chasm and ran to Kat's side. There was no time to check her vitals; all I could do was get her out of there.

I grabbed her under her arms and hoisted her over my shoulder in a fireman's lift, crying out as I did so. Gritting my teeth, I jogged toward the library, away from the crack, which was now more than three feet wide. With my injuries and while carrying Kat, I couldn't risk jumping back to get to the car or the front door, so my best hope of getting us both out of there was to go through the window in the library.

As I reached the door, the floor lurched and started to collapse, making me stumble and nearly drop my precious cargo. I couldn't let myself dwell on the fact that she hadn't yet given any signs of life. I'd convinced myself I could feel a heartbeat against my shoulder blade, albeit faint, and I had no intention of giving up on her yet.

I clung to the doorknob, turning it and pushing against the door. At first, I was appalled to find it would barely open, as I knew my route to the front door was now almost certainly fatally compromised. I probably should have put Kat down, but suspected I would never be able to lift her again if I did.

Again, the floor rippled as a number of mini explosions rumbled dully, and I could feel the heat of the fire on my back—it was too close, and I needed to get into the library right this second if we had any hope of surviving. Gripping Kat's legs, I put my opposite shoulder to the door and pushed as hard as I could, and this time the damage worked in our favor as the door swung open over a sunken floor. I put a foot tentatively on the warped and shattered surface, feeling it give a little but seeming to hold my weight. Encouraged, I carried on into the room, kicking the door shut behind me and made my way unsteadily to the front windows. They may have been glazed with toughened glass, but almost every pane was now cracked in twisted, splintered frames.

The heat was less intense in here, but fissures had opened up in the beautiful, polished oak flooring, through which yet more smoke and fire poured.

As gently as I could, I lowered Kat onto the couch under the window and finally let myself take a moment to check her pulse. As I searched desperately for any sign of life in the relative quiet of what had been my favorite room, I suddenly became aware of sirens in the distance. It was at that moment, as if by magic, that I found a weak but insistent beat when I pressed my fingers to Kat's carotid artery.

I think I might have wept had I not been so damned dehydrated. Instead, I brushed my dry, chapped lips over her forehead and then moved around the couch to release the catch on the sash window. Then, slipping fingers under the pulls at the bottom of the long casement, I yanked hard. The damage to the frame was such that I thought it might not open, and I could see nothing close to hand with which to smash my way through. But then, just as I was about to give up, it suddenly juddered and then slid upwards, letting in blessedly cool, clean air which I inhaled greedily.

The sirens were louder, and I could see blue flashing lights in the distance—I hoped they'd sent an ambulance as well.

Turning, I bent to pick up Kat. I could have waited for the fire department, but I didn't want to stay in that house a minute longer. Taking a deep, agonizing breath, I once again hoisted her onto my shoulder and moved back to the window. I tried to lift my leg over the casement, but the sill was at least three feet off the ground, and, with Kat's weight and my multiple injuries, I knew it would be impossible. Instead, I leaned over, bracing my knees against the wall, and slid her down my body on the other side of the window. She crumpled in a heap, and I had to lean over to make sure she didn't bang her head on the ground as she fell, the maneuver causing me to scream loudly. But she was out.

I straightened up, fighting nausea and dizziness, and watched in blessed relief as a fire truck swung into the top of the drive, swiftly followed by a second one. A moment later, an ambulance tore in behind them, and I felt my body slump as my last reserves of adrenalin dissipated.

A loud roar and crash of glass behind me brought me back to reality, making me realize that I wouldn't be safe until I got outside. Just as that thought passed through my mind, the floor under my feet bulged and cracked, another fissure opening up between my legs. Glancing over my shoulder I watched in agonized astonishment as the bookshelves which lined the room collapsed and toppled, sending all Kat's precious books tumbling. The fissure widened, and the furniture at the other end of the room started to lurch and slide into the gaping maw. Above, the stunning vaulted wooden ceiling feature cracked and sagged, the rafters beginning to shower down to join the destruction below.

I could watch no more.

The gap at my feet widened, and I had to hang onto the window frame to keep myself from falling. Flames shot up a little too close to my most sensitive body parts, and I pitched headlong out the window, twisting awkwardly to stop myself falling on top of Kat.

Hitting the ground, I bellowed in pain, and the next thing I knew two firefighters were grabbing me, carrying me away from the house.

'Kat—get Kat first, not me,' I croaked.

'It's all right, sir, the paramedics have got her.'

I strained to find her, just as I was gently laid on a gurney. I sighed as I saw Kat being similarly cared for, dropping my head in exhaustion.

An urgent voice came from above. 'Sir, can you tell me if anyone else is in the house.' A firefighter stood next to me, his hand on my arm.

I shook my head, unsure if I had the energy to actually speak.

'What the hell happened here? It looks like there's a car *inside* the house!'

Before I could respond, a huge noise filled the night—not an explosion per se, more ... *an implosion*—and the sound of twisting, collapsing masonry, steel, wood and glass rent the air.

I pushed myself up on my elbows as chaos erupted around me. Firefighters were shouting and running around, desperately moving their trucks away from the house, and pulling back the men who had started unfurling hoses.

I say 'house' ... That was probably overstating it.

All that remained of Kat's lovingly restored, mellow brick mansion was random piles of rubble jutting up from a crater in the ground. Even as I looked on, the remaining stone and brickwork shifted and sank deeper, all but disappearing from sight. The last thing I saw was my rental car lurch and then slowly slide down into the abyss.

'Come on, sir, we need to get you out of here.'

I heard the voice, but it seemed to be coming from a long way off. I was vaguely conscious of being moved rapidly over uneven ground, making me feel disoriented and dizzy, and then everything just kind of ... faded away.

There was only darkness and silence—blessed silence.

Chapter Fifteen

When I came to, I was lying in a hospital bed and wearing one of those god-awful gowns which did up at the back. It had obviously been washed so many times that the pattern had faded to a pale blur, and I suspected that at least one of the ties had come off, as it felt like it was only secured by the one between my shoulder blades. Much to my relief, I was still wearing my boxer-briefs, because I was in dire need of the bathroom, and parading my bare ass for all to see was not something I cared to do.

Looking around, I saw that I was alone in a two-bed room, but it seemed I would need to take a walk to find somewhere to relieve my aching bladder. First, however, I needed to free myself of all the medical paraphernalia attached to me. I removed the nasal oxygen tube, pulled out the IV connected to the back of my hand and unclipped the pulse monitor from my finger.

Duly untethered, I planted my hands either side of my hips and pulled myself up, only to let out an involuntary and agonized expletive. Putting a hand to my ribs, I could feel that my torso had been tightly wrapped in a bandage, from just below my pecs to the waistband of my underwear. Also, my left arm was covered from elbow to wrist. Groaning, I threw back the sheets and, as carefully as possible, rotated my body and slid my legs off the bed. I discovered that if I only took shallow breaths and moved at a snail's pace, I could avoid the worst of the pain, although a dull, throbbing ache was ever-present.

Thus, I managed to stand, albeit unsteadily, wincing as my bare feet hit the cold floor. I had to hang onto the bed for a moment while I fought back dizziness and nausea, but eventually I felt clear-headed enough to shuffle across the room and go in search of a bathroom. Only then would I be able to start looking for Kat.

Just as I reached out to open the door it swung open, and only my out-flung arm prevented me from being smacked in the face.

'Ow!' I quickly withdrew my hand, shaking it hard in a vain attempt to sooth the pain in my rapped knuckles.

'Mr. Brodie! What are you doing out of bed?' A middle-aged woman in a nurse's uniform stood in the doorway, holding a small tray with a pill cup on it and glaring at me.

'I need to pee. Where's the bathroom?'

'You should have called for help. Someone could have brought a bedpan.' Her eyes flickered to the disconnected cannula in my hand and over to the bed where I'd abandoned everything. The glare she gave me might have made a lesser man tremble, but I was on a mission and my bladder would brook no interference.

'Look, I'm sorry, but unless you want to see a grown man piss his pants, you better point me in the direction of the nearest bathroom right now. And then I need my clothes and information on where I can find Kat Tregowen.'

Jeez, she looked like she was sucking a lemon, and I could see she was about to protest. I held up my hand.

'The bathroom, please. Or get a mop.' I went to move past her, and thankfully she stepped aside.

'Turn left out the door; it's halfway down the corridor on the right. And I'm calling for the doctor.'

'Whatever.' I waved dismissively and hurried down the passage … well, shuffled quickly anyway.

ജാ

An hour later I was dressed and sitting on the bed, waiting impatiently for the doctor to finish his spiel about taking it easy and to give me my meds. I was wearing faded jeans and a plain white t-shirt which weren't mine, but nevertheless fit pretty well—the nurse who helped me dress told me they'd been dropped off by a friend. That little mystery was one I didn't dwell on as I had more pressing matters to resolve—namely, finding Kat. Finally, the doctor held out a clipboard with the treatment waiver form, which I signed and handed back to him, in exchange for a prescription for painkillers.

'Thanks, Doc. Did you manage to find out about Kat?' I asked, standing up gingerly and looking at my watch. When I'd returned to the room and checked the time, I'd been horrified to discover that more than eighteen hours had passed since we'd escaped that dreadful house. Now, it was nearly eight o'clock in the evening, and I didn't want to waste another minute in idleness.

'Miss Tregowen is in a medical ward on the third floor. I understand she's stable, but you'll need to talk to someone up there to see if they can tell you anything. If you're not family—'

'I am family. Thanks, Doc.' With that, I left the room and went in search of my girl.

It didn't take long to find the third-floor nurses' station, but to my frustration there wasn't a soul in sight. I wandered back and forth for a few minutes but saw no one who could help me. I looked either way down a long corridor, wondering if I could chance checking rooms for Kat, but just then I saw a man emerge from a room right at the end, closing the door carefully behind him. He walked in my direction, and I couldn't help but watch him. His shoulders were slumped, and he looked drawn and exhausted. As he got closer, my fascination with him was explained—I'd recognize those eyes anywhere, even though I'd never met him before.

I stepped forward and he stopped in his tracks, familiar hazel eyes evaluating me.

'Mr. Tregowen?'

He gazed at me speculatively for a moment before responding. 'Yes. And you are?'

'I'm Luke Brodie, sir. I was with Kat—'

His eyes widened slightly. 'You were at the house? Were you the one who got her out?' His voice cracked and his eyes became glassy when I nodded. 'You saved my little girl,' he whispered.

I shrugged uncomfortably and held out my hand. 'I'm Luke Brodie, sir,' I repeated, giving him a small smile. A long couple of seconds passed, my hand wavering a little as he continued to ignore it, his watery gaze locked with mine. I knew the English were all about stiff upper lips and not showing their feelings, but I thought he would at least shake my hand.

Needless to say, I was taken completely by surprise when he stepped forward, brushed my hand aside and wrapped his arms around my shoulders. This was no tentative man-hug, this was the embrace of an emotional and grateful man, and I brought my own arms up to hug him right back. He was a little shorter than me, perhaps a shave under six foot, and I could feel dampness against my jaw; he was weeping.

Oh, God, please don't let her be … gone. No, no, that couldn't be right—he said I saved her.

He tightened his grip, causing a hiss of pain to escape me. He pulled away, holding me at arms' length and giving me a concerned look.

'You're hurt—'

'I'm okay,' I told him, shaking my head dismissively. I had something much more important to focus on. 'Mr. Tregowen, you have to tell me ... is she ... is Kat...?'

He released me to rub the heels of his hands across his cheeks. Brushing aside his tears, he gave me a tremulous smile.

'She's fine, son. Thanks to you, she's going to be just fine.' He rubbed his forehead and looked down at the ground for a moment, before meeting my eyes again. When he spoke, his voice was low, urgent. 'What the hell happened, Luke? The Fire Officer was just here and he said the whole house is gone—literally *gone* ... completely swallowed up by the ground. I can't even begin to get my head around that.'

I ran a hand through my hair nervously. What was I gonna say? Oh, well, the ghost of my great, great, great grandfather seduced your daughter, thinking she was the love of his life, and when she spurned him, he decided to just blow up the house, with the intention of killing her and taking her straight to hell with him.

Yeah, that wasn't going to impress the man I hoped might one day be my father-in-law.

And yes, I really was thinking that far ahead.

'Luke? You were there; you must have some idea.'

'I, uh, I'm not really sure, sir. I had to attend a client meeting in London and didn't get back until late. By the time I got there, the house was already on fire. I, uh, think it was maybe a gas explosion or something?' I didn't mean to make it sound like a question, but I hoped to God that Mr Tregowen would accept it. However, I had no idea what else, if anything, he'd been told.

'Yeah, that's what the Fire Officer thought. He said there's a crater in the ground that looks like a comet hit the Earth,' he said, shaking his head in disbelief. 'He thinks it's possible that an unrecorded mine shaft might have lain undetected beneath the house for two hundred years or more and that the explosion could have ruptured the shaft, causing the entire structure to collapse into the void. Either that, or the house was built over a sinkhole. Jesus, when I think what might have happened to Kat if you hadn't been there...' He squeezed his eyes closed and covered his face with his hands as he took a steadying breath.

I hoped that, in his distraction, he didn't notice my exhalation of relief as I realized I wouldn't need to go into detail about the events of the previous night.

Dropping his hands, he glanced up at me again, once more in control. 'He also said it looked like there'd been a car *inside* the house—you know anything about that, Luke?'

I felt my cheeks heat as he squinted at me speculatively. 'Uh, yeah, I'm sorry about that, sir. I think it was Kat's new car … I, uh, couldn't get in, so I, uh … I kind of used the car as a battering ram. I can certainly attest to the safety claims Volvo make.'

I gripped my hair, wincing at my stupid joke as Tregowen gave me a sharp look. Then I saw his eyes crinkle slightly as a faint smirk lifted the corners of his mouth.

'Well, it would have been insured, and I'm guessing Kat will forgive you.'

I chuckled nervously. 'I hope so, sir—'

'And you can cut out that 'sir' nonsense. My friends call me Nick, and after what you did last night, I think you've earned that right.'

I smiled gratefully. 'Thanks, Nick; that means a lot to me.'

Once again, he pinned me with that sharp, speculative gaze with which I was already becoming familiar.

'I have a feeling my daughter means a lot to you, too.' He put his hand on my shoulder. 'Look, she's been asleep since I arrived, so I was just taking a minute to use the toilet and see if I could find a cup of tea. Will you join me?'

I glanced longingly up toward Kat's room. If she was asleep, then it would be a good opportunity to get to know her father … but, Jesus, I wanted to see her. A squeeze of my shoulder brought my attention back to the man in question.

'It's okay, Luke. Why don't you go up and sit with her? I'll find the gents' and get us something to drink. Tea or coffee?'

'Thanks, Nick, I really appreciate that. And a coffee would be great—black, no sugar.'

'Okay, I'll be right back.'

For a couple of seconds, I watched him saunter away, wishing we could have met under better circumstances, but so glad they weren't worse. Turning away from Nick's retreating form, I made my way as quickly as my aching ribs would allow to the room from which I'd seen him emerge a few minutes earlier. I stopped outside the door and took a deep breath before pushing it open and slipping into the dimly lit room. I wasn't sure what I was expecting to see, but the sight that met me took my breath away.

Looking tiny and impossibly fragile, with small cuts and bruises littering her translucent skin, and wires and tubes seeming to protrude from every visible orifice, she was still the most beautiful woman I'd ever seen. Her dark blonde hair had been brushed and was spread out over the pillow, somehow emphasizing the pallor of her face and arms.

On either side of the bed, monitors beeped steadily, letting me know that all was well. I knew I should probably leave her undisturbed but, like a moth to a flame, I was drawn to her side, finding that I was incapable of keeping my hands to myself. Reaching out, I took Kat's small, delicately boned hand in both of mine and brought it to my mouth. I brushed the lightest of kisses across the back of her fingers—the only place that wasn't enveloped in white surgical gauze. As I did, the sonorous beeping of the monitor at Kat's head accelerated briefly, drawing my eye to the spike in her heart rate and making me smile.

'There you are, my sweet girl. You had me so worried—I thought I was going to lose you before we even had a chance to find out where this … this *thing* between us is going. I feel like I've waited all my life for you, Kat, so don't you dare bail on me. You hear me?'

Behind me, the door squeaked, and I turned my head to see Nick pushing backwards into the room, holding a cardboard cup in each hand. Swinging around to face me, he gave me a smile and held one of them out to me. Very gently, I lowered Kat's hand to the bed and took a step towards her father.

'Coffee—black, no sugar,' he said as I took it from him gratefully. Lifting the lid, I breathed in the welcome scent and took a sip, surprised at how good it was.

'I'm claiming elder's rights and taking the chair, so you'll have to sit on the bed. I doubt that'll be a hardship for you, son, but you'll have to take the flak from the nurse if she catches you.'

He sat down in the only chair, a smug look on his face, and I had to chuckle as I lowered myself gingerly onto the edge of the bed, facing him.

'Fair enough, Nick. And don't worry about me—I've got away with nurses.' I grinned as he nodded sagely.

'Yeah, I just bet you have. Now, do you want to tell me what's going on between you and my daughter that has you giving her goo-goo eyes after just three days' acquaintance?'

I was glad I wasn't taking a drink when he said that, because there's a good chance I would have spat it out in surprise. Still, it was a legitimate question from an anxious father, and he might as well know now as later. I sighed, wondering where to start and what to say without going into the more gruesome details of the circumstances which had led us all here.

'Well, I guess you know we're related?'

'Kat mentioned it—I understand we're second or third cousins, or something.'

'Uh, yeah, something like that—Catherine Tregowen was my great, great, great grandmother and Kat's great, great aunt."

He nodded and waved a hand to indicate that I should continue.

'Okay, well, I'm gonna be straight with you, Nick, because I'm hoping the two of us will be good friends. I know there are those who might say it's ridiculous that Kat and I could feel so strongly about each other after such a short time, but ... *God*, how do I say this? It's like we were meant to be—and I swear to you, Nick, I'm not the kind of guy who's ever thought in those terms before. But from the instant we met, there's been something ... something incredible and honest and ... and so damned right about us. I think I knew it as soon as I saw her, and I'm pretty sure Kat feels the same way. It felt like ... like every single day, hour, minute of my life had been leading up to that one moment.'

I ran both hands through my hair, looking down at the floor for a second before once again meeting his steady gaze. He was a hard man to read, but at least he wasn't staring at me like I was insane. Still, I needed to make sure I left him in no doubt as to the strength of my connection to his daughter.

'Have you ever had that thing where you've run into or met up with an old friend you haven't seen or thought about in years? You walk into a room or a bar and look around, and then you see them and the recognition is instant ... they've changed, of course, but as soon as you clap eyes on them, you realize you would know them anywhere, regardless of the passage of time. Well, that's what it was like when I met Kat ... like I'd known her all my life but hadn't seen her since we were kids.'

I gave him a rueful smile, clasping my hands in front of me as I rested my forearms on my thighs. In the face of his continued silence, I felt compelled to explain myself.

'Look, Nick, I know I'm probably not making much sense, but I don't know how else to describe what's happened. I'm not sure where we go from here, but I won't lie—I'm going to do my damnedest to persuade Kat to come back to the States with me, where she'll be safe.'

I swore inwardly at my slip, thinking I might have fucked up as Nick fixed me with a piercing look that seemed to penetrate my very thoughts. Before he could challenge me, however, a change in the steady rhythm of Kat's heart monitor drew our attention away from my faux pas.

Swiveling my head to look at her, my own heart seemed to skip a beat as I watched her eyelids flutter. I grabbed her hand where it lay on the bed, capturing it with both of mine and holding it gently, like a small, captive bird. Behind me, Nick was on his feet, peering over my shoulder.

'Kat? Wake up, baby.'

Once again, I lifted her fingers to my mouth and kissed them, willing her to come back to me. My prayer was answered almost immediately, as Kat's beautiful eyes slowly opened and locked onto my delighted gaze.

'Luke?' Her voice was husky and broken, and I turned to Nick to ask him for water. He was way ahead of me, though, filling the plastic cup from a jug by the bed. I looked back at Kat, only to see bloodshot eyes widen in fear.

'Is he gone?' she croaked, making my heart clench. 'Oh, God, tell me he's gone…' Tears spilled over, making twin tracks down her cheeks as I bent to cup her face.

'Shh, everything's okay, love, I promise.'

She squeezed her eyes shut, a broken sob wracking her small frame as I stood by, feeling helpless. All I could do was press her hand to my heart while I gently brushed away her tears.

Behind me, I was aware that Nick was standing very still, but I couldn't drag my eyes away from Kat to look at him. The next thing I knew, he was walking around to the other side of the bed, where he bent over and carefully put a straw to her lips. She transferred her gaze to her father, who stood patiently waiting for her to take a much-needed drink.

'Come on, sweetheart, have some water; it'll make you feel better.'

At last, she took the straw between her lips and began to drink, swallowing several mouthfuls before she pulled away.

'Thanks, Dad,' she whispered, her eyes flickering to me and then back to her father. 'What are you doing here?'

He cocked an eyebrow and pursed his lips. 'Well, here's the thing. I didn't have anything better to do, so when a woman with a sexy voice calls me saying she's a friend of yours and you've been rushed to hospital after your house blew up … well, I thought I might as well mosey on down to check on you and say 'hi'. I mean, it's only a couple of hundred miles or so and what else was I gonna do at one o'clock on a Tuesday morning, eh?'

I watched in horror as Kat's beautiful eyes filled with tears and her lower lip started to tremble.

'I—I'm sorry, Dad.' It was all she managed to choke out before her father dropped heavily on the edge of the bed and gathered her in his arms. Her hand pulled out of mine as she clung to him, her sobs muffled against his chest.

'Hey now, sweetheart. It's okay … it's all okay. I'm sorry, Kat love, I didn't mean to make you cry. Shhh…'

He continued to croon soft words of comfort, and all I could do was stand by and watch. After a couple of minutes, I decided that I should maybe leave them alone, and turned toward the door. As I did, Kat pulled away from her dad and, wiping tears away with her fingers, called out to me.

'Luke, where are you going? Please don't leave.'

Moving back to the side of the bed, I once again took her hand in mine. "I was just going to give you some time with your dad, Kat. I didn't want to intrude—'

'Don't be silly. Luke, you're not intruding…' Her voice broke and she coughed, prompting Nick to offer her more water. When she'd drunk her fill, she smiled up at me, and I rejoiced to once again see that sparky, strong woman I'd first met.

Squeezing my hand, she looked at her dad and then back to me. 'I know this wasn't quite what we had in mind, but I still want to introduce you to my father. Luke, this is Nick Tregowen … Dad, this is Luke Brodie. Be nice, he's important to me.'

∞ᄋᏮ

They finally released me from hospital late in the afternoon following my return to consciousness. I was glad to leave, but as I climbed into the back seat of my dad's Bentley the reality of my situation really hit me—I was literally homeless, with nothing but the things I had packed for my trip to London. My friends had all come to visit me that morning, and Josh had told me my room at the pub was available for as long as I—and Luke—wanted it. I accepted gladly, although Luke and my dad had clearly been reluctant to linger in Cornwall. But I wasn't quite ready to leave yet.

They gave in quickly in the face of my intransigence, my dad resigned and Luke apparently aware that this was something he was going to have to learn to live with. Sam immediately offered Dad her spare room and he had followed her and Tom to their place, having grudgingly agreed to finally get some rest after his long, stressful, late-night drive and bedside vigil. As both my new car and Luke's rental had, it transpired, been terminally damaged when the house collapsed, Ruby had offered to return when I was discharged to bring me and Luke back to the pub, where we were all meeting up later.

I was still struggling to come to terms with the devastation wrought on my home and was unable to visualize the level of destruction Luke and Tom described to me. It turned out that Tom's employee, Mark, was a part-time firefighter, the local fire department being mostly comprised of volunteers, and he had attended on the night I had lost everything. Tom had been up there early that morning to see what, if anything, was salvageable, and had the unenviable task of telling me that there was literally nothing left. I had never seen him look so down-in-the-mouth.

The only good news was that, although Luke's car had toppled into what had been described to me as a crater, the rear was still accessible and Tom, with help from Mark and a rope, had managed to scramble down to it. Despite the damage, he was able to pop the trunk with the aid of a crowbar and retrieve Luke's suitcase. It was just as well, because it seemed he was currently wearing Josh's clothes, which Ruby had apparently dropped off for him the day before.

Arriving at the Griffin, Luke and I went straight to my room. He was clearly exhausted and in pain, and, despite my period of unconsciousness and a couple of nights in the hospital, I, too, felt bone-weary. We both had so much to talk about, but it would have to wait. Divesting ourselves of our clothes, we climbed silently into bed and just wrapped ourselves around one another. We didn't speak; we only held each other until sleep eventually claimed us. I don't know if I dreamed; if I did, I remained thankfully oblivious.

When I awoke, it felt quite late. It wasn't yet dark, but the sun had obviously set. Opening my eyes, I found myself gazing into rich, deep violet.

'Hey,' I whispered.

'Hey.' He lifted a hand and gently tucked my hair behind my ear, and then leaned in to place a soft, feather-light kiss on my mouth. He started to pull away, but I couldn't bear it. Wrapping my hand around the back of his neck, I pulled him back to me, covering his mouth with mine. The kiss was full of my desperate need to reconnect, and I was beyond relieved when Luke's response was uncompromising and enthusiastic. Closing what little distance remained between us, he wrapped his arms around me, his mouth opening beneath mine as he rolled onto his back and pulled me with him. I lifted my leg so that I was straddling his hips, looking down at his bandage-covered torso.

'Is this okay? Are you in pain? I don't want to make it worse.'

'I'm fine, don't stop,' he pleaded, giving me a smile which, almost immediately, turned into a wince.

I frowned, knowing that he was in a lot of pain, and even though I was desperate for us to reconnect, I refused to let it be at the expense of his recovery. Dipping my head, I kissed him lightly and then carefully climbed off. His harrumph of impatience made me smile, but further acts of love would just have to wait.

༺༄༻

Without words, we took our time readying ourselves for the evening. With only smiles and glances we were, for the moment, in silent accord, but we both knew there would be some hard questions coming our way, especially from my dad. Preparing to leave the room, I was unsurprised when Luke took my hand and pulled me to sit down on the bed beside him.

'Kat, before we head downstairs, we need to talk.'

I nodded, my eyes never leaving his face.

He sighed and scrubbed his face with both hands. Meeting my gaze again, he took one of my hands in his and held it against his thigh.

'You need to know that I'm mad as hell with you, Kat. What on earth possessed you to go back to that damned house when I asked you—I fucking *begged* you—not to go there alone?'

I shook my head and looked down at our clasped hands. 'I know, and I'm sorry, Luke. You have no idea how sorry I am. I keep thinking I could have lost you…' I had to stop speaking as my voice trembled, and I swallowed around the lump forming in my throat. Thankfully, Luke released my hand and wrapped his arms around me, making me feel safe and secure.

'Jesus, Kat, I was more worried about losing *you*. That … that *fiend* was … I saw him … fuck, Kat, he tried to … to *suck* the life out of you. He wanted you dead! Christ, baby, he wanted to take you with him.' He choked on his words, but I pulled back to look at him.

'You … you *saw* him? Oh my God, Luke … what *happened* in that house?'

I listened in shock and astonishment as he described the events of that night, from the moment he decided to leave his hotel and head down to Port Simon, to battering down the door with my car and seeing me comatose, with his ghostly twin hovering over me. He told me how Merrick had apparently taken on a corporeal presence which enabled Luke to fight him, despite the spirit's superior strength, and cast him down into the fire pit.

Nausea threatened to overtake me as he told me how the floor had cracked open, almost as if an earthquake was moving tectonic plates, so he'd had to carry me into the library and lift me out the window. I already knew from his bandages that he had been badly hurt in the struggle with Merrick, so how he was able to get me out of there I just couldn't imagine. Swallowing hard, I leaned into him, pressing my forehead to his chest.

'Is it really gone, Luke?' I asked softly, my voice muffled against his shirt. 'My beautiful house, just … *gone?*'

He pushed me back by my shoulders and cupped my face with his hands.

'I know you put your heart and soul into it, Kat, but in the end it's just bricks and mortar … just material things. You're alive and you have a chance to start again. We're *both* alive, and I'd like to think that maybe we could make that new start together. Kat, I want—'

His words were cut off by a knock on the door.

'Kat? Luke? Are you awake? Sam and Tom are here with your dad, Kat.'

It was Ruby, calling softly from the passage, and I dragged my eyes away from Luke as he dropped his hands.

'Thanks, Ruby. We'll be right there,' I called, before turning my attention back to Luke.

'Kat—' he started, but I pressed my fingertips to his lips.

'Let's … can we just get this over with first?' I asked. The time for long term plans would come later; right now, we needed to decide what, if anything, we told my friends and, more importantly, my dad.

To my relief, he nodded, and I marveled that he was so in tune with me, as he had been since the moment we met. I knew we had a lot to talk about, but I was pretty sure we were going to find a way forward that worked for both of us. We had more pressing matters to deal with first.

'I, uh, I'm not sure I want to lie to them, Luke—I especially don't want to lie to my dad, but—'

'But you don't want them to think you're crazy either, right?'

'Right. I mean, I know my friends have kind of got on board with the whole ghost thing, but what went down on Monday night is a completely different ball game. And as for my dad…'

'Yeah, that's a tough one. The fire department told him that they think it was a gas explosion, and I haven't denied it, but something tells me he thinks there's more to it than that, especially as I said I wanted to keep you safe, and then you woke up and started asking if 'he' was gone!'

'Shit, yeah, that was pretty stupid, but I just didn't even consider that he'd be there,' I groaned. My father was a very astute man—he'd built up an enormously successful construction business, weathering several recessions, including the last one, which hadn't happened by a fluke. No, I could quite imagine that Nick Tregowen had a lot of questions, many of them I'm not sure I would be able to answer.

Luke brushed the backs of his fingers gently down my cheek, drawing my eyes back to his. He smiled encouragingly and then leaned in to place a soft, too quick kiss on my mouth. Standing, he held his hands out for me to take and pulled me to my feet. Slipping his arms around my waist, he brought his forehead down to mine.

'Come on, beautiful girl. The sooner we get this over with, the sooner we can leave. I'm thinking plausible deniability is the way to go.' He drew back, dipping slightly to capture my gaze. 'Okay?'

I smiled and nodded, although I couldn't quite dispel an odd little niggle at the back of my mind. I could neither explain it nor give it substance—it was just ... *there*. Like when you leave the house and know you've forgotten something, but just can't think what it is. I shook my head to dispel such a silly notion. 'Yeah, let's do this,' I told him, letting him lead me out of the room.

Chapter Sixteen

We were a subdued group when we all met in the pub. Josh had called in extra staff so that neither he nor Ruby would have to work, and I was so glad to be able to properly introduce my friends to Luke and Nick. As expected, this wonderful group of people—my Port Simon Posse, as I'd come to think of them—who had wholeheartedly welcomed me into their midst, were equally accepting of the two most important men in my life. And if I'd had any doubt that this would be the case, it soon became obvious by the easy banter which had already begun to fly between them.

And, truth be known, I strongly suspected my dad had a teeny, tiny crush on Samantha—she of the 'sexy voice'.

Unfortunately, that effortless rapport meant that it was impossible to ignore the ginormous elephant in the room for long.

In the end, Luke and I went with the gas explosion theory because, although I'd told him I didn't want to lie, the truth was just too fantastical to speak of. In fact, even after all we'd been through and with our tangible losses and injuries, the whole debacle had already taken on the quality of a dream ... or, more accurately, a nightmare. Added to that was the more prosaic issue of insurance. I seriously doubted that writing 'paranormal activity' on the claim form would be considered either acceptable or legitimate, and there was no way I was going to throw away all the money I'd poured into Chimneys. I wouldn't be penniless, of course, as I still had my condo in San Francisco, which was worth quite a bit more than my mortgage, and just a couple of weeks earlier Sam had accepted an offer on my behalf for the refurbished cottage, which would net me over a hundred thousand dollars, even after tax and expenses. Added to what was left of my inheritance, it was a substantial sum. Still, Sam had valued my renovated house at a staggering three quarters of a million pounds, which, even at a conservative exchange rate, equated to almost a million dollars.

Some might call that a great return on my initial investment in little more than five months, but I was having a really hard time coming to terms with my loss.

Echoing Luke, my dad pointed out that we were both still alive and relatively unscathed, which was much more important than bricks and mortar. They were right, of course; I knew that intellectually. Emotionally, though? Yeah, that was different. I just couldn't stop myself yearning for my beautiful home, despite all that had happened. Despite what had turned out to be the extremely malign presence of Lucien Merrick.

I kept thinking that if I'd only fought his influence, maybe brought in a priest or some kind of medium...

But it was all stupid and irrational. I mean, didn't you need to be a believer for that type of thing to work? I had little faith in priests, and none at all in so-called spiritualists. Merrick had obviously made me rethink my attitude about the supernatural, but I was unsure what, if anything, I could have done other than leave my house, which, as far as I was concerned, simply hadn't been an option. Besides, how could I, in good conscience, sell it to someone else knowing the dangers that lurked within?

Perhaps, with the benefit of hindsight and distance, I would be able to think a little more clearly about the extraordinary and unexplainable hold Chimneys had had over me, but right now it was an unfathomable enigma.

Nevertheless, I felt bad for lying to everyone, especially Dad. He had, of course, asked who I'd been so afraid of when I woke up in the hospital. I told him it was just a nightmare, which had elicited a frown and a sharp look, but he didn't push it ... at least, not in front of everyone. I suspected he might have some tougher questions for me when we were alone.

As for my friends, a few telling glances between them told me they weren't buying it either, but, again, it seemed they were reluctant to challenge us in front of my father.

'So, Kat, what are you going to do now?'

Jolted out of my morbid reflections by Sam's question, I looked up and gazed around at the somewhat doleful faces surrounding me, feeling a lump forming in my throat at the thought of leaving them. They were a special bunch of people and the connections we had formed in these few short months were unlike any I had previously known. I felt Luke squeeze my hand and shifted my gaze to smile at him, knowing that he understood how hard this was for me.

Turning back to Sam, I sucked in a calming breath and gave her what I hoped was a confident smile, but it felt more like a grimace.

'In the short term, Luke and I are going to head back to London with Dad. We'll stay with him while Luke finishes up his business there. I can't stay here, not now. If the house was salvageable, I might have considered it, but, well...' I glanced at Luke. As I did, Ruby leaned across the table and covered my hand with hers.

'It's okay, Kat, we get it. You have to do what's right for you, and I'm pretty sure that involves Luke here. Which I suppose means you'll be returning to America when he goes.'

Her face fell, and I could detect a hint of a tremor in her lower lip before she looked away. I just nodded, unable for a moment to respond in words for fear my voice would waver and the dam would break. As I was wondering whether I dared speak, Tom made us all jump by slapping his hand down on the table.

'Well, we're gonna bloody miss you, Kat, that's for sure. This town hasn't seen so much excitement in a long time, and we're all gonna be dining out on this story for the next twenty years—it's got everything: a haunted house brought to life, explosions, fire, a beautiful damsel in distress, a handsome hero coming to her rescue … and an even handsomer builder!'

As this point he glanced around the table, a wide grin plastered across his face, and it was impossible not to crack up, our laughter ringing around the bar and instantly easing the rather glum atmosphere.

'I'm gonna bloody miss you too, ya big lummox!' I declared, bumping the fist he offered up. 'But, hey, I'll be back for visits, and you guys have to come out to see us in San Francisco.'

Sam smirked. 'Us? So, you're already thinking in the long term, are you?' She looked between me and Luke, causing me to take a peek at the man beside me, who was positively beaming in my direction. I was pretty sure we were an 'us' and that we'd still be an 'us' in six months or six years … or maybe even sixty, if we were really lucky.

I turned my head to look up at Luke, only to be captivated, as ever, by the warmth and affection in his gaze. I wondered in that moment if I would ever tire of having those beautiful eyes look at me that way; I sincerely doubted it. As we continued to simply stare at one another, it was as if everything and everyone around us faded into the background, until a cacophony of throat-clearing dragged us both back to the present. This time it was Josh who spoke.

'So, I suppose you'll be leaving straight away then?'

Both my father and Luke immediately responded with a yes, but I hesitated.

'Um, I'm not sure, Josh. Why do you ask?' I ignored Luke's sharp look in my direction.

'Uh, well, if you were going to stay until tomorrow, I thought maybe we could all have dinner tonight, or something.' He glanced around the table, getting an enthusiastic nod from everyone and a 'hell, yeah' from Tom.

Luke started to speak, but I put my hand on his forearm to get his attention. 'Please, Luke. I'd like to spend one more night with my friends before we go ... unless you really need to get back to London.' I turned to Nick. 'How about you, Dad—do you need to leave, or can you hang on another day?'

He shook his head, giving me a speculative look. 'I'm not going anywhere without you, Kat. I'd rather we all left as soon as possible, but ... well, I understand why you want to spend a little more time with your friends.' He shot them a quick smile, but I could tell he wasn't too happy about delaying our departure.

Beside me, Luke was ominously quiet, and I was anticipating a good deal more resistance from him to my desire to linger. And, if I was honest, I would find it hard to argue with him ... except that I couldn't shake off that odd feeling of something unresolved which had plagued me since I'd come to in the hospital.

When I finally turned my gaze to him in mute enquiry, much to my relief the expression on his face was one of understanding and resignation. I knew he didn't want to hang around, but he really seemed to get that I needed this. He smiled, bringing his hand up to brush his fingertips across my cheek.

'If that's what you want, love, who am I to deny you?'

In response, I grabbed his hand and pressed my lips to his palm. 'Thank you, Luke. Thank you so much.'

With that, it simply remained to agree a time and place to meet for dinner, and then Luke and I got stiffly to our feet. He winced and put a hand to his ribs, making me frown.

'I'm okay, Kat ... just a bit stiff from sitting for a while. Hey, Nick, I could use a little exercise to get me moving. How does a drive out to the beach and a walk on the pier sound?'

As everyone got up to go their separate ways, my father looked a little lost, so I wanted to kiss Luke for including him in our plans for the afternoon, especially when I saw the grateful smile he gave us.

'Ha, you just want a chauffeur,' he snorted, but I knew he was happy to join us.

As we climbed into the Bentley and set off for the beach, my mind wandered, trying desperately to pinpoint the root of the vaguely anxious feeling which continued to niggle at me, but all I knew was that I wasn't yet ready to leave. I continued to worry at it like a loose tooth while the three of us strolled along the promenade and down the pier. Several times, Luke gave me odd looks, clearly concerned about my obvious distraction, but thankfully didn't probe—probably not wanting to discuss anything in front of my dad. Still, I laughed when he won me a silly purple dinosaur on the rifle range, and again when we found a little café selling cream teas where Nick regaled Luke with embarrassing tales of my childhood and early adolescence. It was a pleasant way to spend the hours before dinner, although I didn't miss the speculative glances Nick kept giving me.

When Dad dropped us off at the pub and headed back to Sam and Tom's to shower and change, Luke and I went straight to our room. We were both still suffering from the after-effects of our experience at Chimneys, and when he suggested a soak in the bath I agreed enthusiastically. I found proper bath salts in Ruby's bathroom and filled the tub with hot, scented water, throwing open the windows to get a nice breeze circulating. We both undressed together before I helped Luke remove the bandages from his torso; I couldn't suppress my gasp of horror at the livid bruises which adorned his body. I climbed into the water first, insisting he sit in front of me so that I was able to cushion his sorely abused ribs from the hard surface. When he laid his head back against my shoulder, I gently washed him with the soft sea sponge Ruby had provided, smiling as he hummed in pleasure at my careful ministrations.

It wasn't long before my touch had a predictable effect on Luke, and he was keen to get out and do something about it. However, I wanted him to soak in the hot water for as long as possible, and when he finally climbed out, his hisses and grunts of pain left me in no doubt that lovemaking of any description was simply not on the cards yet. I just couldn't bear the thought of him in agony, and there would be plenty of time for us to indulge all our desires when we were both stronger. Instead, I made him sit on the bed while I carefully re-wrapped his ribs, before handing him a couple of painkillers and a glass of water.

Dinner was, as expected, bittersweet. It was full of laughter and enormous affection, but it was impossible for me to adequately express my deep and profound gratitude for the welcome and friendship I'd been offered since the moment I'd set foot in Port Simon. Not only was I bereft of words, but my tears were ever close as I thought about leaving this place and these people. I knew, without a doubt, that no matter how short our acquaintance, I had forged a connection with Sam, Tom, Josh and Ruby which would be unbreakable and everlasting.

The food in the little bistro Josh had suggested was excellent and the wine flowed freely, together with several cognacs for my dad. We drew the evening out for as long as possible, but at last it was time to say goodbye, and the dam finally broke as I bid a fond farewell to Sam and Tom. I clung to them each in turn, issuing tremulous invitations to visit, and demands to keep in touch. Nick had driven them to the restaurant because Tom had apparently wanted to ride shotgun in a Bentley at least once in his life, but clearly none of them was capable of driving home, opting instead to call a cab.

While we waited, my mind began to whir as the niggling feeling I'd had for the last couple of days suddenly started to take shape, becoming clearer; it was like rainclouds parting to reveal the sun, the last few pieces of a jigsaw snapping into place. Suddenly, I knew exactly what it was I needed to do.

'Hey, Dad, we came in Josh's car, but Luke didn't drink because of his meds, so why don't we take your car back to the pub and pick you up in the morning?'

Nick merely shrugged, which told me that he really had had too much to drink, as he rarely allowed anyone other than himself or his driver to get behind the wheel of his precious Bentley. He dug out his keys and tossed them to Luke, who caught them deftly, despite his surprise. He gave me a quizzical look, but before he could speak the taxi had arrived, and more hugs and promises to write and skype were exchanged.

Then they were driving away, and I ached at the sight of their cab disappearing around the corner. Because we had to pick up Nick the next day, I would probably see them again, but it would be brief and all too final. I sucked in a deep, trembling breath and fought back the enormous lump in my throat, only to feel the warm comfort of Luke's arms envelop me from behind. Already, he knew me so well.

Turning, I let him hold me for a moment, as the sharp pain of loss pierced my heart. In my head, I started chanting a mantra: *'I will see them again, I will see them again, I will see them again.'* It was hard, but I had to tell myself that it was true.

With that thought in mind, I pulled away from Luke, giving him a soft smile, and turned to Josh and Ruby to give them both a quick hug. As they headed to the parking lot where Josh had left his Range Rover, Luke and I turned and walked up the road to where I could see Nick's car parked. There would be more goodbyes in the morning, but for now I was content to know I had the means to fulfil my last act in Port Simon before leaving for London.

Settling into the sumptuous interior of the luxury sedan, I waited while Luke took a moment to appreciate it and familiarize himself with the controls. That done, he started the engine, but didn't immediately pull out onto the road. When I turned to look at him in enquiry, he was regarding me intently.

'What?'

'You wanna tell me why I'm driving your dad's car to the pub when we could easily have picked it up in the morning?'

I sighed, looking down at my hands in my lap and then out the passenger window.

'Kat? Hey, what's going on?' He reached across to me, gently gripping my chin with his forefinger and thumb to bring my gaze back to him.

'I, uh, wanted ... I mean, I need to...'

'What, Kat? What do you need?'

I grabbed his hand, pulling it into my lap with both of mine, playing with his long, elegant fingers. Even in the dark, I could see that they were bruised and scratched, the knuckles of his right hand still raw and painful looking.

'Your poor hands, Luke...' I whispered.

'Never mind my hands, Kat—they're fine. What gives?'

At last, I looked up at him. We were parked right next to a street light, and I could clearly see the concern etched on his handsome features.

'Do you promise not to be angry with me?' I asked, unable to mask my fear of his reaction to what I was about to say.

Panic flickered across his face, his eyes wide.

'Jesus, Kat, you're scaring me. What the hell could you want that you think I'll be angry?'

I bit down on my bottom lip as I desperately tried to figure out a way to answer him.

'Iwanttogoseethehouse,' I gabbled, the words all running into one another.

His eyebrows shot up and his hand, which had lain prone in my lap, grasped one of mine and squeezed it hard.

'What?! Christ, Kat, for a moment I thought you said you wanted to go see the house, but that can't be right … can it? Please tell me you don't want to go back to that house of horror.'

I took a deep breath and met his confused and anxious gaze.

'I know it probably sounds stupid, but … I just need to see it with my own eyes. That it's actually gone.'

His frown deepened. 'You don't believe me … or Tom … or, or … fuck, Kat, you gotta give me something here, because I'm having a really hard time understanding why you would want to go back there.'

I gripped his hand in both of mine, raising it to my lips before bringing it back to my lap.

'"Oh, Luke, of course I believe you. I know it's gone, I do. I just...' I shook my head and looked out through the windshield before turning back to him. 'It's so hard to explain, but I feel like, even though I know it happened, it doesn't *feel* real … like I won't be able to truly accept it and move on until I see with my own eyes that the house no longer exists.'

I pleaded with my eyes for him to understand, and after a long pause he sighed, a look of resignation beginning to overtake the confusion. Still, he wasn't quite ready to give in.

'Seriously, Kat? You really want to go back there? You couldn't just look at a fucking photograph? Or take my word for it, and the word of a dozen or so firemen and paramedics? You have to actually go there and look at a pile of rubble and steel in a hole in the ground?'

I winced at the thought, but merely nodded.

Without another word, he pulled away from me and faced front, staring at the lamp-lit street ahead, his jaw tense.

I leaned forward, trying to see his face in the dim, synthetic light. My voice little more than a whisper, I tried again.

'I don't mind going on my own—'

'Don't be fucking ridiculous, Kat,' he exclaimed, whipping his head round to glare at me. He was clearly struggling to contain his irritation and frustration, and I knew I was seeing a different side to Luke. In a now familiar, tell-tale gesture, he raked both hands through his thick hair as he huffed out an exasperated breath and focused once again on the empty street.

'Is there *anything* I can say to persuade you that what you want is an exercise in rank stupidity, Kat?'

I cringed at his censorious tone, but I couldn't deny that he was probably right. All I knew was that it was unfinished business, and I would find it hard to leave Cornwall if I didn't do this first.

'I don't think so,' I told him, my voice small.

After what felt like an eternity, he finally turned to look at me again, his expression worryingly blank.

'Okay, but you do as I tell you and we leave when I say. And you stay in the car. Promise me now or I swear, Kat, I'll find a way to lock you in our room before bundling you in the car and driving as fast as I can out of this town.'

I suspected he was entirely serious and knew that this was the best I could expect—in fact, it was better than I had hoped.

'I swear I'll do whatever you say, Luke. I only need a minute— just to take it all in—and then we can go.' I reached out a tentative hand to cup his cheek and was so relieved when he covered it with one of his own, leaning into my touch.

'I'm wondering when you will have had enough of me and all the crap that comes with me,' I told him softly.

He turned his face into my hand and kissed my palm, sending a frisson of undiluted pleasure right through me. When he once again met my eyes, his gaze was intense.

'Well, I figure it really can't get worse than a murderous ghost and property Armageddon, so I have high hopes it can only get better from here on in.' He flashed that devastating smile of his, although it made me feel sad to see it didn't quite reach his eyes … and just a little guilty.

ɞᴄᴈ

Following an emotional farewell to Josh and Ruby, and another one at Sam and Tom's, early morning found us parked in the drive of what had once been my home, albeit briefly. Luke had insisted, as one of his conditions for returning, that we pick up my dad first—I think he was hoping that Nick would try to dissuade me from my irrational quest. Much to Luke's obvious irritation, it seemed Dad was equally curious as well as supportive of my desire to get some kind of closure.

It was a surreal feeling, the three of us enclosed within the insulated interior of the big limousine under a clear azure sky, the air-conditioning keeping us cool, even as another Cornish summer day promised sweltering temperatures.

Luke was behind the wheel, and I was riding shotgun, while Nick nursed his hangover in the back seat. For a while I just gazed out the windshield, trying to take in what I was seeing ... or, rather, not seeing, because where my beautiful three-story brick house had so recently stood, was a vast hole in the ground. Luke had been right when he described it as a crater. From where we sat in the car, there was little else to see, other than a few scorched trees lining the boundary of my property as it sloped down towards the sea.

Before I could control it, a loud sob of grief escaped me and my hands flew to my mouth to stem the tide. Beside me, I was aware of Luke releasing his seatbelt, and I felt my dad's hand grip my shoulder and squeeze it gently. Shifting closer, Luke attempted to gather me into his arms, but in the big car it was awkward at best, and, if I was honest, I wasn't really co-operating because I resisted moving toward him. Instead, despite the spacious interior, I experienced a growing sense of claustrophobia. As Luke tried to pull me towards him, I suddenly lunged toward the door, wrenching it open and clambering out.

'Kat!—'

I wasn't listening, intent only upon getting a closer look at the devastation wrought on my home. I started moving, the sound of car doors opening behind me barely impinging on my senses.

'Kat, wait. You fucking promised me!'

He was right, of course—I had promised him, and now I was going back on my word. That thought alone was enough to make me think twice. Why was I so compelled to get closer? Was Merrick's malign influence still at work, even now? Were the forces which had originally pulled me to the house—and kept me here, when any sane person would have run away—still weaving their dark and potent magic?

I stopped my forward momentum, finally listening to both my inner voice, which was screaming at me to stop, and Luke's entreaties to go no farther.

Tearing my eyes away from the devastation, I slowly turned, feeling only relief when I realized he was mere steps away. He closed the distance quickly, his arms encircling me and holding me tight. I clung to him desperately, appalled at my selfish actions.

'I'm sorry, I'm sorry, I'm sorry, I'm sorry...' I chanted over and over.

'Shh, it's okay,' he murmured, kissing the top of my head.

He continued to hold me for a moment or two, gently rocking me from side to side until I felt calmer. I started to pull away, thinking this was probably a good time to return to the car and leave this desolate place, but he tensed, tightening his embrace. I could feel his heart beat a rapid rhythm against my chest and glanced up at him.

'I'm ready to go now, Luke. I'm sorry I was such an idiot.' I tried a tentative smile, but it quickly dropped when a frown marred his handsome features, and I began to fear I had really fucked up.

'I really am sorry, Luke. I know I broke my promise, but I just want to leave now ... please?' I was a little surprised to find that I meant it. It was as if whatever hold the house had had over me was finally gone ... the link broken, and I felt free.

My joy almost overwhelmed me when his frown disappeared, to be replaced by a radiant smile which lit up his face like the sun coming out.

'Me too. I've had my fill of this place, and I'm ready to start a new life with you. Let's go.'

With that, he pulled away and turned, throwing an arm around my shoulders as we walked back to where Nick waited anxiously next to the car.

ᛈᚲᚱ

The next couple of weeks flew by in a whirlwind. True to his word, Luke had persuaded his company to let him extend his trip, insisting that they owed him a lot more than that in vacation time and overtime worked—in that, it seemed we had even more in common than we realized. His boss had been unable to refuse, especially when Luke offered to make himself available to the client for some of that time.

Inevitably, our time together was dominated by discussions of our plans for the future and my return to San Francisco. A fly in the ointment was getting a new passport from the American Embassy, as I needed proof, in the form of a report from the Fire Department, that it had been destroyed. This, in turn, had become problematic, as I was required to attend an interview with the Fire Officer, which necessitated a return to Cornwall. Luke had been dead set against it, but the report was critical, both in terms of obtaining a new passport and to settling my insurance claim, so we had reached a compromise. I arranged to meet both the Fire Officer and the Insurance Assessor in Bodmin rather than on site, and Luke would go with me.

He had been quiet and somewhat introspective since we'd arrived in London. We were staying with Nick, whose large four-story townhouse had a completely self-contained apartment on the top floor. It meant we could spend time with my dad, but still have our privacy, which was something we really needed and appreciated. I had been concerned at first that Nick would baulk at the idea of Luke and me sharing a bedroom, especially considering the newness of our relationship. However, he seemed utterly unfazed by our closeness, and it was never even an issue—I guess the guy who saves your daughter's life gets some kind of special Dad-dispensation.

If Luke had turned in on himself a little, I put it down to his concerns about work and the possibility of having to travel home without me whilst I waited for my replacement passport. I imagined he was also worried about our return to Cornwall, but if he was, his concerns proved to be groundless. We went, we attended our scheduled meetings—which went without a hitch—and then drove home; we didn't even stay the night, both of us keen to keep our time there to a minimum.

Regardless of how he was during the day, at night Luke more than made up for it. There was a new intensity to our lovemaking which took my breath away. He was clearly a quick healer, his injuries barely seeming to affect him as he took me over and over in every conceivable way. It was both enthralling and exhausting—especially as I didn't seem to possess the same super-healing properties. But I couldn't help but revel in our ever-growing intimacy and the conviction that Luke and I were true soulmates.

The days sped by at lightning speed as the date of Luke's departure loomed ever closer and still there was no sign of my passport. In the end, I decided I needed to go to the US Embassy, which, having moved from its conveniently central location in Grosvenor Square, was now a pain in the neck to get to at its new location in Vauxhall. Nevertheless, on a day when Luke had to meet with his client, and with time running out, I opted to take a trip south of the river and sit in the Embassy until I got my hands on that precious dark blue booklet. However, much to my annoyance and frustration, they pretty much kicked me out at four in the afternoon, telling me to call them the next day.

With little more than a day to go before Luke would have to fly home, I could barely contain my nerves as I hung on the phone, listening in mounting irritation as a teeth-grindingly perky Californian fuckwit kept telling me in a recorded message how happy she was that I'd called the Embassy and that her co-workers could hardly contain their excitement at the mere thought of talking to me and were practically peeing their fucking pants over being able to help me … well, obviously not in those words, but that was the implication. God, I wanted to punch the stupid bitch in the face!

At last, an hour before they were due to close, a real person came on the line and told me my passport was ready. Ten minutes later I was in a black cab, offering a twenty-pound tip to the driver if he got me to Vauxhall in less than half an hour. There were many things I loved about London, but black cabs were pretty close to the top of my list. There wasn't a street or short-cut they didn't know. I'd read once that London taxi drivers have a more well-developed hippocampus—the area of the brain responsible for long-term memory—than the average person because of the huge amount of information they had to store. They had to learn every single street, significant restaurant, store and landmark within a four-mile radius of Charing Cross, one of London's major train stations—and that was in one of the most built-up, higgledy-piggledy cities in the world. They called it The Knowledge, and the sheer scale of the task was mind-boggling … quite literally. I was therefore delighted but unsurprised when, with time to spare, my cab pulled up beside the newly built US Embassy in Nine Elms.

Half an hour later, I was clutching my crisp new passport and was in another taxi on my way back to Regent's Park.

The following day, I clung to my dad like I was never going to see him again as we said our final goodbyes in Heathrow's Terminal 5. Luke stood back, letting father and daughter have their moment. My rather was a pretty stoic guy, but I could feel the depth of his love for me in the tightness of his embrace, and it made me squeeze him one more time before we broke apart.

Holding on to my hands, he gazed intently at me.

'I know you haven't told me everything about what happened in Cornwall, sweetheart, and maybe I don't need to know anything other than that you're safe and alive. I hope you know that if you ever decide to tell me the truth, I'm open-minded enough to listen and not judge. Okay?'

I nodded, uncertain I'd be able to speak without breaking down. My father was basically telling me that he knew something … *otherworldly* had occurred and that he would believe and accept whatever I chose to tell him. That knowledge compelled me to throw my arms around his neck again and hug him one more time.

'Come visit me soon. I promise I'll tell you everything, Dad,' I whispered.

And then Luke and I were heading through to security and to our future.

Chapter Seventeen

I reached for Luke's hand as we stood in the ascending elevator, on our way up to his parents' apartment. We'd arrived in San Francisco the previous afternoon and spent the night at Luke's place, just chilling and enjoying being alone together. I had worried all the way over on the flight that I would feel disconnected from the city where I'd spent most of my life, but was both surprised and ecstatic to discover I was right where I wanted to be. I missed my friends, of course, but I knew that I'd managed to get Cornwall and Chimneys out of my system merely by putting five thousand miles between us.

I realized as soon as I stepped through the automatic doors at SF International that I had been carrying the mantel of Lucien Merrick's influence across my shoulders like an invisible but heavy yoke from the moment I found his ruined house. But as a cool fall breeze wrapped itself around me, I felt free in a way I hadn't for what seemed a very long time. I was home ... and it felt better than I could ever have imagined.

Luke and I had both called our mothers once we were settled in his apartment, and Helen had got her invitation in first. It would be Luke's turn to face the parental inquisition at the weekend, but right now I was the one in the firing line.

That was unfair, of course, because, truth be told, I was as excited to meet Helen and Richard as they apparently were to meet me. And as we stepped out of the elevator, a squeeze of my hand brought my attention up to sparkling blue eyes and a radiant smile that I suspected would never fail to wield a very special power over me—not the malignant, emasculating kind that Merrick had used to render me stupid and vulnerable; no, Luke would raise me up, make me strong, empower me in a way no one and nothing had before.

I returned his smile just as he stopped in front of a door. Tearing his gaze from mine, he lifted his hand to ring the bell, but before he could do so the door was flung open and I found myself looking into dancing blue eyes set in a beautiful, smiling face.

'Mom, have you been standing there peering through the spyhole for the last half hour?'

'Oh, Luke, don't be mean to your poor mother,' she pouted, but there was laughter in her eyes as she stepped forward and threw her arms around her son. She was no taller than me, and he seemed to envelop her.

I stood back, taking in the deep affection that obviously existed between them. But then she was pulling back, holding him at arms' length as she looked him up and down.

'How are you, darling—I suspect you didn't tell me everything on the phone.'

'I'm fine, Mom, really. Much more importantly, this is Kat—'

Before he could say more, she released him and turned to pull me into a tight clinch.

'Oh, Kat, my dear girl, forgive me!' she blurted, before withdrawing to give me a similar perusal. 'I was just so worried when Luke told me about the fire, because I know he probably down-played what happened.'

I smiled, giving her hands a squeeze as she continued to hold onto me.

'I totally understand, Helen. I'm just so happy to finally meet you.'

With that, she hugged me again, only letting go when Luke chuckled beside us. Putting his arm around her shoulders, he turned his mother and guided her in through the door. With his free hand, he reached for mine and pulled me in behind them.

'Come on, Mom, let's talk inside. Where's Dad?'

As if he'd conjured him with his words, a tall, middle-aged man seemed to materialize in the spacious entryway, a wide smile on his face. As tall and handsome as his son, he had the exact same blue eyes and black hair—although his was starting to turn silver at the temples, giving him a decidedly sexy-distinguished air. I couldn't help but think of Lucien Merrick and Catherine Tregowen, and the superior gene pool they had initiated.

'There you are! I thought you'd all decided to go nightclubbing without me.'

'Watch it, Dad—don't put ideas in Mom's head.' Luke and his father laughed, the sound blending, as they hugged one another.

'Don't start, you two. Richard, come say hello to Kat, my new ally in this Boys' Club you've had going for the last thirty years.'

Again, I was enveloped in a warm embrace as Luke's father greeted me like a long-lost daughter.

'You're very welcome in our home, Kat. I'm so happy to meet you at last.'

With greetings over, I was led into a large room with stunning views over Sausalito Bay. Helen excused herself to check on dinner, and I immediately offered to help, keen to get to know her better. Linking her arm through mine, she grinned at me.

'I knew I was going to like you,' she announced, leading me into a chef's wet dream of a kitchen and pointing me at the island, where various vegetables were awaiting preparation. We quickly fell into easy conversation, as if we'd known each other for years, and I had no doubt that we would become fast friends.

Luke had, I knew, given her the bare facts of what had happened in Port Simon—that we'd met, made an instant connection and were going to pursue a relationship. He'd told her that, while he was at a meeting in London, there'd been a gas explosion at my house and that he'd returned in time to help me escape before it was destroyed. That was the extent of her knowledge, but her intuition clearly told her there was more to it than that. We were chatting generally about all our family coincidences and connections when she paused, causing me to look up from the carrots I was cutting into batons.

'Kat, I know it's probably too early for you to trust me enough to confide in me, but … well, I have a strong feeling that something … not quite right happened in Cornwall. It all seems too bizarre that you found that house and then found me, and met Luke, with whom you've formed this instant and extraordinary bond—and don't get me wrong, I totally understand it because the same happened to me when I met Richard; I knew the moment I saw him that I would marry him one day. It's odd, isn't it, how sometimes you just know? But there is more to it than what Luke's told us, isn't there?'

I gave her a wry smile and put down my knife. 'You're right, Helen, there is more to it than that. And it's not that I don't trust you, because I do. I felt it right from our very first contact … and that's all part of it, I think; part of the whole fantastical story of the Merricks and the Tregowens and the Brodies. It's like a kind of celestial chess game, one of those stories by Homer, in which the gods on Mount Olympus move around the pieces and we mere mortals unknowingly do their bidding—if you believe in such things, which I'm still not sure I do.'

She stood on the opposite side of the island, regarding me with an open expression on her face, silently inviting me to continue.

I sighed. I wasn't ready to talk to anyone about Merrick yet, not even Luke, so I really didn't want to get into it with his mother within minutes of meeting her.

'I'm sorry, Kat, just ignore me. I promise I'm not the nosy, interfering mother-in-law type. I just want you to know that I'm a good listener. When we know each other better, I hope you'll remember that if you ever need to talk to someone. Now, let's get these vegetables in the steamer.'

I smiled, grateful that she'd read me so well and stepped back without making me feel awkward. Then, as if tuned into his mom's remarkable intuitiveness, a pair of strong arms encircled me from behind and I felt Luke's breath on my ear. I leaned back instinctively, reveling in his closeness.

'Hmmm, I think you two have had enough bonding time. I'm getting withdrawal symptoms.'

I chuckled, not missing Helen's smirk as she set the steamer on the stove. 'Oh, we've definitely bonded—your mom just referred to herself as my mother-in-law.'

My chuckle turned to outright laughter as I felt Luke tense against me, his head snapping up to look at his mother, whose face was a picture of shock and mortification.

'Mom!'

'Luke, I was … I didn't mean … that's not … oh!'

Luke released me as I descended into snorting hysterics, which only worsened as I got my first glimpse of his face, which ran the gamut from confusion to suspicion, speculation to disappointment.

It was this last that finally tempered my mirth, and I immediately reached for him, slipping my hands round the back of his neck as I stood on tiptoes to kiss away the pout he was now sporting. Pulling away, I gave him an apologetic smile.

'I'm sorry—I wasn't laughing at the idea of Helen being my mother-in-law, just the way she said it, and then your face … which is gorgeous, by the way … forgive me?'

I gazed up at him under my lashes, turning on the doe-eyed disingenuousness to full effect, and was rewarded with that smile which made my insides turn to goo. Behind us I heard his mother sigh dramatically.

'Oh, you've definitely taken on a handful with this one, son!'

His smile grew as he continued to gaze down at me.

'But she's such a delicious handful, Mom,' he replied, without taking his eyes off me.

Helen's answering chuckle told me she bore me no grudge for making fun of her ... and Luke's soft kiss confirmed that he, too, had forgiven me.

℘つଓ

Dinner was great—wonderful food, delicious wine and great company. By the time Luke and I were preparing to leave, I felt like I'd known his parents all my life. When they discovered that my mother and stepfather also lived in San Francisco and that my dad was planning a visit soon, they immediately suggested hosting a small party for friends and family while he was here. It could have been a pretentious gesture, but from Helen and Richard it was clearly a genuine and warm-hearted offer which I was more than happy to accept.

Heading home—and Luke's apartment had already become just that—we held hands in the back of the taxi as I rested my head on his shoulder. Wending our way through the late-night traffic, I couldn't help but dwell on all the changes that had occurred in my life in such a short time—some good, some bad. I smiled to myself at that major understatement. But for all the bad—much of it very bad indeed—the good made up for it tenfold. My English friendships were ones I would cherish for the rest of my life, and the new closeness which had developed between myself and my father was something I had never expected, but was all the more precious for that.

And then there was Luke.

How could I ever quantify what he meant to me? Our relationship was still in its infancy, yet our bond was already beyond anything I could have imagined in what I now regarded as the half-life I had lived prior to my fateful trip to Cornwall.

Would I change what had happened at Chimneys? If I'd been able to see into the future when I first set eyes on that house, would I have run? Would I merely have collected my inheritance from Derek Best, instructing him to sell my grandmother's house and send me the money? If I had, I wouldn't have met Sam, and that, in turn, meant that I wouldn't have met Josh, who set me on the path to finding Helen and, through her, Luke. Would I go through hell, almost die at the hands of a psychotic ghost—not just once, but three times—and lose the house I'd poured my heart and soul into?

If my reward for dancing with the Devil was this incredible man, there was only one answer.

In a heartbeat.

The only hell I could conceive of now would be a life without Luke.

Turning my head slightly, I found dark eyes regarding me. Sodium streetlights may have robbed them of the rich blue that reminded me of wild blueberries, but they couldn't disguise the humor and affection which shone from them.

'Penny for your thoughts,' he murmured, just as the cab swung into the curb outside his building.

'We're home,' I smiled, giving him a quick kiss and climbing out of the car.

Upstairs, Luke unlocked the door to his apartment and stood back to let me precede him inside. I barely heard the door close before he'd grabbed my hand and pulled me to him. Turning us, he pressed me against the door, his intense gaze flickering across my face, almost as if he was familiarizing himself with my every feature.

Then his mouth was on mine, his tongue demanding entrance, kick-starting my own passionate response. We kissed like it was our last night on earth; we devoured each other … a final meal to be savored, consumed with relish.

He pushed my jacket off my shoulders, letting it fall to the floor where it lay, unheeded, while his hands cupped my ass, lifting me so that I was forced to wrap my legs around his waist. For a brief moment I wondered about his injured ribs, but he didn't even flinch as I clung to him. Without even being aware that we were on the move, I realized a second before he lowered me onto the bed that we'd left the hallway and he'd carried me to the bedroom.

He remained standing and, without taking his eyes off me, quickly stripped. As he did, I noticed that he hadn't re-taped his ribs after his shower. The only illumination in the room was the light bleeding through the open door from the hall, but it was enough to see that the bruising was miraculously reduced.

Before I could ponder this oddity he knelt on the mattress and crawled slowly up to me, forcing me to scoot back until my head met the pillows. Wordlessly, he slid his hands beneath my light sweater, pushing it up. I lifted my arms and he pulled it over my head, throwing it carelessly to the floor. He reached behind me, dexterously unsnapping my bra one-handed, making me smirk as I arched an eyebrow at him. His attention, however, was elsewhere as he peeled the lacy garment from my skin and sent it in the same direction as my sweater. He paused, staring at my breasts as if he'd never seen them before.

'Luke?' I whispered.

He didn't look up, instead resting one hand on my chest as he continued to gaze at me.

"So beautiful." His voice was so low I barely heard him.

He said nothing more as he moved back in order to remove my shoes, skirt and underwear. Then he was back between my legs and I reached up to bury my hands in the thick hair at the nape of his neck. As our mouths once again collided he pushed into me, making me gasp with the pure pleasure of it. We didn't need words now as he moved inside me, urgent and deep.

I might not believe in a god, but making love with Luke had become a religious experience for me, never more so than on this night. No longer just a feast of sensual carnality or even an act of love—my orgasm was a truly rapturous thing, a moving, profoundly emotional event. Even as tears of joy slid from my eyes and into my hair, I held on tight to Luke, feeling him surge into me.

'Oh God, so good. Catherine, my love, my angel...'

Beneath him, it seemed that my heart stilled for just a second as he collapsed on top of me, burying his head in my neck.

Both breathing hard, I could do nothing but cling to him, my mind in uproar.

Say something, a voice inside my head screamed.

But what *could* I say?

Who are you?

What do you want?

Do you mean me harm?

Is my Luke in there?

As if he was aware of my confusion and distress, he lifted his head and propped himself on his elbows. Looking down at me, a soft smile lit his handsome features.

'Hey, sweet girl, where'd you go?'

I could ask you the same question, I thought.

But then he seemed to notice the tracks of my drying tears and his brow knitted in consternation. Using his thumbs to gently wipe away the dampness from under my eyes, he continued to gaze down at me.

'Are you okay? It feels like I lost you there for a moment.'

'Yeah, me too … I, uh, I thought I heard you call me … Catherine.'

He narrowed his eyes, looking confused.

'Katherine? Did I? Well, it is your name.' He chuckled softly

I nodded, keeping my eyes fixed on his. It was dark, but I could detect no artifice.

'Is that what your mom calls you? I've never heard anyone else call you that, but if you want me to, I guess I could. I'm not sure it suits you, though.' He frowned. 'Do you want me to call you Katherine? I kind of prefer Kat … 'cause you're like a beautiful feline.'

'No, Luke, I don't want you to call me Katherine. No one calls me that. I hate it. I must have misheard you. I love the sound of my name on your lips.'

He grinned, dipping his head to brush his lips against mine. I wanted more, but before I could free my hands to pull him back to me, he was rolling off me. I immediately felt his absence, the lack of skin on skin, but he didn't go far, merely moving to lie on his side next to me. He propped his head on one hand, splaying his other hand across my stomach. As I looked up at him, at my Luke, a lazy smile played across his face.

'I'd say I'm sorry I attacked you before you even got your coat off, but I'm not … sorry, that is. You're amazing, do you know that?'

I smiled, shaking my head. I reached my hand up to cup his face, rubbing my thumb across his cheek. He immediately covered it with his own, turning his face to kiss my palm. When he turned back to once again meet my eyes, we just stared at each other for a moment, before he lowered both our hands to his chest, where he held mine over his heart.

'Kat, I know it's probably too soon, and I don't know if you're ready to say it back, but I don't care, because I love you and I'm pretty sure I always will. This past week has taught me that life's too short to worry about other people's ideas of what works and what's right—this feels right … you and me. Like I say, there's no pressure to say it back, I just need you to know that that's where I am.'

I continued to simply gaze up at him in wonder.

Who are you?

The answer came instantly.

You're my Luke. You're the man I love. I couldn't leave you now if I tried.

Is there more in there than I bargained for?

Possibly.

Does it matter?

'Say something, love … you're making me nervous.' He smiled uncertainly.

I won't let it matter.

'Don't be nervous. Wherever you are, that's where I am, where I always want to be. I love you too, Luke … every part of you.'

As the smile I adored lit up his face, I slipped my hand from under his and pulled him down to kiss him. He came willingly, our mouths meeting and molding together.

We made love then, Luke Brodie and me.

Epilogue

At last, I had been set free ... free of that house that held me captive for so long, and free of the anger and bitterness that had flourished within like a cancer, consuming me and robbing me of my humanity.

My beautiful Catherine ... oh, how I loved her. But can it possible that my parents lied to me all those years ago?

Ha! Of course they did. They would never have accepted a mere servant girl as a daughter-in-law. Their bigotry and snobbery took everything from me, and for what? In the end, it was all for naught. But along the way, they infected me with their prejudices, such that I forgot why I fell in love with Catherine in the first place. I forgot that it was her honesty, her kindness and her proud spirit that first captivated my heart. The spirit that burned inside her and would never let anyone believe they were better than her—and she was right, for surely I was her inferior in all but social rank and money. And what use those meaningless accoutrements in the face of a cataclysmic war and an influenza epidemic that killed more people than had died in the trenches, and what good were they when my skin and lungs were destroyed by gas?

The woman who looks so much like my lost love—everyone calls her Kat, which seems so strange and yet so appropriate—she told me once that Catherine had come back, that she had a child—our child, whom she'd named Sarah. It seems that the young man, who looks so like me, is Sarah's great, great grandson—which, of course, means he is my three-times great grandson.

I did not believe her at the time—surely what she said was impossible! And so I hurt these two young people—my bitterness at all that I had lost did far more damage than that scorching gas attack. Indeed, the evil I perpetrated over so many years had surely damned my soul to the very fires of Hell itself.

And yet, here I am—neither in nor of this world, nor in Hell. I have no understanding of why I have been saved, nor do I yet comprehend how it has come to pass. All I know is that Kat is my liberator, and that salvation—if such is my path—lies with her and the love she feels for the boy called Luke.

Ah, Luke—precious blood of my blood and the vessel through which I might serve my penance and achieve the peace that I craved for more than one hundred years. I wronged him so grievously, but in that brief moment when his heart and soul opened as he embraced his beloved Kat, he became the conduit for my escape and my redemption. I cannot, of course, right the wrongs of the past, but perhaps I have been offered a second chance to be something better than the sum of my past deeds. My great, great, great grandson is a good man, and he is loved by an exceptional woman, and therein, I believe, is the salvation that I have striven to deserve.

Most of the time, it seems that Luke is unaware of me and, indeed, my power over him is minimal—perhaps even waning over the five years since the ghastly events of that fiery night in Cornwall. Occasionally, though, it seems that he shakes his head, as if to clear it of a thought that was not his own, but more and more these days I feel myself being subsumed by his stronger lifeforce. How ironic, when it was I, in my madness, who tried to rob Kat of her own lifeforce over that fateful summer in Port Simon.

For her part, I know that Kat sometimes looks into the eyes of her lover and sees beyond them to where I hide, that she knows I'm here but has accepted my presence. I will never betray that trust nor the incredible gift she has given me.

Of one thing I have no doubt; that one day I shall be gone, that I shall no longer exist as a separate entity to the one called Luke Brodie. He and I shall be one—one body, one mind, one eternal love. I believe that day may come sooner rather than later.

But not quite yet. For today, I will receive the greatest gift of all. The gift of a life—one more precious than any other. Today, my son—or, rather, Luke's son—is being born; my four-times great grandson. Four years ago, I watched through Luke's eyes as Kat walked towards him on the arm of her father in a little church on a hill in Sausalito. And, over the last nine months, I have watched as their son grew in her womb. And now, on this fine day, beautiful Kat strains and cries out as he pushes his way into the world. I have become inured to her cursing—it seems to be the modern way for women to speak as men these days. But I feel Luke's pain as her grip on his hand seems out of all proportion to her delicacy. I suppose, in that, too, I am out of step.

It has been a while since I have felt so ... separate from Luke. Perhaps it is a sign, I am not sure.

Oh, but here is the child ... screaming and bloody and so full of life—he is glorious, and I am so hap—

'Oh my God, Kat, you did it. God, I love you, I love you so much—'

'I love you too. Is he okay?'

'He's perfect, beautiful, just like his momma.'

I was exhausted but only let myself relax when the midwife gently laid my son—our son—on my chest, as she invited Luke to cut the cord.

His grin was infectious and, tired as I was, I could only answer it with a wide smile of my own as my baby stopped screaming and snuffled against my breast, a shock of tufty black hair contrasting vividly against my own pale skin.

'Looks like he's got his daddy's mad hair,' I said, gazing up at my husband. As I did so, I was surprised to see a brief frown mar his features as he shook his head.

'Luke, what is it, are you okay?'

For a moment, he looked confused, and then that smile I loved so much returned.

'Yeah, sorry, I'm fine, I just felt weird for a second there."

He leaned over and kissed me, then oh so softly kissed his son's dark head.

'Weird how?' I asked, still a little anxious.

He chuckled. 'I dunno, I can't really explain it, just ... like ...' He shook his head again and laughed. 'It's nothing, it's gone now, I don't even know what it was.'

I looked at him carefully but he just grinned, open and guileless. There was nothing in his eyes but love and happiness. Nothing at all.

THE END

Printed in Great Britain
by Amazon